# THE
# CHRISTMAS
# QUILT

PATCHWORK MYSTERIES

# THE CHRISTMAS QUILT

## KELLY ANN RILEY

**Guideposts**

New York

This book is dedicated to my mother, Evonne Leiske, who always makes Christmas extraspecial.

*Family Patterns*
*Time to Share*
*Muslin Mystery*
*Timeless Treasures*
*Homespun Holiday*
*Pieces of the Past*
*Threads of Truth*
*Secret in the Stitches*
*Bound in Love*
*Yesterday's Secrets*
*Squared Away*
*Mystery on the Midway*
*A Quilt of Memories*
*The House on Lookout Mountain*
*To Have and to Hide*
*Nothing to Hide*
*The Christmas Quilt*

# THE CHRISTMAS QUILT

 CHAPTER ONE

S now drifted in sugary waves across the street and glistening icicles hung on the eaves, but Sarah Hart felt snug and warm in Wild Goose Chase, her favorite fabric store in Maple Hill. She turned from the frosty window, and took another deep sip of the spicy tea the store owner Vanessa Sawyer had offered on her arrival.

Sarah moved to a nearby table and lifted a bolt of velvet fabric with a pattern of pale blue and delicate white flowers, which would make lovely pillows for the sofa in her daughter-in-law Maggie's parlor. Now if only she could figure out what to get Liam and Martha.

A tiny flutter tickled her stomach at the thought of the handsome Irishman who owned The Spotted Dog Café and Bookstore. Liam Connolly and Sarah had been friends for a long time, but over the last year they had grown closer and had begun to date. She had searched several shops but nothing really struck her as right. She wanted to get him something meaningful but maybe not too personal. Not yet. Both of them had been happily married before and were taking their time, enjoying their blossoming relationship.

Sarah gave herself a little shake and focused back on the fabric she had twisted between her fingers. She smoothed out the cloth. She would think about Liam's gift later and concentrate on what to get her best friend.

She had known Martha Maplethorpe for most of her life. They had been through a lot together from grade school to marriage: raising kids, Sarah's husband's death, Martha's husband's Parkinson's disease and, most recently, the passing of Sarah's father. Sarah wanted to give Martha something unique this year. Something that came from Sarah's hands and heart.

She gazed around the shop seeking inspiration and spied a small stack of yellow flyers on the counter proclaiming "Christmas Mystery Quilt." The ad gave a Web site address and stated that daily sewing instructions would be blogged for fourteen days in December. If the sewer followed directions, she would have a quilt in time for Christmas Day. Perfect!

She would make the quilt as a gift for Martha. The project would be fun and keep Sarah busy, plus Martha would love the idea of a mystery quilt. She could even catalog each step in a little booklet to give Martha along with the finished quilt.

It was eleven days until Christmas, which didn't give Sarah a lot of time, but with her sewing experience she should be able to catch up.

She studied the list of fabrics required to start the quilt. She needed two and a half yards each of dark-, light-, and medium-colored fabrics and three and a half yards for the border to make a queen-size quilt. Taking the list with her, Sarah began perusing the shelf of holiday bolts in the front of the store.

"I don't know what else to tell you, Annie," Vanessa said, her portable phone stuck against her ear as she came out of the stock room, "but if I were you I'd call the police."

Police?

Sarah set the fabric down and glanced at Vanessa. She smiled and held up a finger indicating she would be another minute.

"I know, I know," Vanessa continued, "but just to be on the safe side, I'd make a report. If it turns out to be a mistake, so what? No one would be upset if you err on the side of caution."

Sarah tried to concentrate on matching up the red ornaments pattern with a bolt of solid burgundy fabric, but Vanessa's conversation piqued her curiosity, and she found herself straining to hear every word.

"You may also want to consider putting in a better alarm system. There's a new guy in town who used to be a cop. He's supposed to be really good. He stopped by here and offered me a free estimate. You can't be too careful." Vanessa paused and then said, "Okay, let me know how it goes. Merry Christmas, Annie."

She set the phone in the base unit. "Whew. Sorry about the interruption."

"I couldn't help overhearing. I hope everything's okay."

"So do I. Annie is missing part of a shipment. It may just be a mistake, although the shipping company is denying it. She's out quite a few bucks."

"How awful for her," Sarah said. She rarely shopped at the Crystal Unicorn, Annie's New Age shop, but she had met Annie a few times.

"Unfortunately, with so many customers at this time of year, shoplifters aren't as easy to spot. In truth, Wild Goose Chase doesn't attract that kind of crowd. I don't have many items easy to conceal, at least not valuable ones. It's not like someone can just stuff a bolt of fabric under their coat."

"I suppose someone would have to be pretty desperate to steal a pack of pins or a roll of binding," Sarah agreed.

"Exactly. Shoplifters are rare in here, but I do worry about someone breaking in looking for cash."

Vanessa glanced at the paper clutched in Sarah's hand. "Oh, you found the flyer about the mystery quilt. Doesn't it look like fun?"

"It does," Sarah agreed. "Do you know who put it together?"

"No clue. The flyers showed up on my doorstep. It's a mystery all around." Vanessa grinned. "I did check out the Web site. It's a daily blog. It started on December fifth, but you won't have trouble catching up, that is, if you're going to do it. The quilt instructions so far look pretty basic."

"I think it'll be fun. I don't have any restoration projects at the moment, and I'd like to keep busy this season."

Vanessa nodded with understanding. Sarah's father had passed away a few months ago, and a shadow seemed to hang over the holiday season. But Sarah was determined to make the best of the situation for her children's and grandchildren's sake. William would've wanted it that way. She thanked God every day that her son Jason and his family had moved back to Maple Hill. And that she had good friends like Martha and Vanessa.

Vanessa picked up another flyer. "Well, let me see. Will you need more fabric? Or do you have enough at home?"

Sarah smiled. "I have some, but I think I'm going to splurge since it will be a Christmas present for Martha."

They spent a lovely ten minutes chatting about holiday plans as Vanessa measured and cut the fabrics Sarah had picked out for the quilt and Maggie's pillows.

"Is Jenna coming home for Christmas?" Vanessa asked.

"Not this year," Sarah said with regret. "But we *do* have family coming in. Maggie's folks are arriving today."

"What fun. The girls must be thrilled to see their grandparents. They're from California?"

"Los Angeles."

"I knew it was someplace warmer than here." Vanessa rubbed her arms and shivered. "Hope they know what to expect."

"Maggie reminded them to bring heavy coats and snow gear." She glanced out the frosty window again. The local meteorologist had predicted a northern cold front would arrive this afternoon.

"Wish they could bring some of that California sunshine with them," Vanessa said. "Did you hear that with the wind chill the temperature is supposed to drop below zero tonight? I just hope we don't lose power. I put in an order with the Barclay brothers for another cord of firewood just in case."

"Barclay? As in Tim Barclay who works at the courthouse?" Sarah had met the bored young man in the Register of Deeds office and found him generally unhelpful when she was seeking information.

"No, I think one of them said his name was Peter or Paul."

"Might have been Paul. That's Tim's cousin." Paul worked at the Chamber of Commerce and was about as helpful as his cousin Tim.

"Anyway, there were two of them. One looked about high school age. They came by in a pickup loaded with wood and are offering the best price in the area if you need more." Vanessa named a sum.

"That does sound reasonable. I'll have to let Jason know too." Although Sarah's son and Maggie had spent lots of time and money remodeling and updating their old Victorian, the house could still be drafty in the winter. Utilizing the fireplaces helped to cut down on the utility costs.

The phone rang, and Vanessa made a face. "Excuse me again. I'm sorry."

"That's okay. It'll give me time to decide between these fabrics." Sarah ran her hand over the two prints. Tiny holly berries splayed over a rich green background on one. The other consisted of a poinsettia pattern. Both had the shades of red that would go great with the cranberry solid she had picked out.

Sarah decided on the holly pattern as Vanessa rattled off some stock numbers from a clipboard. Sarah returned the other bolt to the rack. Vanessa sent her another apologetic smile. As Sarah waited she thought about the first time she had met Maggie's parents. Because of the distance, Sarah hadn't had a chance to meet the Robertses until the wedding rehearsal dinner after Gerry and she had flown out to California.

Lawrence, whom everyone called Larry, had got on famously with Gerry. The two of them had found a mutual interest in fishing. Larry had offered to take Gerry deep-sea fishing on a boat he kept in Newport Beach. Unfortunately they had planned to stay only for the weekend and there was no time for the ocean. Gerry had accounting work piling up at home.

Patricia, "Patty," on the other hand, had been cordial but cool toward Sarah. Sarah had attributed it to nerves before the big event. After all, the mother of the bride carried tremendous responsibility. Sarah had offered to help in the months prior to the wedding, but Patty had insisted everything was under control. Gerry had paid for the rehearsal dinner as is customary, but when that event was over,

Sarah had felt like a distant acquaintance at her own son's wedding.

Vanessa returned. "Just had to check on a stock order." She glanced at the cutting table. "So, you decided on the holly berries? That's one of my favorite Christmas patterns."

As Vanessa cut the specified number of yards and bundled up Sarah's purchase, the door opened and a woman entered with a gush of frigid air. She wore a brown wool overcoat and a green hunter's cap crammed over long, curly brunette hair shot with grey. She stomped her black boots on the floor mat. "Helping Hands Services," she called.

"Come on in, Kathleen. With the wind being so strong, I thought the bin might blow over," Vanessa said, referring to a tall, narrow plastic box near the door. "I moved it inside until the storm passes." Helping Hands was printed on the side with an invitation to give goods to the needy. Some of the merchants, like Vanessa, had posted signs advertising that they would match their customers' merchandise donations from their stores. Sarah had seen similar bins on stoops outside stores and public buildings throughout downtown.

"Thanks. I wish others were as thoughtful," Kathleen said. "At my last stop, some idiot knocked the bin out from under the porch awning and water dripped over the donations. Ruined several packages of cookies and some books. Such a waste, especially with people being so stingy these days."

"Are donations down?" Sarah asked, trying to think of some things she could give. The Helping Hands charity had started in Maple Hill five years before. It collected items and distributed them to needy families who were referred to its center. "More so than usual." Kathleen reached into the bin and lifted out several pairs of scissors, a packet of needles, and three skeins of blue yarn. "There's really something wrong with a society where some have so much and others so little, especially at Christmas. This is America. No one should go without basic needs. We have to—"

"Do you have time for a cup of tea?" Vanessa interrupted. "It's so cold out. You must be freezing."

"Thanks, but no. Running behind, and I'm trying to beat the storm. Roads will get nasty. I'll be back later this week."

Vanessa stared at the items in Katherine's hands. "Oh, wait a second. I owe you another skein of yarn." She darted toward the rear of the store.

"And I need another pair of appliqué scissors." Kathleen held up a pair of expensive silver curved scissors that Sarah had been thinking of buying for herself someday.

Kathleen extracted a large plastic bag from her coat pocket and stuffed the donations into it. She glanced at the fabric Sarah was holding. "Pretty. Making Christmas gifts?"

"Yes. Some pillows and a quilt." Sarah smiled. "Do you sew?"

Kathleen laughed. "No, although my aunt tried desperately to teach me to quilt long ago. I'm all thumbs and don't have a creative bone in my body. I'm more suited for handing out blankets than making them."

Vanessa returned with the items. "I don't remember selling any of the appliqué scissors recently."

"Do you want them back?" Kathleen dipped her hand into the bag.

"No, no, I'll donate them. I just need to make a note if I didn't record the scissors earlier. The scissors are easy to mix up."

"Well, thanks either way." Kathleen threw the bag over her shoulder and stomped out the door. "Call if the bin gets full. Ha!"

Vanessa shook her head and gave Sarah a wry smile. "I hope I didn't sound too rude when I interrupted her. Once Kathleen gets going on her causes, it's hard to get a word in edgewise."

"She seems...zealous."

"She's that." Vanessa gave a little laugh. "I suppose that's a great quality for someone working in charity. You should hear her stories sometime. She was very politically active in her time. Protests. Sit-ins. Even now I can imagine her leading a march on Washington, DC."

Sarah smiled. "She must find Maple Hill rather boring." Sarah loved that her small hometown was generally peaceful and the citizens friendly. With more people moving to the area, she just hoped it stayed that way.

The door opened and two women rushed in. "It's starting to really come down," one said, brushing snowflakes off her coat.

"I better get going." Sarah handed Vanessa her debit card. "Maggie's expecting me over at the store. Thanks for the help."

"Let me know how the mystery quilt turns out," Vanessa said before turning to assist the other two women. Sarah tugged open the shop door and the wind nearly blew it out of her hand. She had to grip it hard to keep the door from slamming against the wall.

The Helping Hands truck idled at the curb. Kathleen came down the sidewalk, plastic bags in each hand. Sarah gave her a little wave and ducked her head as she hurried to her silver Grand Prix. She jumped inside and fired up the engine. Her breath fogged the windshield. She flipped the heat to high, although the air coming out of the vents was still cold.

The streets were beginning to ice some. She hoped Maggie's parents were getting close to Maple Hill. Maggie said her parents would stop by the store if they got there early enough. Sarah had offered to pop in to see if Maggie needed help with afternoon customers. Her daughter-in-law's store had grown in popularity over the last year thanks to Maggie's excellent eye for antiques.

Snowflakes swirled in the wind, and Sarah braked gently as she approached the town square. Tiny colored lights adorned most of the shop windows. Wide swaths of red holiday ribbon wound around the lampposts, which were hung with giant glittery snowflakes. Despite the cold snap, holiday shoppers were in evidence as they scurried down the sidewalks from one shop to the next in the quaint downtown.

A police car idled by the sidewalk in between the Crystal Unicorn and the Galleria, gift shops near Magpie's Antiques. A crowd filled the sidewalk and judging from the agitated expressions on several faces, something awful must've happened. Sarah slowed even more as she rolled past. She recognized several of the adults. Five teenage girls were lined up against the store window facing two uniformed policeman, obviously being questioned.

Sarah gasped and slammed on the brakes. Two of the frightened-looking girls were her granddaughters.

"Grandma!" Amy called as Sarah hurried up the sidewalk at the same time Audrey cried, "Mom."

Maggie was pushing her way through the small crowd from the opposite direction. "What's going on? Are you all right?" Maggie asked. The wind whipped her auburn hair around her face. She was coatless, having just run out of her shop as Sarah was parking her car.

There were three other girls huddled close to Amy and Audrey. One of them was Martha's granddaughter Lexie. The other two, Zoe and Claire, were schoolmates of Audrey and Amy.

Audrey swiped her glove across her pink nose. "They think we stole something." Her voice quavered.

"Stole something?" Maggie's voice rose to a squeaky pitch.

"Ma'am, would you please step to the side until we finish our questions," one of the officers said. Sarah didn't recognize the short, balding man, but the way he paced back and forth in front of the girls reminded her of a bantam rooster her grandmother used to own. The bird would puff out his chest and strut about establishing his rule over the hens.

Maggie wrapped her arms around her daughters' shoulders, her green eyes glaring at the balding policeman. "I will not. My husband's a lawyer and I know you can't question a minor without a parent present."

The policeman sighed noisily. "They're not charged with anything. Yet. We're just gathering information, Ms..."

"Mrs. Hart. Margaret Hart. Audrey and Amy are my daughters. I know these other girls as well, and I can vouch for them. They're all good kids. I'm sure this must be some kind of mistake."

Sarah pressed in closer to Amy and recognized the face of the taller policeman. "Officer Hopkins?"

"Mrs. Hart." The worried wrinkles in his forehead smoothed when he smiled at her. "Thank you for the Christmas cookies you dropped off at the station. They were delicious."

"I'm glad you liked them. I'll be baking more this week with my granddaughters here," Sarah said. "I'll bring more by. Is there something I can do to help right now?"

"Well—"

The other policeman cleared his throat. "Officer Hopkins."

Hopkins jerked to attention. "Sorry, Chief. This is Mrs. Sarah Hart."

He raised his eyebrows. "Another Hart?"

"I'm Audrey and Amy's grandmother. And you are?" Sarah asked.

"Chief Halliday."

"Chief Halliday is filling in for Chief Webber while he's on vacation. It's only for a couple weeks. He's from Pittsfield," Hopkins explained, earning another glare from his superior. The officer closed his mouth and stepped back.

"Nice to meet you, Chief Halliday. Welcome to Maple Hill." Sarah shot him a friendly smile, but the stern-looking policeman didn't reciprocate. "What's happened here?"

"There have been two reports of theft today. And from what I gather, these girls have been in both stores."

"So...someone other than Annie was hit?"

"Annie?" Halliday asked.

"I think she means Annie Harper at the Crystal Unicorn gift store," Officer Hopkins said.

"That New Age place?" The chief jerked his chin in the direction of the store.

"Yes, that's it," Sarah interrupted, growing annoyed at the officers for carrying on a conversation as if she weren't standing there. "I'd heard some of her items were missing, I just assumed that's what you were referring too."

Chief Halliday glared at Officer Hopkins. "Is there a report?"

Hopkins shrugged. "First I've heard of it."

"Maybe she found whatever was missing," Sarah said. She spotted C. J. Wyatt, the owner of the Galleria. A rangy stranger dressed in faded jeans and army drab jacket murmured something to C.J. His hands were stuffed in his jacket pockets and he had a confident, almost insolent, expression as his pale blue eyes returned Sarah's gaze.

"We were just looking," Lexie spoke up.

Zoe nodded vigorously in agreement. "We didn't do anything."

"Or take anything," Amy added, clutching Sarah's arm. "Look in our stuff if you want." She proffered her one shopping bag.

The stranger stepped forward, ignoring the bag. "You look like smart girls. You could've stashed or dropped the merchandise someplace. Statistically this is the age group that starts to—"

Maggie turned to him, her face flushing red. "Excuse me. I don't care about statistics. If these girls say they didn't steal, then that's the truth."

"They were with a group of kids that came in my store twice today," C.J. said. "When there are that many, I can't keep an eye on all of them. Who knows what they were up to?"

"I'll need the names of the other kids," Halliday said.

Lexie and Audrey exchanged anguished glances as Officer Hopkins produced a small notebook and wrote the names of four other girls the reluctant teens gave him. A tear rolled down Claire's face and Audrey turned her face into Maggie's sweater. Maggie hugged her close.

"They're going to hate us for ratting on them," Amy whispered to Sarah.

"Honey, they'll understand."

The stranger cleared his throat. "I have a solution—other than what I think would be best, a good security system—that might be worth pursuing—" "Who is this?" Halliday asked Hopkins.

"Gordon Leftfoot. Retired Boston PD," the man said. To Sarah, he looked much too young to be retired. His mussed blond hair led Sarah to estimate he was only in his midthirties.

Chief Halliday ignored Gordon's extended hand. "Leftfoot, Leftfoot. Why does that name sound familiar?"

Officer Hopkins leaned close and whispered something to the chief.

The frown slipped from Halliday's face. "Oh yes, Officer Leftfoot. I remember now. I've heard great things about you. What brings you to Maple Hill?"

"I'm opening a security firm. As you can see, there's a huge need here. Things are subpar in this town safetywise. People leaving their homes and cars unlocked. Purses left unattended in shopping carts. Children and teenagers roaming stores unsupervised. Statistically, youth ages thirteen to seventeen are the second most likely group to shoplift. I have some ideas that may make this town safer."

"Such as?"

"I suggest that a strict curfew be imposed and that children under the age of eighteen not be allowed in stores without a chaperone. I was thinking of proposing this safety measure at the next town council meeting."

Halliday stroked his chin. "Good idea. I've seen it done in other places, particularly malls."

"Are we finished here?" Maggie asked loudly. "You have our information and know where to find us. I want to get these girls out of the cold."

Halliday glanced at her and grunted, "Go."

"Your mom's here, Lexie," Sarah said as Christine Maplethorpe arrived and took charge of the other three girls. Sarah turned and headed toward Maggie's store.

The chimes on the door jingled as they hurried inside. The shop sign had been flipped to "Closed." "I ran out of here so fast, I forgot to lock the door. Talk about shoplifting. Anyone could have walked in here and helped themselves," Maggie said with an almost hysterical laugh. Her hand trembled as she ran it through her wet hair. "I'm going to go heat up some water for cocoa and tea."

"I can get it, Maggie, if you want to change. Your sweater is soaked." The snowflakes that had dotted Maggie's black sweater had turned to sparkling droplets and then dark wet stains.

Maggie looked down. "I hardly noticed. Must be all the adrenaline. I have another shirt in the back. I can change while the water heats. Do you mind keeping an eye on things out there for few minutes?"

"Not at all," Sarah said, helping Audrey yank off her pink parka. Amy shed her blue coat and unwound the white scarf from her neck.

"I left the "Closed" sign up but if anyone comes to the door, you can let them in," Maggie called.

"We got it, Mom." Audrey plopped on the sofa in the cozy sitting area Maggie had created for customers in the back of the store. It was Sarah's favorite spot when visiting the store during the Christmas season. Maggie had decorated a small tree and set fragrant cinnamon-apple candles on the end tables between the comfortable couches and chairs. On a nearby cherry wood table, cookies adorned pretty china platters and a pot of Christmas tea simmered over a warmer. Cocoa and coffee were also available. Customers tended to linger in the friendly atmosphere and consequently bought more antiques.

Sarah swiped a dry mop over the wet footprint trail from the door. The store seemed extraquiet without Jordan, Maggie's part-time assistant, but Jordan had begged for two weeks off during the holidays to go to a family reunion. Normally Christmas was Maggie's busiest time. She had talked about hiring temporary help, but Maggie's mother insisted that she wanted to work every day with Maggie in the shop while they were visiting. Quality mother-daughter time, as Maggie had repeated to Sarah.

"It's not fair." Audrey pulled off her cap in a dramatic sweep, and her long blonde hair flew up in a bright halo. "Why should we be punished for something we didn't do? It could've been an adult who snitched those things. Why blame us just because we're teenagers?"

"I agree. Age shouldn't be a factor, but, unfortunately, Chief Halliday may have heard about last Christmas' incident," Sarah said referring to when two of the twins' friends had been caught shoplifting.

"That wasn't even here. That was at the Pittsfield Mall. Ashley and Megan never did it again," Audrey said. "Just when Mom finally lets us go shopping by ourselves, that dumb policeman ruins it. How am I supposed to get presents for Mom and Dad? I feel like such a dork when they have to take me. I'm *thirteen*."

Sarah smothered a smile. "I can take you Christmas shopping, sweetheart, but let's hope things will simmer down soon."

"Maybe you can find out who's stealing stuff," Amy said, her blue eyes sparkling. She seemed to have rebounded faster from their encounter with the police and she shared Sarah's penchant for sniffing out mysteries.

"I'm sure it won't have to come to that. The police will probably catch them soon." Or maybe the ex-cop security expert would. Gordon Leftfoot seemed determined.

"But what if it takes too long? If you find out who did it, then maybe they won't impose the curfew before Christmas," Audrey said.

"You have a good point," Sarah said. "I can't promise it'll do any good, but I'll see what I can find out."

"Here we go," Maggie said, coming out of the back room with a tray of Christmas mugs and placing it on the table she had set up with cookies for customers.

She had combed her hair and traded her damp sweater for an oversize plaid flannel shirt she kept around for working on the furniture.

Amy and Audrey grabbed a couple of sugar cookies and their cocoa and settled down on the couch. Audrey animatedly spoke into her cell phone, no doubt commiserating with one of her many friends. Amy pulled a YA paperback out from under the couch, where she kept a stash in case she hung out at the store after school.

Maggie flipped the door sign back over to "Open" and smiled at Sarah. "I feel better now. My heart about stopped when I saw the police car out front and Amy and Audrey standing there. At first I thought they'd been in an accident."

"Took me by surprise too. I was driving past and almost slid into a mailbox."

They both gazed out the window. A car passed, its headlights reflecting the thickening curtain of snow and tires throwing slush. Maggie glanced at her watch and frowned. "It's already after four."

"What time did your parents leave the Boston airport?"

"Ten. They wanted to sightsee along the way, but they said they'd be here in time for dinner."

"If you want to go home to get ready for them, I can hang around until six and close up the shop. If someone asks something I can't answer, I can always call."

Maggie hesitated. "I appreciate the offer, but you know what? With the weather changing, I doubt there'll be that many more customers out this evening. The sidewalk is practically empty now. I think I'll close an hour early. In fact, if there are some things you need to do, I'll be fine here with the girls until five."

"Is there anything you need for dinner?" Sarah asked. "I need to run by the market anyway."

Maggie thought for a moment. "I could use some fresh mushrooms and cilantro for the salad. I can get by without them if it's too much bother."

"No bother at all," Sarah said, although she anticipated the market would be crammed with people buying milk and bread as they usually did when a big storm approached. "I'll be over at your place by six then."

Sarah wound her powder blue scarf tighter around her neck. She had parked across the street in her haste to get to the girls, and her car was rapidly becoming a snowy bump in the landscape. She stepped off the curb and glanced up the dusky street. The cop car had departed. Lights shone from the Galleria's window, creating bright squares on the whitening sidewalk.

She hopped back on the curb. She would drop by the market before heading home, but first she had another stop to make.

# CHAPTER TWO

Sarah pushed open the door to the Galleria. A couple of customers wandered about the store that featured paintings, framed scenic photographs, and sculptures made from a variety of colored glass, metal, and wood. C. J. Wyatt stood behind a counter near the front of the store talking with Gordon Leftfoot.

"If you place a video camera there," Gordon pointed to the wall behind the counter, "it'll cover the area from the cash register to the front door. Another camera in the back corner will cover the rest."

"So I need two cameras?" C.J. asked with a frown. "Won't that be expensive?"

"Another option would be one camera that rotates and sweeps the store, but in that case it might miss someone pocketing items."

C.J. sighed. "I just don't know..."

"Meanwhile I'd suggest keeping your smaller merchandise, anything that can be easily pocketed, behind the counter and away from the entrance."

"That I can do." C.J. nodded and leaned over to look around Gordon. "Hi, Sarah. I'll be with you in a minute."

"Take your time," Sarah said, hoping to get a couple of minutes alone with C.J. to discuss the shoplifting. She wandered toward the back and studied a wood carving of a bear and two cubs. She recognized the artist as local. She wondered if Liam might like one of the sculptures for Christmas. She wasn't sure if it would fit his style. She would have to think about it. Art was such a personal taste.

Liam's store was filled with spotted dogs, including a live one, a delightful black-and-white corgi, Murphy. However, much to Liam's consternation, the dog had suddenly taken to chewing things lately, including boots, a wood cane, and Liam's wool hat and scarf. Luckily he hadn't snacked on any books or customers' shoes yet or he would be banished to home. She wondered if the situation had improved. Liam had made an appointment to take Murphy to the vet to see if there was anything seriously wrong.

"I can bring you estimates tomorrow and outline the different options," Gordon said as he wrote in a leather-bound notebook.

"Well, I suppose that'd be helpful," C.J. said. "I'm still not sure what I want to do. I already have a security system."

"Which works fine for intruders after hours, but as demonstrated today, it doesn't guard against shoplifting. You could tag your items with electronic strips or buttons that will trigger an alarm at the door. Of course that option can be costly and more labor-intensive." C.J. rubbed the back of his neck. "Okay, write up an estimate with the video cameras."

Gordon smiled. "Good choice. Do you mind if I poke around the store some more? I want to see where your electrical lines run, which would make a difference in the cost of installation."

"Go right ahead," C.J. said, distracted as an elderly gentleman with a cane entered and stomped snow off his boots on the mat.

Gordon pulled out a tape measure and limped to the back wall.

C.J. joined Sarah by the bear cubs. "I'm sorry your granddaughters got involved in the mess this afternoon."

"Thanks, C.J. What exactly happened?"

"I'm not sure." C.J. sighed, glancing at Gordon again. "Unfortunately, I wasn't paying as much attention as I should have. Customers have been coming in all day."

He pointed at a sign in the window. "I've been advertising free standard shipping until tomorrow. People were trying to beat the storm, and I was stuck behind the counter processing orders."

"The tour buses probably pulled out early then too," Sarah said, referring to the companies that transported people around New England to the numerous small towns touting antiques and Americana merchandise. Maggie had managed to get on their list of stops, which had resulted in a great increase in the store's revenue.

"Yep. Everyone was in a rush. I suppose the thief might've been someone from the bus. Anyway, the group of girls came in earlier today which was unusual since I don't sell merchandise that attracts that age group."

"Unless they're shopping for Christmas gifts," Sarah pointed out.

"Well...yes. There's that," C.J. conceded. "But when the police asked if anybody unusual had been in, I saw the girls passing by the window and mentioned they'd been in here earlier. They were quick to question them."

"What was taken, if you don't mind my asking?"

"Some of those crystal angels on the tree by the door. They're worth about forty-five apiece. I estimate maybe six are missing."

"Which, again, is why they should be moved away from the door until we get a better security system in," Gordon said, walking past them to another wall with his tape measure and notebook.

"Right." C.J. grimaced. "And I'm not the only one caught unprepared. An electronics store and a drugstore got burglarized a couple of weeks ago."

"Sir, could you give me the price of this painting?" the elderly gentleman with the cane asked.

"Excuse me for a moment," C.J. said to Sarah and hurried over to assist the gentleman.

Sarah looked over her shoulder. Gordon was watching her. She returned Gordon's speculative gaze and joined him by the wall.

"You're Sarah Hart, the twins' grandmother—Amy and Audrey," Gordon said. "Their mother owns the store next door."

"That's right." He either had a detective's memory for details or he had done thorough research on potential clientele. Probably both. "And you're Gordon Leftfoot. Welcome to Maple Hill. How long have you been in town?"

"A couple of weeks," Gordon said, marking a spot on the wall with a pencil.

"How do you like it? You mentioned you're retired from Boston. This small town must seem quiet compared to the city."

He shrugged. "It's big enough to need a good security firm. Nice to meet you." He stuck his pencil in his back pocket. "C.J., I'm finished. I'll be back in the morning with your estimate."

Gordon retrieved his jacket and went out the door, his limp becoming more pronounced when he hit the icy sidewalk.

Was the limp the reason he wasn't on the police force anymore? Sarah glanced at her watch and then out of the window as Gordon Leftfoot climbed into a black Wrangler Jeep. The snow continued to come down in thick swirls.

Maggie's parents were due any time. She had better get over to the market. She waved to C.J. and headed out into the storm. Her boots slipped some as she hurried across the street to her car.

Chances were a stranger from one of the tourist buses had taken the angels. Here and gone. There would be no way to track them now if that was true. But what about Annie's loss of supplies and the other thefts C.J. had mentioned? A rash of thefts might indicate the thief was someone local. For Audrey's and Amy's sake, she would do some more investigating.

"Dinner's ready. Let's go ahead and eat." Maggie breezed into the kitchen where Sarah was cutting a chocolate sheet cake into portions.

"But we can't." Audrey looked up from the kitchen table where she had listlessly been drawing on a sketch pad. She set down her pencil. "Grandma and Grandpa aren't here yet."

Maggie lifted a slim shoulder in a half shrug. "It's after seven, and if we wait any longer the lasagna will turn into rubber. Don't worry, sweetheart. We can save them leftovers. And who knows, they might still get here in the next couple of minutes. Go tell Amy and Dad that we're ready. I think Amy's still watching the game in the parlor. I'm just going to slide the garlic bread under the broiler."

"Can you try calling them again?" Audrey asked.

"I just did. They must be in an area where there's no service. Now go on and wash up. We'll all feel better if we eat something."

Audrey slowly slid out of her chair and after she left the room, Sarah said, "I hope the weather isn't giving them problems."

Maggie shoved the baking sheet with the bread onto the top rack in the oven. "The news said the highways are still clear. They probably got distracted on the way and forgot the time. My parents tend to be … free-spirited."

"Is that what they're calling it these days? I'll remember that the next time *I'm* late and forget to call," Jason said, coming in the door with firewood tucked under his arm. He grabbed Maggie with his free hand and swung her against him, planting a kiss on the top of her head.

"Eek, you're so cold." She playfully pushed him away. "Go on. You're getting bark all over the floor. Besides, it's time to eat."

"Good. If we wait much longer I might be tempted to start gnawing on one of these logs." Jason grinned at Sarah and strode out the door toward the parlor where a fire blazed in the fireplace.

Sarah grabbed the bowl of salad and took it to the dining room. A set of china with a red holiday pattern that Maggie had found at an estate sale brightened the table. Amy and Audrey had made a banner that read "Welcome Grammy and Grandpa" and hung it on the wall.

Jason lit the pine green candles and the candlelight reflected off the crystal goblets. "You did a great job setting the table, Amy," he said as the teen entered the room.

"Thanks." She gave him a small smile that didn't reach her blue eyes. She glanced at their welcome banner before settling in her chair. Audrey joined them, a pout on her pretty face.

Sarah sighed inwardly. Where were the Robertses?

"Bread is done. I think that's everything." Maggie set down a basket and the scent of garlic wafted over the table.

Jason offered a blessing for the food and the safe arrival of Maggie's parents.

Silence stretched as they passed around the salad. Amy dug into her food, but Audrey merely stabbed at the lasagna with her fork.

"We can celebrate that it's Christmas vacation, well...at least for two-fifths of us at this table," Maggie said. "I realize it's getting off to a rocky start, but we have two weeks to make up for it."

"Zoe's mom grounded her from hanging with us, unless we have a grown-up watching us." Amy made a face. "She said where there's smoke there might be fire. I don't get it."

Jason scooped salad on his plate. "Guilt by association."

"But we didn't do anything!" Audrey dropped her fork on her plate with a clatter and Maggie shot her a warning look.

"I'll talk to Zoe's mother," Maggie said. "Maybe Zoe can come over here to play on the weekend when we're home."

Audrey scowled. "It's still not fair. I want to go shopping."

Jason reached for the salad dressing. "You know it isn't uncommon for stores to make such policies, especially during the holidays. If someone asked me if the rule seemed prudent, I'd tend to agree."

"Dad!" Audrey said.

"My point is that it's better for you if there's an adult around for your safety and reputation."

"But seventy-five percent of all shoplifters are adults," Amy said. "I looked it up online."

"I'm not saying it's fair, but right now it's the cautious thing to do. I advise it as your lawyer and your dad."

Audrey rolled her eyes.

"What about the other girls?" Sarah asked. "Have you heard from them? Have their parents said anything?"

Amy shrugged. "Don't know. Zoe's the only one who texted."

"How am I supposed to get ready for Christmas now?" Audrey asked. "It's going to be so boring if we can't go out with our friends."

Jason and Maggie exchanged an amused look. Nothing much had changed from the previous year other than that the girls had turned thirteen and been granted a little freedom.

"You'll have time for the stores. I'm sure Grammy and Grandpa will want to take you shopping as well as sightseeing," Maggie said.

"And there are others things to do with your friends besides hanging out in the stores," Jason said.

"And don't forget we have the church party and caroling," Maggie added. "You'll be so busy that time will fly by. Christmas is only eleven days away."

Maggie turned to Sarah before the girls could protest further. "Are you still helping with the home tour this year?"

"Actually, Rosemary Walsh stepped up and volunteered to run it. Martha is still on the committee but mostly as a consultant." Sarah's, Martha's, and Maggie's homes had all been on the home tour last year. It had been a hectic time but fun, and they all agreed they would do it again. However, the committee liked to feature different historical houses each year if possible, and this Christmas enough other families had volunteered that the Hart and Maplethorpe families were off the hook.

"I'm helping at the first home with raffle tickets," Maggie said. "I tried to get out of it, but they're shorthanded and it *is* a good cause. The money raised for the raffle baskets goes to the Needy Children Fund."

"And it doesn't hurt that it'll be an advertisement since you stuffed those baskets full of stuff from the store," Jason quipped.

"That's not why I'm doing it!"

"I know." Jason grinned at his wife. "But like I said, it doesn't hurt."

"I'll be happy to help out at the store if you want to spend more time with your parents," Sarah said.

"Thanks. I'll call if I do. My mom's been dying to get involved in the store ever since we opened."

"Is she into antiques?" Sarah asked, remembering the Roberts home as being quite modern.

"Not really, but she loves decorating. They've been talking about moving into a smaller place closer to the beach. My dad is more the history buff. I take after him in that respect."

After dinner, Jason helped clear the table, letting the girls go wait in the parlor for their grandparents while Sarah and Maggie filled the dishwasher. As Maggie was packing the last leftover into a container, Audrey called, "They're here!"

A sound of laughter and squealing arose from the front hall. Maggie tossed down her dishrag and dashed to the entryway.

"Maggie, sweetie!" The petite, short-haired woman turned from the twins and hugged her daughter. "You look wonderful, although a bit pale. I suppose that's to be expected now that you're out of the California sunshine."

Patty stepped back. "Sarah, how nice to see you again."

"Likewise. I hope you had a good trip," Sarah said with a smile.

Jason had gone out the door to help Larry bring in the luggage and a deep voice boomed from the doorway, "Where are my grandchildren? Surely these beautiful young women can't be Audrey and Amy."

"Oh, Grandpa!" Audrey threw her arms around a tall man with a soft middle.

"And which one are you?" he asked.

"Audrey!"

"Should have known." He eyed Amy's green jersey. "Celtics fan? You haven't changed loyalty, have you, Amy?" he asked with mock astonishment.

"I still like the Lakers," Amy said quietly as Larry gave her a hug.

"Now, Larry, leave the poor girl be," Patty said. "Of course she's going to cheer for a Boston team. She wants to fit in here after all."

Maggie's eyes sparkled. "Mom, Dad, are you hungry? We have lasagna in the fridge."

"Oh, sweetie, when we saw how late it was we stopped at this quaint little restaurant near Amherst. Did I tell you that your father and I have gone vegetarian, and we try to eat only organically grown fruits and vegetables?"

"No, you didn't," Maggie said faintly.

"Anyway, we were in Amherst because there were a couple of caches we wanted to find," Larry added.

"Caches?" Maggie asked, looking even more bewildered.

"Yes, we were geocaching."

"What's geocaching?" Jason asked, bringing in another suitcase from outside.

"It's GPS treasure hunting," Sarah said, as Maggie shooed everyone into the parlor by the fire.

Amy stared at Sarah. "How'd you know that?"

"I read about it in a magazine," Sarah said. "Apparently thousands of people are into it."

"We discovered it about a year ago," Larry said, "although geocaching has been around for a long time. People hide things and then put the location coordinates online with clues." He pulled a gadget that looked like a walkie-talkie from his pocket. "You plug the coordinates into the GPS and it'll lead you to the spot."

"Awesome," Audrey held up her hand. "Can I see it?"

Larry gave her the unit. "Sometimes the treasures, or geocaches as they're called, are easy to find, but sometimes they're hidden so you have to use the clues."

"I even brought a travel bug from California." Patty gave her coat to Maggie.

"A *bug*?" Audrey's voice rose. "Eww."

Patty laughed and pulled a small toy dump truck from her purse. "It's not a bug really. It's an object that people stash in geocaches to see how far they travel. People log onto the Web site and record where they found it. I know of one that went around the world three times. It took several years. And there was another one that went to Hawaii five times with five different people."

"Hawaii would be heaven right now," Larry said, gazing at the frosty window. "We'll all have to take a vacation there someday."

"That'd be so cool. I wanna learn to surf," Amy said.

"Well if you come to visit us in California next summer, you can learn there too." Patty shot a glance at Maggie. "In fact, I'd love it if you could come out for the whole summer sometime. I was hoping you could visit last summer but..." She gave a little shrug as she sat on the couch.

"We talked about it," Maggie said, her voice starting to have a strained note in it.

Jason clasped his hand over Maggie's. "I wish we could've too. It's just been so hectic trying to set up two businesses. Maybe next summer."

"Oh, I have a big surprise for you, Maggie," Patty said, her eyes shining, "but we'll talk about it later."

Audrey looked up from the GPS she was holding. "Can we go geocaching while you're here?"

"Of course. In fact, there are several geocaches right around Maple Hill. I think we should all go."

"Sounds like fun," Jason said.

Larry reached into one of the suitcases and extracted some boxes. "I brought you all a GPS."

"Cool," Amy said, sitting cross-legged in front of the fire and opening the box.

Larry glanced at Sarah. "I'm sorry. I'm afraid I only brought four."

"We didn't think you'd be interested in tramping around town and through the woods. A lot of people your ... I mean *our* age aren't," Patty said.

"Sure she would." Amy shot Sarah a grin. "Grandma loves mysteries."

Patty raised her eyebrows. "Oh, really?"

"Don't worry, Grandma," Audrey said holding up the little device. "I'll share with you."

"I can get another one. No problem," Larry interjected.

"Oh, that's quite all right," Sarah said. "I don't mind just watching."

Larry smiled. "Actually we need only one GPS per group going out. I just got extras for fun."

The topic turned back to California and Maggie's friends and how much they missed Maggie and Jason. "Caroline asked if you'd grown tired enough of the cold to come back," Patty said to Maggie with a titter. Maggie's smile seemed forced in return.

Sarah shifted in her seat and tried to ignore the underlying pool of tension that had seeped into the room. She typically avoided family arguments and wanted everyone to be happy and relaxed this Christmas. The girls had been so excited about their grandparents coming. They had made that lovely banner and planned a wonderful welcome dinner. So what if Patty and Larry had kept them all waiting while they played a game? They seemed carefree and fun-loving, and now the girls were excited about geocaching.

She glanced at Maggie's tight-lipped expression. Surely Patty didn't mean to make Maggie feel bad about not visiting more. She was probably just speaking without thinking. Poor Patty. It was understandable that a mother would want her children close. Sarah missed Jenna every day. Texas was just too far away.

Jason caught her eye and winked. A smile tugged at the corners of Sarah's mouth as gratitude flowed through her. She thanked God she was blessed to have Jason and his family in Maple Hill now. She would do her best to make the visit with Maggie's parents go as smoothly as possible so they could enjoy being together. After all, their differences made life much more interesting. It was going to be a great family Christmas.

Meanwhile, she had a quilt to sew and a mystery to solve. As soon as it was polite, she would head home and get started.

## CHAPTER THREE

Sarah lined up the burgundy fabric along the grid on the cutting mat and unlocked the safety on her rotary cutter. The familiar exciting tingle she got when she started a new project tickled her spine.

She picked up the blog printout and reread Day Two on the mystery quilt. Each blog entry began with an anecdote or advice about the holidays.

*Christmas can be such a hectic time. It always helps your stress level to be organized. Plan now what you will eat, what parties and community events (that sneak up on you!) you'll attend, which Christmas programs you don't want to miss on tel@vision. Music plays an important role in this holiday. Gather together mus@c that brings Christmas into your home. Be prepared. Perhaps you need to invest in a new CD pl@yer. Before you begin cutting your strips today, go get your music organized and turn it on while you are working. Sing along and feel the spirit of Christmas come over you.*

Sarah noticed a few typos in the passage, but the instructions that followed were typo-free, and Sarah ran her rotary blade along the fabric to make a precise cut. Quilting had a calming effect on her. She loved the feel of the fabric under her fingers, and the slick sound of the blade as it first made strips, then squares, and finally triangles.

Sarah had already turned on Christmas carols. She agreed with the blogger that music was important. Carols always evoked in her a homey, cozy feeling. Gerry used to play them starting the day after Thanksgiving and all through the Christmas season. He would stack records, later tapes and CDs, in the stereo and the family would drift off to sleep to the familiar, happy tunes.

She had kept the music volume low. Danielle Park, her current boarder, was probably asleep. The door to her room upstairs had been closed when Sarah passed it earlier and all was quiet. The young Korean-American woman had just finished her last credit, student teaching at Hawthorne Middle School, for her degree in education, and was returning home to Pittsfield in the morning.

Sarah counted and stacked her red triangles and was just starting on the green strips when the kitchen phone rang.

"Hi! It's me," Martha said, although Sarah already knew from her caller ID. "Sorry I didn't pick up earlier. I turned my phone off while I was at the home tour committee meeting. When they asked me to stay on and advise the director this year, I didn't realize how much time it would involve. You'd think they'd pick a director who'd at least attended the tour last year," Martha huffed. "Anyway, did you hear about the run-in that Lexie, Audrey, and Amy had with the police?"

"I was there. That's why I was calling you, but it wasn't something I wanted to try to explain to your voice mail."

"I got some garbled story from Christine. She said that the new temporary police chief was just trying to throw his weight around. What's your take?"

"Could be. I got the impression Chief Halliday's not used to small town living. Neither is the new security specialist." She described Gordon Leftfoot to Martha and his presence in The Galleria. "But as far as the girls were concerned, none of them had the stolen merchandise on them, so for now they're in the clear."

Silence hovered on the other end of the connection and then came a "*But*?"

Sarah grinned. Her friend knew her so well. "*But* I'm still going to look into it."

"I thought you might," Martha said with a chuckle. "What do you have so far?"

"The items stolen from C.J.'s store were small crystal angels. Small enough to be easily pocketed. They were near the front door. C.J. said that an electronics store and a drugstore were hit last week. But I did learn when I was at Wild Goose Chase that part of a shipment to the Crystal Unicorn was missing."

"Well, no wonder Chief Halliday is grouchy, and Gordon Leftfoot wants to impose a chaperoning rule. For Maple Hill, this is a crime wave."

"I'm going to talk to Annie tomorrow. I need to pop in there anyway and see if I can find a Christmas gift for Maggie's parents. They're vegetarian and want only organic food."

"If anyone would have any ideas, it'd be Annie Harper," Martha agreed. "Want to meet at The Spotted Dog tomorrow morning for breakfast?"

"I'd love to, but I'm baking Christmas cookies in the morning with the girls. Maybe later in the afternoon. Like three?" Sarah said. It would give her a chance to see Liam. Sarah found herself missing him if too much time elapsed between their visits. The length of time before she missed him seemed to be shrinking too.

Sarah returned to her sewing room and straightened the stack of blog pages. She had printed out two copies of each day and planned on putting one copy in a pretty binder to give Martha. Martha would enjoy reading anecdotes and advice related to New England Christmases past and present. Some of the pages contained photographs of holiday scenes and Christmassy clip art.

She set the stack on her desk and noted some numbers and symbols at the bottom of the first page. Looked like gibberish. Was her printer acting up? She brought up the Web site again on her laptop.

No, it wasn't her printer. The numbers and symbols were at the end of the blog. Probably some technical problem since they were on each page. She supposed she could just cut a strip off the bottom before she put them in the binder. The few typos in the stories she couldn't help unless she re-typed the pages herself. Martha wouldn't mind. The quilt was the real gift.

She glanced at the clock hands approaching midnight. Time to wrap it up and get to bed. She reached for the notebook she had started with the quilt and jotted a reminder to pick up another accent color.

She tapped a pencil on the paper. Her schedule was packed tomorrow. She wanted to do some Christmas shopping. Maggie might want her help at the shop in the afternoon, and of course there was the sleuthing she had promised the girls.

She tidied the kitchen and put glasses in the dishwasher. She had left her jacket on the back of a chair and as she lifted it to put it away, Gordon Leftfoot's business card fell out of the pocket. He called himself a security specialist and listed phone numbers, an address near downtown, and a Web site.

Sarah grabbed her laptop and took it upstairs with her. After she had changed into her warm, flannel pajamas, she pulled back the quilt on her sleigh bed and settled in with her computer. She connected to her wireless Internet and tapped in the Web site for Gordon Leftfoot. A photo of Gordon in a police uniform appeared in the upper lefthand corner of the page and one of him dressed as she had seen him today in jeans and jacket was at the bottom left.

His services were listed as security analysis, system installation, and monitoring service. Five references were included. Two were local numbers, one for Ted's Electronics on the other side of town and one for a jeweler's shop. The rest had Boston area codes with names beside them, people who, she assumed, were character references.

He had a section on safety tips for the holidays, which included putting bought gifts in car trunks when shopping, locking one's vehicle, being aware of your surroundings at all times, and carrying a cell phone. Also, he suggested for peace of mind that businesses and homes consider putting in an alarm system. Gordon was offering free security evaluations for new customers and on existing systems, and providing estimates for new installations or upgrades until New Year's Day.

He also listed statistics of home and business break-ins in towns of varying sizes in Massachusetts. Although Maple Hill appeared comparably quieter than other towns of similar size, the number of break-ins was surprisingly higher than Sarah would have anticipated.

Jason had wanted her to get a security system, but with her boarders coming and going at different hours, it seemed to be more of a hassle than it was worth. She had quality locks on the doors and windows and neighbors that watched out for each other. Still, maybe the many years in her home had caused an overdeveloped sense of security.

Sarah shut down the laptop and turned off the lamp on the nightstand. The house creaked and groaned under the onslaught of the wind. She shivered and snuggled under the warm quilt, and although she knew Danielle slept only a room away, she felt suddenly very alone. As always she missed Gerry, but tonight thoughts of her father kept drifting through her mind as well.

Christmas at the Drayton house had been somewhat chaotic and bursting with fun activities and laughter. William had loved Christmas. Sarah's mother, Ruth, catered to his every whim during the holidays, baking enormous quantities of goodies and adding her special touch to decorating their old house. When Sarah and Gerry were first married, they had celebrated Christmas by alternating between their parents' households. Gradually as Jason and Jenna grew older, Gerry and Sarah developed their own special holiday traditions. Now Jason and Jenna were grown and doing the same thing.

Her thoughts turned to Maggie's upbringing in southern California. Different from Jason's, but Sarah thought Larry and Patty had done a wonderful job with Maggie. She was a good mother, a smart business woman, and a loyal, compassionate wife. When the pressures from Jason's job were risking his health, she had uprooted her family and transplanted them in Maple Hill.

That must've been upsetting for Patty and Larry, although Maggie had never said anything about it. The holidays had to be tough now. Until they moved, Jason,

Maggie, and the twins had spent holiday time with the Robertses. But anyway, Patty and Larry were here now, the family all together again, and this Christmas was going to be wonderful.

She patted her goose down pillow and turned on her side. Fatigue tugged at her, but her mind still raced. A dozen different worries flitted across her mind, ranging from the twins being accused of shoplifting to not getting the right gifts for Maggie's parents. And what was the big surprise Patty had for Maggie? She had mentioned it again later in the evening.

Jason had taken Larry and Patty on a tour of their home. He and Maggie had put a lot of work in the Victorian, but Patty hadn't seemed impressed and kept talking about the new condos she and Larry had been looking at. She did approve of the colors Maggie had chosen for the walls, though.

Larry was more interested in the remodel and offered to take over a closet expansion project Jason had been saving to do next spring. Maggie tried to dissuade him, pointing out that Larry was supposed to be on vacation, but she finally caved under her father's enthusiasm.

Oh, how Sarah wished Gerry was there with her. He would tell her she was worrying for nothing and everything would be just fine. Holidays were hard without him. And even harder this year since she didn't have her father to talk to.

A loud crack sounded outside the window. Sarah jumped, her head hitting the headboard. No doubt a branch from one of her oak trees had broken in the howling wind and under the weight of the snow.

Sarah sat up, listening. After half a minute passed with no new cracking noises, she sighed. This was ridiculous. She was no nearer sleep than she had been half an hour ago. She turned on her lamp. Her devotion book lay on the nightstand. She flipped through it until she came to a page with one of her favorite Bible texts from John 14.

*Peace I leave with you, my peace I give unto you: not as the world giveth, give I unto you. Let not your heart be troubled, neither let it be afraid.*

The words were a soothing balm. She would just have to live in the moment and tackle one problem at a time. Starting *tomorrow*. She turned out the lamp and squeezed her eyes shut. Tonight she was going to dream about her family and Christmases past.

Sarah wiped the dust off the last cookie cutter and set it on top of the box containing flour, sugar, softening butter, spices, baking powder, cookie sheets, and an extra rolling pin.

After a restless night Sarah had awoken to sunshine streaming over her bed. The world outside her window sparkled under the sun with such sharp brightness Sarah's eyes ached. She had hustled to get the baking items ready in time to take everything over to Patty and the girls. She had even rushed up to the attic and found more of her grandmother's cookie cutters.

Besides the traditional sugar cookies, she planned to make pinwheels, fruit drops, sandies, and peppermint chocolate chip.

They would make enough cookies for Maggie to give out to customers at the store and some to take over to the nursing home for the nurses and Leland, a gentleman the family had befriended since William passed away.

A thud sounded in the living room and Sarah hurried out to see Danielle dressed head-to-foot in what she called her "ultrachill" defense. Danielle had dropped a box on the floor and, with so much snow gear on, she was struggling to bend over.

"Let me get that for you." Sarah laughed and felt a pang of regret. She was going to miss the young woman's company. She set the box on the arm of the sofa and asked, "Are you all ready to go?"

"I think so. I cleaned the bathroom and vacuumed the room. The bedspread and sheets are by the washing machine."

"I appreciate it. You've been such a wonderful housemate. If you ever need a reference, just have them call me."

"I will." Danielle gave Sarah a big hug. She stepped back and picked up her box.

"You going to be okay? Do you need any help?" Sarah asked, trying to ignore the tears stinging her eyes. She knew she was sounding like an anxious mother sending her kid off to college for the first time, but she couldn't help it. She had grown fond of Danielle.

"Yeah, Spencer is going with me to help me move stuff into my apartment on the other end, so I'm all set." The town librarian, Spencer Hewitt, and Danielle had been dating, and Sarah was glad that the relationship wasn't ending with Danielle going home.

Sarah walked Danielle to the door and waved as she got in her car. She was closing the door when the phone rang. She raced back to the kitchen.

"Sarah, it's Maggie. I'm glad I caught you before you left. I'm sorry for the late notice, but my parents decided to take the girls out to a late breakfast and then they got involved with geocaching. They ended up halfway to Pittsfield and decided to go there to do some shopping. I would've called you sooner, but I didn't know until a few minutes ago."

Sarah glanced at the box full of baking items. "It's okay, Maggie. No harm done. I'm sure they're having a great time."

"If you're not busy, I think the girls would like to bake cookies this afternoon. My mom wants to help me in the store today, and Dad plans to finish knocking out that wall for the closet."

"I'll be happy to come over in the afternoon. I'll run some errands this morning."

"That would be great. Thanks for understanding," Maggie said, relief in her voice. Door chimes rang in the distance. "Gotta run. Customers."

Sarah put the butter back in the refrigerator. Everything else would keep in the box until the afternoon.

She wiped her hands. Now what? The house seemed des-
olate with Danielle gone, although Sarah knew it was just
psychological. Danielle had hardly ever made noise while
she was living there. Sarah assured herself she was just tired
from tossing and turning last night.

She felt an urge to pop in at the nursing home. Leland
Montgomery Mercer II had been friends with Sarah's father
and the family had sort of adopted him. She had wanted
to wait to visit until she could take him Christmas cookies,
but a visit now would be nice. She could go back later with
cookies.

She picked up the phone and called Martha who was delighted Sarah had some free time. They decided to meet at
the Crystal Unicorn in an hour, which would give her time
for her visit with Leland.

Sarah checked the outdoor temperature, which was still
hovering below freezing, and changed out of her jeans and
long T-shirt into warm wool slacks, a fluffy burgundy turtleneck sweater, and black snow boots. Before she headed to
the door she grabbed a blank notebook from her office and
dropped it into her purse. Since she was going to be out and
about in the local shops, there was no harm in doing some
sleuthing, was there?

The tires crunched over a small berm of frozen snow
as Sarah turned her Grand Prix into a parking spot by
the Crystal Unicorn. The roads were surprisingly clear
considering how the wind had pushed the snow into drifts.

She spotted Martha's green minivan two parking spaces down.

Martha leaned forward in the driver's seat and waved at Sarah. She jumped out of the van and Sarah met her on the sidewalk. Her friend's cheeks had a rosy hue and her smile reached her lively hazel eyes.

"Hi!" she said with a puff of steam. She rounded her lips and blew out another stream and then grinned.

Sarah grinned back as they headed for the store. "You look happy for it being so cold."

"Oh, I am. I am. You know Ernie hasn't been doing so well the last couple of weeks? Well on Monday, the doc started him on some new med and it seems to be working. His hands hardly shook this morning. Before I left the house, he even said he was going out to the garage to work on Lexie's car."

"I'm so glad," Sarah said. Martha's husband loved fixing up old cars for his grandchildren, but his Parkinson's disease had been slowly worsening with time.

"The repair has been slow going, but she's only thirteen so he has lots of time to get the old clunker working."

"Lexie will be thrilled." Sarah wondered how long they had before Audrey and Amy wanted to drive. At fourteen Jenna had begun begging Gerry to learn to drive. With Jason it had been at twelve.

"How's Leland?" Martha asked as they climbed the steps.

"I didn't get a chance to see him. The doctor was in the room and he'd been having some tests done this morning."

"Nothing serious, is it?"

"They told me it was just routine. I waved at him from the door. He was fussing at the doctor as usual so I know he was feeling okay." Sarah smiled. Leland gave the impression of being a grumpy old man with his rough, deep voice, but he really was a teddy bear. "I'm going to try to see him tomorrow or the next day."

Martha pushed open the shop door. Annie Harper looked up from behind the counter where she appeared to be sorting colored candles. Annie's smile creased into a slight frown when she caught sight of Sarah.

"Good morning, Annie," Sarah called. The scent of jasmine incense tickled her nose.

"Mrs. Hart, good morning," Annie answered in a cool tone and resumed sorting.

Martha raised her eyebrows at Sarah. Sarah lifted a shoulder indicating she had no idea what was bugging Annie.

Martha and Sarah were the only customers in the store. Soft, lyrical music with the sounds of ocean waves played in the background. Sarah wandered along the many shelves trying to find something that might please Patty or Larry.

Annie sold a variety of wind chimes, candles and holders, incense, stationery and greeting cards made from recycled products, polished stone paperweights, essential oils and lotions, locally handmade jewelry, and other unique gifts.

A table in the center of the store was devoted to the winter solstice with a nod toward Christmas with ancient-looking Santa Clauses. Sarah steered clear of a small section with tarot cards and crystals and headed over to the three jars of loose tea on the counter. The chamomile jar had only a few leaves on the bottom.

Martha picked up a jar of tea and took a sniff. She made a face and set it down.

Sarah turned. "Annie, do you have any of your organic chamomile tea?"

"All out."

"Will you have any more before Christmas?"

"Couldn't say," she said, her gaze not meeting Sarah's eyes. "I could give you a call if I get some."

Sarah studied the younger woman. "Annie, have I done something to offend you?"

Annie blew out a big sigh. "Why did you have to mention my lost shipment to the police? Not only did they stop by but so did a very annoying man claiming my store was not secure. It's not like I don't have enough to worry about. I don't even know if the shipment was stolen. The delivery company could've made a mistake."

"Annie, I'm sorry. I assumed at the time you'd made a report." She explained the situation with the police and the teens.

"But how did you know about my stolen shipment?"

"I overheard Vanessa at Wild Goose Chase talking to you on the phone. Please don't blame her. It's my fault. I can be a nosy busybody at times."

"I can verify that," Martha said in a teasing voice.

The lines in Annie's face softened as she glanced from Sarah to Martha. "I'm sorry. I'm just in a bad mood. The box that disappeared could mean a week's profit lost."

"Don't you have insurance?" Martha asked.

"Yes, but it's not worth having my rates go up, and I can't blame the delivery company. I signed off that it's okay to leave deliveries by the back door if the store is closed. I'm rarely gone more than a few minutes during business hours."

"And you're sure it was on the back step?"

Annie nodded. "The delivery company got back to me this morning. The driver electronically logged the delivery at 8:17 AM. I'd popped down to the café to get a muffin and was gone about fifteen minutes."

"The driver didn't see anything unusual?"

"Nope. Just left it on the step with the other box, which held these candles."

"If you don't mind my asking, what was in the other box?"

"Pottery. Incense holders. Handcrafted by Isaac Haines." Annie pointed to a table along the far wall. "There are some over there."

"They're pretty," Martha said, stepping closer to examine the beautifully glazed globes. Various symbols and designs were cut out of the walls, each unique in shape and color.

"Who usually uses the alley?" Sarah asked. "Could someone else have gotten your shipment by mistake?"

"Some of the store owners park back there. Sometimes kids run through." She shrugged. "Anyone can wander down it if they want." She unwrapped the last candle and set it carefully with the other blue ones. "Enough about my troubles. Is there something I can help you with? If you want I can try to get some chamomile tea for you."

"Well, now that I think about it, I don't even know if Patty likes tea," Sarah said, explaining how Patty and Larry had recently begun eating organic vegetarian food. "I thought maybe you'd have some ideas. The tea was just the first thing that came to mind."

Annie thought for a few moments. "I think I have just the thing." She turned to a small cabinet and took out some boxes. "Like the tea, I grow these herbs in my garden. They're sun-dried and organic." She lifted a fragrant branch with a pungent odor.

"Oregano," Martha said.

Annie smiled. "Yes, and I have dried rosemary, thyme, sage, basil, coriander, and mint. Do you think your son's mother-in-law would like these?"

Sarah took a sprig and sniffed the rich aroma.

"The herbs make a unique gift since they come from Maple Hill," Martha said. "You can find some pretty tins to put them in. In fact, I'd like a bag of each kind."

"Me too. Thanks, Annie," Sarah said. "I think Patty will like them."

Annie bagged up the herbs and they paid.

"Now where to?" Martha asked.

"The alley."

They put their bags in their vehicles and then walked to the end of the block and around the corner to the narrow alley behind the stores. It hadn't been plowed yet, but tire tracks ran down the middle to a truck parked by the rear entrance to The Spotted Dog. Maggie usually parked out front with most of the other store owners.

Sarah moved forward, examining the ground.

"What are you looking at?" Martha asked.

"Footprints." There were two sets of prints. Someone with large feet had walked down the alley between the tire tracks. The other set was smaller. Sarah motioned for Martha to follow as she tracked the footsteps. The smaller set ran the length of the alley, zigzagging from one side to the other for the entire block and then turning back toward the main street.

"Was this person drunk?" Martha asked. "They couldn't walk a straight line to save their life." Martha paused by one of the garbage bins by the café. The lid had been knocked off and Martha wrinkled her nose. "Good thing it's so cold, or it'd really stink back here."

Sarah turned and surveyed the alley. The footprints seemed to stop by each set of garbage bins, or maybe someone had been casing the back doors to see if they were unlocked.

A burst of wind whipped down the alley, blowing up fine snow that stung Sarah's cheeks.

"*Brrr.*" Martha stamped her feet and wrapped her scarf tighter over her mouth.

Sarah pushed down her glove to glance at her watch. She still had a couple of hours until cookie baking.

"Want to go to The Galleria with me? I want to talk to C.J., and there might be something I could pick up as a gift for Larry." And Liam. She had decided against the wood carving, but maybe there was something else in the store that would strike her as the right present.

"I'd go anywhere to get out of this wind tunnel," Martha said. They carefully trod over the crusty snow until they reached the shoveled sidewalk and zipped into The Galleria.

An unfamiliar young woman with cropped, curly hair was wiping a glass case. "Can I help you?" she asked, setting the bottle and rag on the floor.

"Is C.J. here?"

"He's in his office."

Sarah left Martha to browse and headed to the back. She paused in the doorway. C.J. was on the phone and he held up a finger indicating to give him a minute.

"Do you think Larry would like these?" Martha walked over to Sarah and held up what looked like greeting cards. Instead of a printed front, each card had a black-and-white photo of a scene around Maple Hill or the Berkshires. The inside of the cards was left blank so they could be used for a variety of purposes.

"These are really nice," Sarah flipped through the photos. "I should go Christmas shopping with you more often."

"I keep telling you with four kids and ten grandchildren, I've learned to make snap decisions, or I'd never get anything done. Of course I have no clue what to get Ernie this year. He has almost every tool imaginable. He doesn't need clothes. Maybe I should just get him a jar of car wax."

"Wait, that's what I was going to give him," Sarah said with a laugh. "No, seriously, I thought I might give him some strawberry jam that we canned last summer."

"Oh, he'd love that!" Martha exclaimed. "He and the grandkids ate every last jar of mine. I should've hidden a jar for Christmas dinner. Nothing like the sweet taste of summer on hot biscuits when it's nasty weather outside."

"Then I'll give you two jars or more if you'd like. The girls had such fun making it last summer I still have two dozen," Sarah said.

Liam would probably appreciate some jam too, but Sarah still wanted to get him something else for Christmas. She glanced around the store, but nothing jumped out at her. She could ask Martha for advice if she got desperate, but right now she wanted to keep her choice close to the heart. Surely she would know the right present when she saw it.

"Aren't those cards nice?" C.J. asked from behind Sarah. "They're handmade. The photographer is a friend of mine."

"They're lovely. I'll take a box," Sarah said. If she found something else for Larry, she could send these to Jenna for her birthday.

"Great choice." C.J. took the cards to the counter. "Is there anything else I can help you with?"

Sarah reached into her purse for her wallet. "Do you have any decorative tins or pottery jars about so big? I want to put dried herbs in them." She held her hands up to demonstrate the size.

"Nothing that small. You might try the China Cup."

C.J. glanced at Martha who was examining the wood carvings. "The China Cup store lost some merchandise yesterday too. The teens were in there before they came here."

"How'd you hear that?" Sarah asked.

"Mr. Leftfoot. He was over there doing a security review. I'm having him put in security cameras."

"Back entrance too?"

"No, that door is rarely used, and I keep it bolted."

"So you don't park back there?"

C.J. nodded toward the front windows. "I like to keep my car out front, so I can keep an eye on it. Liam and some of his employees sometimes park back there. Why all the questions?"

"Sorry." Sarah smiled. "I was in the alley earlier and I noticed a set of footprints going from door to door."

"Footprints?"

"I know it sounds strange, but I'm trying to figure out if anyone accesses the alley frequently."

"Oh, I see. Annie's missing shipment," C.J. said. "I ran into her last evening and asked her about it. I had told her before that she shouldn't leave deliveries on the steps. It's a crime waiting to happen. I even offered to let her deliveries be dropped here if she wasn't in. Maybe now she'll take me up on it."

He sighed and rubbed the back of his neck. "Maybe I'm overreacting, but times are changing in Maple Hill. You can't trust anyone anymore. Or as Mr. Leftfoot said, 'You can't *afford* to be trusting these days.'"

"He does have a point, although I hate to admit it," Sarah said, remembering the fear in Maggie's voice the time she thought someone had broken into her store.

"Hey, Mr. Leftfoot said that he'd give me a discount for a referral. Do you think Maggie might be interested?"

"I don't know. She hasn't had any problems that I know of." At least not since the break-in over a year ago. Her car had also been broken into, causing Jason great concern for the safety of his family.

"With the way things are going, it's just a matter of time," C.J. said in an ominous tone as Martha sidled up.

"All done?" she asked.

Sarah nodded as C.J. handed her the change.

"You ladies have a great day." C.J. closed the cash register drawer with a firm click.

Sarah returned the sentiment and turned to leave. She paused, glancing up at the place where Gordon was going to put in the video camera. "Hey, C.J. Do you know if Mr. Leftfoot was in the alley this morning?"

"Could have been. He's been drumming up business all over town."

# CHAPTER FOUR

"Why did you ask if Mr. Leftfoot had been in the alley?" Martha asked, nearly plowing into a Helping Hands bin set under the awning. She sidestepped it as they walked toward Maggie's store.

"Just a hunch. The tracks going down the middle of the alley were deep and had ridges. I noticed Mr. Leftfoot was wearing that type of work boots with the deep tread."

"From what Lexie said yesterday he was acting awfully superior," Martha said as they came upon The Spotted Dog Café. "Imagine insinuating our grandkids would shoplift. I have a mind to—hey, isn't that Amy?"

Amy, Audrey, Patty, and Larry sat at the table by the foggy front window. "I thought they were in Pittsfield until after lunch," Sarah said.

Amy spotted Sarah and waved at her.

"I think she wants you to come in," Martha said.

Sarah waved back and hesitated. "I don't want to intrude."

Martha giggled. "Looks like you're outvoted."

The other three had spotted Sarah. Audrey waved as Larry mouthed, "Come in." Patty pursed her lips together but then smiled.

Sarah sighed. "Looks like it. Do you mind stopping in for a few minutes?"

"Not at all. A hot drink would hit the spot after our alley adventure. My toes are like ice cubes."

They entered the café's steamy, aromatic warmth. Liam's corgi met them, tongue hanging, tail wagging. Sarah bent to rub his soft ears.

"Murphy, you are such a happy dog today. Are you behaving?"

The little spotted dog whipped his tail back and forth harder, and then dashed behind the counter to his bed and a Murphy-size pile of dog bones and toys, obvious enticements to keep Murphy away from temptation. Sarah wondered what the veterinarian had to say about Murphy's change in chewing habits.

Sarah glanced around the store, looking for Liam. Today only two people roamed the bookstore side and the café tables were only a third full. No doubt the frigid weather was keeping some people indoors. Liam was nowhere to be seen, but since Murphy was in the bookstore, he couldn't be far.

Audrey was almost bouncing in her seat. "Grandma!" she called as Sarah joined them at the table. "We had such fun geocaching. It is the coolest thing. You have to go."

"We'll go out again soon." Larry stood. "Let's push together the tables."

"Oh, don't go to any trouble," Sarah said. "It looks like you're about done eating."

"We're not in any rush," Patty said as Larry snagged the table next to theirs. Audrey scooted out of her chair and they slid the tables side by side. "That's what's so great about being on vacation."

Larry pulled out a chair for Martha and then Sarah. "The more the merrier."

Sarah introduced Martha to Patty and Larry. "I was surprised to see you here. Maggie said you were heading for Pittsfield."

Patty gave a little shrug. "We were but then changed our minds. Decided to stick close to Maple Hill today."

"We went over to the courthouse and I found this." Amy held out a coin. "It was hidden in a small chest in a planter. Someone from New York must've left it."

Sarah took the gold plastic coin. One side was stamped with the Statue of Liberty and the other with a number.

"It's a geocoin," Amy explained. "It's like a travel bug. If you log into the computer and enter the number on the coin, you can see who it originally belonged to and who's had it since."

"We had to leave something in its place," Audrey said.

"You don't *have* to," Amy insisted.

"But it's considered proper etiquette for geocachers." Patty took a sip of her coffee.

"What kinds of things do you find?" Martha held the coin up to the light.

"You can leave anything you like. Small toys, marbles, baseball cards, coins, or any other kinds of trinkets. Larry and I are going to make our own geocoin when we get home. I wish we'd had time before we left, but this trip was a bit last minute after we found out Maggie and Jason couldn't make it out to visit us."

"We were supposed to go to California?" Audrey asked, her eyes growing round.

"It was just an idea," Larry said. "Instead we came out here and aren't we having fun? Show your grandma what else you found."

Audrey looked like she wanted to ask more questions but then shrugged it off. "This is from Patriot Park." Audrey showed Sarah and Martha a bookmark with a cute kitten on it and a Bible verse. "We left Grammy's travel bug there. You know, the Tonka truck?"

"This sounds like a great game, and it gets people outside and moving around." Martha glanced at Sarah with a gleam in her eye. "I bet Ernie would enjoy geocaching. My husband loves tools and gadgets," she said to Patty. "We have a GPS we use in the car which he tinkers with."

"The car models or the GPS on cell phones can work okay, but you can get a portable unit like I got the girls for fairly cheap. It's more convenient for taking in the woods." Larry went on about the various brands on the market.

"Well now, I see the table has expanded while I was in the kitchen." Liam's rich Irish brogue caused Sarah's stomach to flutter. She looked up at his twinkling green eyes and smiled.

"Would you ladies like to try the special today?" Liam asked. "It's chicken enchilada soup and Mexican cornbread."

"That sounds yummy," Martha said. "I was thinking of just a latte, but soup and cornbread is too tempting. I've got to try it."

"I had the cornbread and it's excellent." Patty dabbed her mouth with her napkin.

"I'll have a bowl too," Sarah said to Liam.

"Two orders coming up," Liam said as his waitress Karen Bancroft approached.

"Thanks, Liam. I can take it from here." Karen pulled her order pad and pencil from her pocket. "Would any of you like to try a dessert? We're featuring gingerbread cake with warm caramel sauce."

"Oh, that sounds wonderful, but I'm watching my calories," Patty said, patting her stomach.

"I like to think that when you're on vacation calories cease to exist," Martha said with a wink. "They go on vacation too."

"She does have a point." Larry chuckled. "Loosen up a little, Patty."

Patty frowned and opened her mouth as if to argue, but then shrugged. "Fine, I'll have cake."

They all ordered gingerbread cake except Amy who wanted a hot fudge sundae. The conversation turned back to geocaching. Martha peppered them with questions, and Larry regaled them with some funny geocache stories until the food and dessert arrived. Sarah was finishing her last spoonful of the creamy soup when Patty touched her arm.

"Sarah, I need to ask a favor."

Sarah set her spoon down. "Sure. What can I do for you?"

"Well, I wanted to get away for an hour or so to do some Christmas shopping before I head over to the store to help Maggie. Can you take Larry and the girls back to the house?"

"I'd be glad to. I was going over there anyway to bake cookies this afternoon."

"Oh yes, the cookie baking. Drat. I forgot." She glanced at the twins and lowered her voice. "I'm sorry I won't be there. I was looking forward to baking with the girls. I wanted to take pictures too."

"Well, we could wait until another day," Sarah offered.

"No, no, I don't want to change your plans. If Maggie isn't swamped at the shop, I'll be back in time."

"Tell you what, we'll start baking and just save some cookies to finish up this evening."

"Marvelous." Patty beamed, setting her napkin on her dessert plate and rising. "I'll be right back. I want to freshen my lipstick." She headed for the restrooms down the hall.

Martha pushed back her chair. "I'll be right back too." She grabbed her purse and followed Patty.

"I think that's our cue we're done." Larry grinned at the girls. "How about we check out the books?"

Karen carried the check and money to the cash register as Larry and the girls headed for the bookshelves. Sarah gathered up her coat and walked over to where Liam stood on a stepladder hanging rope lights along the top shelves.

Liam stepped down when he saw her. "I'm glad you stopped in. I wanted to ask you if you're free Saturday evening. My cousins, well, they're actually my third cousins, are dropping in to visit. I haven't seen them in about twenty years. I think I'll take them to The Old Mill, and I was hoping you'd come too. I better warn you though before you decide that you might find them find a wee bit different. Nice guys but full of blarney."

Sarah smiled. "Sounds like fun. I'd love to. Maggie's folks are in town until after the holidays, but I don't think there's anything going on this Saturday."

Liam glanced over at the group in front of the young adult bookshelf. Audrey showed a cover to Larry and they laughed. Excited, Murphy circled their feet, drawing Amy's attention. She knelt down and gave him a hug.

"How's Murphy doing with the chewing?" Sarah asked.

"Other than leaving a couple of teeth marks on my best belt, he's better this week."

"Did the vet say anything useful?" Sarah asked.

"He couldn't find anything wrong with Murphy physically but suggests he might be bored."

"Bored?" Sarah gazed at the little dog chasing the ball Amy rolled across the floor. "But he spends most of his time with you."

"That's what I said, and the vet just looked at me." He raised his eyebrows.

Sarah laughed. "I can assure you you're not boring."

"I'm glad someone thinks so." He grinned. "So, is the visit going well?"

"They just got here last night," Sarah said. "They're very…"

"Compulsive? Spontaneous?"

"I was going to say energetic." Sarah laughed, although she tended to agree with Liam's quick assessment.

Liam's gaze shifted over Sarah's shoulder. "And very generous."

Audrey and Amy arrived at the counter, each with an armload of books. Larry pulled out his wallet as Liam stepped over to the register to ring up the books.

"Thanks, grandpa," Audrey said with Amy echoing. Sarah glanced over the popular teen novels. Amy's pile had a couple of sports books mixed in.

"Larry, now what are you buying the girls?" Patty asked as she rounded the corner and entered the bookstore with Martha.

"Just a few books. Never can read too much." Larry handed over a credit card.

Patty clapped her hands together. "Oh, look at all these little dogs. Aren't they adorable? I have to take one back to my friend Clarisse. She's always looking for unique toys for her grandchildren. Girls, help me pick one out."

"This may take a while," Larry said with a wink. After Liam gave him his receipt, he moseyed over to the shelf with the newest releases and picked up a hardcover mystery.

"That was fast." Martha nudged Sarah and pointed to a flyer on the counter, announcing the proposal of establishing citywide chaperoning rules and a curfew. Voting would be next week at the town council meeting.

"Who gave you the flyer, Liam?"

"This security expert," Liam said, bagging the girl's books. "He said there have been several thefts. Shoplifting. He wanted local business input."

Sarah glanced at Martha. "That'd be Gordon Leftfoot. Did he offer to give you a security evaluation?"

"As matter of a fact he did. Was quite insistent. Do you know this Mr. Leftfoot?"

"I ran into him yesterday. Amy, Audrey, Lexie, and some of their friends were questioned by the police," Sarah said, explaining what had happened with the twins, C.J., and Annie.

Liam's eyes softened with concern. "Poor girls. Are they okay?"

"Christine said Lexie was shook up some, but she's okay now," Martha said.

"Audrey and Amy seem fine too, other than being upset that one of the other girls isn't allowed to visit without supervision. Of course the arrival of their grandparents distracted them."

Liam sighed. "I'd assume it was an outsider before accusing any of the kids around here. I haven't had any trouble with shoplifting, but . . . something strange *is* going on. Don't know if it's related, but someone stole my umbrella stand the other night."

"I didn't even notice when I came in. I'm sorry," Sarah said. In late November Maggie had discovered the unique statue at an estate sale and called Liam to see if he was interested. A spotted dog sat beside a large cast-iron basket which could have had a variety of uses. Liam had bought the statue, set it under the front door awning, and popped an umbrella in the basket.

"Maybe we should be looking for someone with a hernia," Martha said. "That thing must've weighed a ton."

"About fifty pounds. If it weren't so heavy and awkward to move, I would've brought it in at night. Never thought someone would nab it, so I can only blame myself. The dog wasn't an antique, so it's not that big of a loss."

"But I liked it," Sarah said.

"So did I," Martha echoed. "And it was out there in plain sight, so you'd think it'd be safe, not like Annie's box that disappeared in the alley."

"I know you park out there, Liam, but who else uses the alley?" Sarah asked.

"Karen does sometimes, but most people park out front."

"Uh-oh, I heard my name. Did you need something?" Karen asked with a smile. She set a plastic tub down on the table closest to the bookstore.

"Sarah was asking about who used the alley," Liam said.

"I park back there sometimes," Karen said, filling the tub with empty water glasses and dirty plates. "Why? Is there a problem?"

"I'm just wondering if you saw anyone back there snooping yesterday."

"Didn't work yesterday." Karen moved the tub to a chair and wiped the table down with a big white cloth. "Oh, but there is this poor homeless lady who sometime collects stuff out of the garbage. I see her if I come in early."

"Oh dear, I didn't think we had homeless people in Maple Hill, at least not out on the streets," Martha said.

"Is this someone who needs help?" Sarah asked, concerned. "I can let Pastor John know and get her on our community service list."

"That'd be a good idea," Liam said with a warm smile for Sarah. "I'll see what I can do too. We'll need to get her name."

Martha shook her head. "I hate to think anyone is going hungry in Maple Hill."

"Whoa." Karen waved her dishrag to interrupt them, her face flushing a pretty pink. "I'm sorry. I shouldn't have called her homeless. I really don't know her situation. Her clothes are old, like she's poor, and she pokes around in the trash. She could just be someone looking for things to recycle. Next time I see her, I'll try to find out more about her."

"Thanks, Karen," Sarah said, although she still planned on trying to talk to the woman from the alley personally. Maybe those weaving footprints belonged to her.

"Decision made," Patty said, coming toward the counter with the girls. She held a fluffy stuffed spotted dog that resembled Murphy. "Wait until I tell them back home about this place. So quaint and fun."

Martha and Sarah said good-bye to Liam and Murphy and headed out into the bright cold. Martha buttoned up her coat as they stood on the sidewalk, waiting for the girls to get their things from their grandparents' rental car.

"What are you thinking about?" Martha asked.

"That the incidents of Annie's missing shipment, C.J.'s stolen ornaments, and the other stores could be unrelated," Sarah mused. "Maybe there's a separate explanation for each."

"Yes, you could be right," Martha agreed, but there was a dubious note in her tone.

They stood silent for a few moments and then Martha asked, "Want to meet tomorrow and check out the China Cup and see if there are any more clues? You know, just in case it *is* someone from around here?"

Sarah nodded. "I think we should."

The crash reverberated throughout Jason and Maggie's house. In the kitchen where they had been baking cookies, Sarah, Amy, and Audrey looked at each other with wide eyes and then bolted through the doorway. They raced through the dining room bumping into each other and stopping short at the sight of Larry lying on the hall floor beside an overturned stepladder, coated in white dust and with a big chunk of plaster on his chest. His eyes were shut in his ghostly pale face above the dust mask that covered his mouth and nose.

Audrey gasped and knelt beside him. "Grandpa, are you all right?"

"Larry, can you move?" Sarah asked, helping Amy pull the plaster off his chest.

"Should I call 911?" Amy's voice shook as she patted her pockets for her cell phone.

Larry opened his eyes and groaned. "No need to do that." He struggled to sit up.

"Anything hurt?" Sarah asked, her heart still tripping.

"Just my pride." Larry tugged down his mask and grinned. He brushed the dust and plaster crumbles off his shirt. "Takes more than a short fall to damage the rest of me."

Sarah let out a relieved breath as she stepped back and took in the disaster scene. Holes in the plaster indicated Larry had used a sledgehammer to bust out the wall above and on either side of the small closet.

"Grandpa, you made a huge mess," Audrey said.

Larry got to his feet with the help of Amy. "Didn't I though?" He gazed around at the rubble littering the floor with a look of satisfaction.

Sarah studied the craters he had made. The closet opening looked much larger than what Jason had described the other night, but she refrained from saying so.

Larry rubbed his lower back. "I think that's enough de-molition for today. I can get the rest of the wall tomorrow. How's the cookie baking going? My stomach's been growling from all the yummy smells."

"Oh, the cookies!" Sarah said. They had left sugar cookies in the oven.

Amy ran to the kitchen ahead of Sarah. The timer was buzzing. She pulled open the oven door. "They're not too bad."

Sarah grabbed pot holders and pulled the two sheets out. The little stars, bells, and Santa Clauses were a dark toasty brown with blackened edges instead of being golden yellow. They were going to be as hard as rocks too.

"Grandpa is going to take a shower," Audrey said, coming into the room. She studied the burnt cookies and wrinkled her nose. "Those are ruined. Throw them out."

"No. I'll eat them. I like them burnt." Amy carefully picked up a hot star and nipped off a corner.

Audrey rolled her eyes.

Sarah scooped up the cookies and put them on a cooling rack. She wiped the sheets and set them on the table. "Don't worry. We can make more."

They finished another batch of sugar cookies and decided to save the oatmeal cranberry cookies for when Patty got home, since they seemed the healthiest of the cookies. Sarah glanced at the clock. It was after four already.

The cordless house phone rang and Sarah picked it up.

"Hart residence."

"Is my mother there?" Maggie asked in a strained voice.

"No, she said she had some shopping to do and was going over to the shop after."

"She's not answering her cell, and I'm swamped. A delivery of glassware just arrived and it's blocking the aisles, and a bus just dropped a load of antique hunters from Boston."

"Oh dear. Is there anything I can do to help?"

"Hold on a second. Someone's asking me a question." Maggie's voice became muffled. "I'm sorry. The delivery men moved the bin. If you give me a couple of minutes, I have some things I'd like to send to Helping Hands."

"Sorry," Maggie said, her voice clear again.

"I can be there in a few minutes." Sarah took off her apron.

"Could you? I hate to take you away from the baking."

"The girls have been doing a great job as usual. Larry is here, and he can help them finish up."

"Thank you. Oh ... wait. Never mind. There's Mom now. I'll put her at the cash register, and I should be fine now."

"Can we help by starting supper for you?" Sarah asked. "I'll be here for at least another hour."

"Sure, you can have the girls make a salad. I was going to heat up the beef stew I have in the freezer, but I didn't realize my parents had changed their eating habits so drastically. I'm going to stop and buy some risotto at the market on the way home. Would you like to stay for supper too?"

"I'd like to but I really need to work on a Christmas gift tonight," Sarah said, thinking about the mystery quilt.

Besides she also wanted to make sure Maggie and her parents had some alone time. She said she would help the girls make a salad, and Maggie thanked her before signing off.

"Everything okay?" Amy asked, smearing yellow frosting on a star.

"Yes. The store's busy, but your grandmother is there now."

"I can't resist any longer." Larry walked in with damp, silver hair and the pleasant scent of soap and piney aftershave.

"Do you want some?" Audrey asked, holding up a plate of frosted creations.

"You did such a terrific job decorating them they look too good to eat." His blue eyes gleamed as his gaze roamed over the piles of goodies on the counter. "But I think I can manage."

Sarah handed him a small plate and he took one of each kind. "I'll have some of these to tide me over until dinner. Just don't tell your grandmother. She's had me eating sugar-free tofu cookies." He spied Amy nibbling one of the over-baked sugar cookies. "I used to eat all the cookies your mom burnt too." He bit into a crispy Christmas tree and sighed. "These bring back memories."

Amy shot Audrey a smirk.

"I think I'm going to go relax in the parlor. You don't want me around all these cookies. Trust me," he said with a wink.

Sarah spent another hour with the girls finishing up the sugar and peppermint chocolate cookies. They made a huge green salad throwing in all the fresh vegetables they could find in the refrigerator. Audrey chatted about what her friends were doing over the holidays. Amy added a comment or two but as time passed, she grew even quieter.

"I'm going to go see what Grandpa's doing," Audrey said after they had cleaned up the counters and washed the dishes. Amy lingered, watching Sarah finish drying her cookie sheets and put them in the box.

"Something bothering you, Amy?" Sarah asked.

Amy shifted her feet. "Can I tell you something in secret?"

"It depends what it is. You know I can't keep something from your parents if it's something they should know. But if not, I won't share it with anyone else if you don't want me too."

Amy made a face. "It's not a big secret or anything. I don't know if Mom or Dad needs to know. I just heard Grammy talking to someone on the phone. She was telling them why she was in Massachusetts in the middle of winter. She said that Dad gave up a big career to move back here. He could've been someone important. That there are no opportunities here. Is that true, Grandma. Did Dad make a mistake?"

"No, of course not," Sarah said a little too sharply. She paused, choosing her words carefully. "He *did* make some big changes, but that doesn't mean he can't be successful here. Being successful also can mean being happy. And you all are happy here, right?"

"I guess."

"Your grandmother misses you, and sometimes adults say things when they don't think anyone else is listening."

"She knew I heard because she saw me. She also said that Dad could've been more ambitious, and he's just lazy."

Sarah set a mixing bowl down harder than she intended. What was Patty thinking? Sarah could understand them being upset that their daughter and grandchildren had moved clear across the country, but sharing these things around Amy was uncalled for. And calling Jason lazy was a downright lie.

A wrinkle marred Amy's forehead. "She wants Audrey and me to go to California for college. Grammy said she and Grandpa went to the University of Southern California, and she thinks we could get scholarships."

Sarah took a deep breath. Even if she was irritated, she needed to be supportive of Amy, not angry at Patty. Amy obviously took this all to heart.

"That's a good school, but you have lots of time to talk to your parents about it and consider your options." Sarah smoothed back Amy's bangs. "No need to worry about college now, sweetheart. And if this continues to bother you, talk it over with your mom or dad."

Amy nodded again. "Maybe." She snagged a cookie. "Did you find out anything about the shoplifting?"

"Not much yet." She told Amy about the footprints in the alley. "I'm trying to find out who might've been in the alley and took Annie's box. Karen Bancroft said that sometimes a lady goes back there, looking in the trash cans."

"Oh! I saw her once when we stopped by the store before school one day."

"Do you know anything about her?"

Amy shook her head. "Mom wanted to talk to her, but she comes really early in the morning. Mom thought the lady might be collecting aluminum cans, so we brought a bag of them from home and left it out there for her. It was gone later."

"It was really nice of you to try to help her out."

Amy chewed on her cookie. "Is that all you've found out? The footprints?"

Sarah smiled at Amy's impatience. Although some inklings were forming in her mind, it had only been a day. "Don't worry. I'll keep working on it."

Amy smiled. "I know you will."

# CHAPTER FIVE

Sarah's sewing machine hummed as she stitched triangles together to form two- by two-inch squares. Faster and faster the fabric flew under the presser foot until the needle nipped her index finger. She jerked her foot off the pedal.

The needle had snagged only a little skin. Nothing serious, but she needed to focus. Ever since she had left Maggie and Jason's, the conversation with Amy had kept churning in her mind. It wasn't Sarah's place to get involved. Patty was entitled to her opinions, but when they had the potential to cause hurt and confusion, should Sarah say something? Maybe she should wait for Amy to talk to her parents. What good would it do to bring this all up now, especially during the holidays?

As her pile of green and burgundy squares grew on the other side of the sewing machine, her anxiety lessened. At least when she was quilting she had control over the outcome. She finished the row and pulled the squares onto her lap.

She finished the required assignment and then added the instruction sheet to the binder with the others. The anecdote was about organizing recipes, obtaining ingredients, and getting out the required cooking and baking equipment before the big day. The copy for today still had some typos such as p@t and knive# and a string of random numbers at the bottom even longer than before: *20111214%20:15&&1342####@@N42°XX26.648** W074°++15.299.*

She had compared the different blog sheets and each day the bottom numbers consisted of the same symbols, but different numbers.

She turned to the next day's instructions for sewing the squares together. The directions weren't clear. Which sides of the squares were to be sewn together? The green fabrics with the burgundy or the greens with the greens? How the squares were joined to each other would change the quilt's pattern.

It was as if the author had skipped a line or two. Sarah turned on her laptop and brought up the home page of the blog. An e-mail address was listed to contact the blog owner if there were any questions. She wrote a friendly note asking for clarification and sent it off into cyberspace.

Sarah stood and stretched. Her shoulders and neck ached from being hunched over the sewing machine. But she felt pleased. She had gotten a lot done. She wandered into the kitchen to put the kettle on for tea.

The *Maple Hill Monitor* still lay on the kitchen table. With getting the cookie baking equipment together that morning, she hadn't had a chance to read it. She wondered how Patty and the girls were doing with the cranberry oatmeal cookies. She had left the ingredients and recipe on Maggie's counter before she left. She hoped Patty was enjoying the experience and time she obviously missed having with her grandchildren.

Sarah skimmed the letters to the editor section, her gaze stopping at a letter titled *Mayberry No More?*

*Dear Editor,*

*In regard to Friday's story concerning the recent burglaries in Maple Hill and the need for more patrolmen, I wanted to express my opinion as a former police officer.*

*We would all love to live in the fictional TV town of Mayberry where crime is the exception and the sheriff doesn't have to carry a gun, but unfortunately real life isn't that simple anymore.*

*Crime is on the rise even here, but it can be held in check if citizens take a few precautions such as locking doors, being aware of their surroundings, and safeguarding valuables.*

*As an outsider and ex-city slicker, I like Maple Hill with its hometown values and people who are friendly and, for the most part, honest.*

*Considering I own a security business, some will think this letter is self-serving, but the fact is I do care about continuing to make Maple Hill a safer place to live for all of us. Even if you don't need my services, please at least check into the other security options out there and be proactive against crime. Prevention will help preserve our wonderful town.*

*Gordon Leftfoot*

The man was certainly getting his name out there. Sarah wondered how long he had actually lived in town. She turned the pages until she came to the police blotter column that had recently been added in a campaign to make citizens aware. Every Tuesday the column listed local arrests and crimes from the previous week.

She skimmed the page. There was one arrest for drunk driving and then a list of local thefts that had occurred since the previous Tuesday.

*The Galleria—ornaments—$270*
*Joe's Drugstore—shampoo and hairclips—$35*
*The Lonely Cricket—misc merchandise—$150*
*The Spotted Dog Café—umbrella stand—$125*

Annie's theft was unlisted, which didn't surprise Sarah since the woman seemed dead set against making an official report. C.J. had mentioned that the China Cup had lost some merchandise too, but it wasn't listed in the blotter either.

Sarah retrieved her notebook and jotted down all the businesses and the stolen items. She tapped her pencil. Was there a connection between all of them? Kids might find the items in the stores tempting but stealing an umbrella stand? Of course these thefts might all be unrelated. Still . . . why so many now?

Sarah ventured into the frigid garage, quickly sorted through her recycling pile, and dug out all the recent Tuesday editions of the *Monitor* she could find. She rushed back inside, shivering, set the stack on the table and tore out all the police blotter columns from November to that morning's. She laid them side by side on the kitchen table.

One or two stolen items were listed each week, with a sharp increase after Thanksgiving. Naturally more people were shopping during the holidays, but surely Maple Hill hadn't had a big problem like this before.

Sarah tapped her pencil on the table. How fortunate for Gordon Leftfoot's business. He seemed to have arrived in Maple Hill just in time for a crime wave.

Snow crunched under Sarah's boots as she crossed Main Street to meet Martha in front of The Spotted Dog Café. She had awakened to a glorious sunny winter day. Although the temperature still hovered around thirty, the wind had died, and Sarah didn't mind the cold nipping at her nose and cheeks. She waved at Martha who stood on the sidewalk, holding two paper cups with lids.

They had decided to go to the China Cup and then have lunch. Sarah came armed with her Christmas list and also the notebook where she had been jotting down information. Despite her worries last night, she had fallen into a deep sleep and had awakened eager to do more investigating. She might not uncover anything to help with the chaperoning rule, but to keep her promise to her grandchildren, she needed to try to find the true culprits. Besides, she was curious and concerned. Maybe Gordon Leftfoot would consider her naive, but she had spent her life in Maple Hill and she felt safe here. She wanted it to remain that way.

"I brought you some of the Christmas chai tea I'm making for gifts," Martha said by way of greeting. "I got the idea yesterday when you bought those herbs for Maggie's mother. I wanted something nice but inexpensive to give the ladies helping on the home tour this year. Only I may have goofed it up. See what you think. I may have put in too much ginger, but I wanted that warm feeling like you get from ginger ale. So I doubled what the recipe called for."

Sarah reached for the cup which heated her fingers through her light gloves. She breathed in the heady spicy scent and took a cautious steaming sip. Finding it not too hot, she took a gulp. The liquid flowed down her throat, spreading tingling warmth throughout her chest.

Martha watched her with a worried expression. "What do you think? It's too strong, isn't it? Should I make a new batch?"

"If you're going for that warm feeling, you've got it," Sarah said, taking another drink. "It's great. I don't think you need to change anything. What else do you have in it?"

"The usual. Cinnamon, cloves, and cardamom with instant tea, French vanilla nondairy creamer, and powdered milk," Martha listed as they strolled toward the China Cup.

A large, brown-paneled Helping Hands van idled in front of the Crystal Unicorn. Sarah recognized the employee, Kathleen, standing on the sidewalk talking to someone who had her back to Sarah and Martha. Kathleen was waving her gloved hands as she emphasized her points.

"I can't believe some of the things people give away," Kathleen said, holding a bundle of dingy socks between two fingers. "I mean look at these. Someone donated socks that are so worn you can almost see through them. I guess it's better than nothing if you have no socks, but can't we as a society do better? Why can't the more fortunate share with the less fortunate?"

"I agree. I just heard a news commentator the other day talking about how selfish capitalist pigs have taken over this country. You'd think there should be plenty to go around for everyone," the other woman said. Sarah recognized Patty's voice and stopped so suddenly Martha nearly plowed into her.

"I think I can understand how frustrating it can be," Patty continued. "I work at an animal shelter in California and walk the dogs. Such sweet creatures abandoned by people who never should've owned animals in the first place. And money … we're always trying to raise money for these creatures that can't help themselves. I really admire what you do. Helping people is even more important than helping pets."

Kathleen smiled. "Well, that's what's great about Helping Hands. I love working for them. Our mission is to help those who can't help themselves." She spotted Martha and Sarah behind Patty. "I'm sorry. Are we blocking the sidewalk?"

Patty looked over her shoulder. "Good morning! I've just been in some lovely shops and literally bumped into Kathleen here. I was texting Audrey and almost ended up flat on my face on the sidewalk. Kathleen kept me from falling."

"I just happened to be in the right place at the right time," Kathleen said.

"Do you two know Kathleen?" Patty asked.

"We haven't officially met," Sarah said. "I saw you at Wild Goose Chase the other day doing a pickup."

"I do get around." Kathleen's steely gray-eyed gaze swept over Sarah and Martha. Sarah got the uncomfortable feeling Kathleen was assessing their income level.

Patty introduced Sarah and Martha to Kathleen as if the woman was her dearest friend.

"You're the quilt lady, aren't you?" Kathleen asked Sarah. "Vanessa told me about you. She said you could repair quilts."

"That's my business."

"My aunt who left me her house quilted up until the day she passed away. She used to e-mail me photos of her quilts back before I got rid of my computer." Kathleen eyed Sarah. "We get ripped quilts at Helping Hands sometimes."

"Give me a call and I'll be happy to take a look," Sarah said, reaching in her purse for a business card.

"We couldn't pay you."

"That's okay. I'd love to help if I can."

"Thank you so much. Every little bit helps, especially in these small towns. I used to work in the larger cities and in some ways I think it's easier because there are more people to make donations. I just hope I'm making a difference in people's lives," Kathleen said in a wistful voice.

Patty patted Kathleen on the arm. "I think you're making a difference already, and I really want to help too. I just bought these sweaters for my granddaughters, but I'm thinking someone less fortunate may benefit from them more." She shifted the three bags between her hands and gave one to Kathleen.

"Great! I can tell you you're doing the right thing. Let me get your address, and the office will send you a receipt for your taxes." Kathleen reached through the door of the van and snagged a thin box off the seat. She tapped her fingers on it and Sarah realized it was a computer touch pad keyboard.

Kathleen saw Sarah watching and grimaced. "I hate this thing, and I don't trust it. More technological intrusion into our lives."

"What do you mean?" Martha asked.

"Do you realize that when you go on the Internet, someone can track everything you do and buy? It's a conspiracy! I won't even let a computer into my house anymore, but they make me use this electronic pad for work. Some hotshot donated the entire system. Why he didn't just donate the money, I'll never know. Pens and paper still work."

"Well, now, I don't need a receipt if it's a bother," Patty said.

"I still have to make a record of the pickup, so you might as well take it. The receipt may come in handy."

Kathleen tapped in Patty's address and the price of the sweaters and then shifted her gaze at Sarah and Martha. "Anything else?"

"I put some things in a bin last week," Martha said.

"I might have some things this spring when I clean my attic," Sarah said. "But give me a call if Helping Hands needs any help with sewing repairs in the meantime."

"Every little thing helps, right, Kathleen?" Patty said, shifting her packages again.

Kathleen pressed her lips together in a thin line, tossed the touch pad back on the passenger seat, and said to Patty, "The receipt should be mailed to you in a few days. Thanks again for being so generous." She trotted around to the driver's side and slid open the door. "Have a good day."

"Merry Christmas!" Patty called and then smiled at Sarah and Martha. "I've been having such a marvelous time in the stores this morning. I found the most wonderful organic dried herbs in that unique store right there. I almost bought out the store." She held up a bulging paper bag. "I can't wait to use some of them for dinner tonight. What are you two up to?"

"Doing a little shopping," Martha said, "and then having lunch at The Spotted Dog."

"You're welcome to join us if you'd like," Sarah said.

"Oh my." Patty lifted her watch. "Is it getting that late? I told Maggie I'd only be gone an hour. I wanted to spend the morning with her in the store while Larry and the girls hung out together. I'm just terrible with time, but Maggie is used to that." She gave a little laugh. "I better head over there now. I have such a wonderful surprise for Maggie and it's so hard to keep it quiet, but I'm just waiting for the right moment to spring it on her, if you know what I mean." Patty waved and took off without explanation.

Martha shook her head slightly. "At least now you know she likes the herbs you got her for Christmas."

"That she does." Sarah said as Patty darted into Maggie's store. "Maybe I'll try to find something else since she seems stocked up."

They continued down the walk and turned on a side street. "What do you think Patty's surprise for Maggie is?" Martha asked.

"I have no idea. This is the third time she's mentioned it," Sarah tilted the mug of lukewarm tea to her lips.

"Maybe they plan to move here."

Sarah nearly choked on the tea. "What?"

"When she passed me, I noticed a real estate brochure sticking out of her purse."

"I can't imagine them relocating here. She didn't like Maggie and Jason's moving away from California." Plus she had been talking to Amy about going to college near Los Angeles. "But Amy and Audrey would love having them closer." Sarah held open the door to the China Cup for Martha.

"Good morning," the owner of the quaint shop, Mrs. Kloche, called. "Let me know if I can assist you in any way."

Martha and Sarah returned the greeting as they carefully made their way around a stoneware display in the doorway. Boxes of the dish sets were piled around and under the table.

Martha paused. "These are pretty. I wonder if Kate would like these. She mentioned her set is getting chipped and the kids have broken some plates. Look. They're marked thirty percent off. I'm going to call her." She pulled out her phone and hit a speed dial button.

Sarah moved toward the back of the store. She always felt slightly claustrophobic when she browsed in the tiny shop, which wasn't often. The place did hold fond memories, though. She and Martha had each gotten their wedding china here. Jenna had registered here, too, for kitchen items, although she had gotten her china from Sarah's mother.

The walls were lined with shelves displaying china sets and crystal goblets. The middle tables held various pieces of dishware such as casseroles, serving trays, silverware sets, and fancy kitchen gadgets.

Christmas music played softly from a radio on the counter where Mrs. Kloche's snow-capped head was bent over a ledger. The lines around her hazel eyes crinkled with her sweet smile as Sarah approached.

"Hi, Mrs. Kloche. I know this may be an odd question, but have you had anything stolen recently?"

"No, dear, I haven't had any problems. I have an alarm system I turn on at night."

"Someone mentioned you'd had some merchandise stolen yesterday."

"I did?" Her forehead wrinkled. "Oh, that! My, how word gets around. No, dear, it was all a mistake. I was carrying a box of silverware and some dishes to the counter when I checked the Helping Hands bin to see what my customers had donated. I'm supposed to match their donations. When that security man was here, I noticed I was missing the silverware from the counter and assumed the worst. He got all excited and jumped to conclusions. Actually, I'd accidentally dropped the box in the bin and had a senior moment." She tapped her pen on her temple and giggled.

"I have those too at times," Sarah said with a laugh. "Well, I'm glad everything turned out okay. There've been several thefts around Maple Hill lately."

"Well, I've been in business for forty-four years and find that the majority of people are honest, at least here in Maple Hill," Mrs. Kloche said as a young woman carrying a bread machine came to the counter.

Sarah stepped back. Martha stood in one of the aisles examining some decorated plastic canisters. Outside brakes squealed and the Helping Hands van stopped across the street near the clothing store the Lonely Cricket.

"Be right back," Sarah said to Martha and trotted out the door. She waited for a car to pass and then darted across the street.

Kathleen came out of the shop door and opened the lid on the Helping Hands container and began bagging the brightly colored contents. A sign on the bin indicated that the Lonely Cricket was also matching any items donated from their store.

"Kathleen," Sarah said with a wave.

"Well, hello again ... Mrs. ...."

"Hart. Call me Sarah."

"Did you change your mind about giving a donation?"

"Actually I wanted to ask you a couple of questions."

"It's your dime, if you know what I mean." Kathleen pressed her lips together. "I help those who help others."

Kathleen continued to load up the donated clothing from the bin. Sarah sighed. She didn't feel guilty about not donating to Helping Hands right now. She had always been generous with donations to the church and various charities, but in the interest of time and solving the mystery she pulled out her wallet. "Here's a ten."

"Well that's kind of you," Kathleen said, straightening. "I'll have to get the doohickey from the van so you can get a receipt."

"It's okay. You can do it later if you want. You have my business card. All the information you need is on there."

Kathleen shoved the cash into her coat pocket. "What can I do for you?"

"You spend a lot of time driving up and down these streets, right?"

"During the holidays, every day except Sunday," Kathleen said, pulling the drawstrings on her plastic bag. "What about it?"

"Maybe you've heard that there has been an increase in theft around here. I was wondering if you've noticed any unusual activity. People loitering or anyone looking suspicious."

"There are lots more people on the streets, but I can't re-call anything stranger than usual happening. Why?"

"I'm just concerned. My granddaughters shop in the area and my daughter-in-law owns Magpie's Antiques, and—"

"I know that place. Patty's daughter. Maggie's real nice. Offers me cookies and something hot to drink whenever I pop in there. Saw her girls once too. Thought I was seeing double for a moment." Kathleen laughed.

Sarah smiled. "Yes, they do catch some people off guard. They're good girls, and I'm concerned that they and their friends might get blamed for the shoplifting around here. There's going to be a town council meeting about not allow-ing the teens to shop without chaperones."

"Isn't that a little extreme for Maple Hill?"

"I think so."

"Well, I can keep an eye out for anything different, but I generally mind my own business."

"Thanks so much. I'd appreciate a call if you notice any-thing." Sarah turned to cross the street and then paused, one foot still on the curb. "Kathleen, do you ever drive that alley behind the Crystal Unicorn and the Galleria?"

"Nope, I don't like alleys. Too easy to get trapped in."

# CHAPTER SIX

I assure you, Mrs. Hart, that a good security system will save you money in the long run. Not to mention giving you peace of mind and sound sleep knowing your business is in good hands. Right now I'm offering a special deal for all the businesses downtown." Gordon Leftfoot leaned again the counter in Magpie's Antiques where Maggie was wrapping a vase with Christmas paper.

Sarah took off her coat and slung it over her arm. After leaving the China Cup where Martha had found the perfect containers for her tea, they'd had a lovely lunch at the Spotted Dog. The place had been hopping, and Sarah only got to speak to Liam briefly to confirm their dinner date.

Martha headed home to work on her chai mix, and Sarah decided to check on how Maggie and Patty were doing. Sarah scanned the store. The shop bustled with business as customers browsed the antiques. But where was Patty?

"Maggie, I can't find the price tag on this lamp," one of the customers called.

"Be right with you, Mrs. Greene." Maggie turned back to Gordon. "My mind is fairly peaceful already, Mr. Leftfoot, but thank you for the information. Now, if you'll excuse me, I have to assist a customer."

"Certainly. I see that you're busy. I can leave you brochures outlining my services." He passed a couple of colorful brochures to Maggie.

She set them on a stool behind the counter. "I'll try to look at them later."

"That'd be great," Gordon said as his keen gaze surveyed the shop. "Since I'm here, why don't I take a look around? Work up an evaluation and estimate."

Maggie shoved a strand of hair behind her ear. "Mr. Leftfoot, truthfully, I'm not interested right now."

"Won't cost you a thing." He smiled brightly. "Can't hurt."

Sarah stepped closer and tapped the man's shoulder. "Mr. Leftfoot, what kind of deals do you give on homes?"

Gordon turned. "Well I have a few accounts in the residential areas, and I'm hoping to expand."

Maggie shot Sarah a grateful smile and hurried toward her customer.

"Have you had any problems with security lately?" he asked.

"I had an estimate written up last year, but then decided it wasn't worth the hassle with people coming in and out so frequently. I take in boarders, and I was afraid we'd be setting off the alarm all the time. But perhaps you may have something simple and user-friendly that would be easy and quick to teach my boarders."

"I could run by your place and take a look."

"You could," Sarah agreed.

He leaned close and lowered his voice. "Or perhaps you're just trying to run interference for your daughter."

"Daughter-in-law," Sarah said with smile.

"She has a nice shop here."

"Yes, she does, and she's really busy this time of year."

"Unfortunately that's when the risk goes up. I don't know a lot about antiques but I can spot quality when I see it. Be a shame for stock to be damaged or stolen." He stroked his chin and Sarah noticed a long, thin scar that snaked under his jaw.

"Were you this intense when you were a police officer?"

He leaned back against the counter and crossed his arms over his chest. "More so."

"You must've been a good cop," Sarah said.

"I was, which makes me perfect for my new job here. I try to help, but unfortunately some people have to learn the hard way. And I'd hate that to be the experience for your daughter-in-law or you. As my grandmother used to say, an ounce of prevention is worth a pound of cure."

"You're right, Mr. Leftfoot, but we also shouldn't put the cart before the horse," Sarah quipped back. "I'll think about a security system as I'm sure Maggie will."

Gordon smiled. "Tell you what. I'll check back here in a week or so. But if anything should happen between now and then, you can call me. I'm at your disposal." He handed her his business card.

"Thank you for your time," Gordon called to Maggie. She gave him a wave without pausing in her sales pitch over a maple headboard. The chimes rang as he went out.

Sarah moved behind the counter as a wisp of a teenager, dressed in a long fuzzy green sweater dress over black tights and boots, examined the charm bracelets. "How much is that one?" She pointed to a delicate silver chain.

Sarah slid open the back of the glass cabinet and removed the jewelry. She examined the tag. "Seventy-five."

"Can I try it on?"

Sarah handed the bracelet over and helped the girl close the clasp. She held it up to the light, examining each charm.

"Ma'am?" someone called.

Sarah turned as a middle-aged woman approached the counter. "I'm looking for one of those rollaway desks that have all the little drawers. There's one in the back, but it's not quite what I'm looking for. I was wondering if that was the only one you have."

"I'm not sure what Maggie has in stock right now. I'll have to ask her," Sarah said. "I'll be just a minute."

She turned back to the girl, but she was gone. So was the bracelet. Sarah's heart thudded, Gordon's warning rolling through her mind. She spun and spied the teen behind her, studying brooches.

She flashed Sarah a smile. "I'm going to take the bracelet, but I still want to browse for a while." She unclasped the chain and handed it over. Sarah set the bracelet by the cash register with relief.

"Be right back," Sarah said to the desk lady. She hurried over to Maggie who was still answering Mrs. Greene's questions about the bed set. Her voice was soft and patient, but her hair bun was unraveling and a wrinkle had formed between her eyebrows.

"Maggie, the customer at the counter has some questions about rollaway desks. She wants to know if you have any more in stock."

"I don't have any more right now, but I did notice one in a catalogue for an estate sale next week. I could order it for her if she's interested."

Sarah relayed the information and assisted Maggie where she could for the next hour. The customers kept them hopping, and Sarah didn't have a chance to question Maggie on what had happened to Patty who was supposed to be helping.

The grandfather clock near the front door had just chimed three times when the phone rang. There was only one customer left in the store by then, and since Maggie was closest to the counter, she grabbed the receiver.

Sarah picked up some hats that had fallen off a rack as Maggie said, "I can't come right now, Dad, and I don't know where Mom is. She said she was going to run to the grocery store. Something about Kasha milk and she hasn't returned. Did you try her cell?" Maggie glanced over at Sarah with a grimace. "She must have accidentally set it on silent again."

Maggie sighed. "I know, I know, but what can I do? Jason won't be off for a couple of hours."

"Is there something I can do?" Sarah asked softly.

"Hold on, Dad," Maggie's hand covered the bottom of the phone. "Dad needs to go to the hardware store, or he won't be able to finish the closet."

"I can take him," Sarah said. "Unless you need me here more."

"I think I'm okay. Mom's supposed to be coming back here. I'm sure Dad would appreciate the ride, *if* it's not too much trouble."

"Of course not. I'm happy to help out," Sarah said. "I wanted to pick up some of that stuff that seals windows anyway."

"Great," Maggie said with a whoosh of breath. "Dad, Sarah will be over." She hung up the phone. "Thanks, Sarah, and thank you for this afternoon. I'll make it up to you."

"You already do in more ways than you'll ever know." Sarah reached for her coat and purse. "Call me if you need any more help."

Sarah counted her blessings every day that Jason and his family were back in Maple Hill. Just the look of relief on Maggie's face was reward enough for Sarah. She glanced up and down the street. Patty's rental car was nowhere to be seen. What was that woman up to?

"Patty says I'm always getting overzealous with my projects," Larry said as he, Amy, and Sarah stared at the rectangular hole in the wall. The wood and metal parts Jason had bought for the shelving and door lay on the closet floor amid the rubble. It was obvious even to Sarah that Larry had made the closet too wide for the parts Jason had purchased.

"I'm going to need more wood and bigger sliding doors," Larry said. He yanked on the end of the measuring tape roll and held it up again. "Probably need to get paint too."

"Dad has paint in the garage," Amy said.

"Good, good. One less thing to try to match."

"Can I go to the hardware store with you?" Amy asked Sarah.

"Sure. What about Audrey?"

"She's on the computer IMing with one of her friends. She won't want to go."

"I better check just to make sure," Sarah said. She left Amy holding one end of the measuring tape as Larry jotted down measurements. Audrey was hunched over the computer, typing away. There were two small boxes on the screen with several lines of text.

"I'm taking your grandfather and Amy to the hardware store. Do you want to come?"

Amy shook her head. "I can't. I'm talking to Courtney and Kimberly. I haven't talked to them in ages."

"Ages? But school just got out last week."

Amy laughed. "No, these are some friends from California. Grandma got their screen names and hooked me up."

"How nice!"

"Yeah, I didn't remember how much I missed them. They're having so much fun. Wish I was there," Amy said with a sigh and then typed in another line.

"You going to be okay here for an hour?"

Amy nodded and gave her a look that clearly implied that was a silly question. She was thirteen after all.

"Call me if you need anything," Sarah said, but Audrey didn't even look up. She giggled at the screen and started typing furiously again.

Sarah got Larry and Amy and led the way to the car. The drive to the hardware store took less than ten minutes. The only parking space was on a patch of salted, pitted ice, and the tires made a crunching sound as she rolled the car to a stop.

Dave Diamond stood by the Christmas trees in the covered side yard with the store owner Hubert Rollins. Mr. Rollins held a clipboard and was flipping through the pages.

Dave was a handyman with his own business, but from time to time, he worked at the hardware store when they needed additional help. This must be one of those times.

Dave looked up and grinned. "Amy, hi! Mrs. Hart, how are you?"

"Doing well, Dave. How are those darling babies of yours?"

"Growing fast. Davie is running around so fast I can hardly keep up with him and Mia is getting so big. What can I help you with today?"

"I'm here with Maggie's father," Sarah said as Larry walked up beside her. "Larry, this is Dave Diamond. Dave worked on the house for Maggie and Jason shortly after they moved in."

"Ah yes, you did a fine job too. Jason was showing me some of your handiwork. I'm doing a bit of remodeling in that grand old house too." Larry explained what he was looking for and Dave sent them off in the right direction.

While Larry and Amy roamed aisles studying their options, Sarah lingered near the gated entrance, looking over the Christmas yard decorations. A pair of wire deer, their silhouettes outlined with white lights, caught her attention. The doe and stag slowly lifted their heads from where they appeared to be grazing and then lowered them again.

"I don't get it," Dave said to Mr. Rollins. "According to this invoice there should be twenty more boards. I checked them in last Tuesday and just assumed they were moved to the back lot."

"I'm positive they're not back there," Mr. Rollins said. "You must've miscounted."

"No way. Not that many. Besides, there are boards missing from two different shipments. See? Jeff checked in the other lot."

Mr. Rollins scowled. "Then someone had to take them. But who would want low-grade lumber? And how did they get it out of here without anyone noticing? These were eight-foot-long boards."

Someone cleared his throat. Sarah looked over her shoulder as an elderly man in insulated coveralls towed a wagon loaded with two-by-fours to the counter.

"Mr. Graham, did you find everything you need?" Dave asked.

"These will do." The older man glanced from one man to the next. "Couldn't help but overhear, and I probably should be minding my own business, but I saw some of them boards like you're talking about. Passed them coming to town yesterday. Those whippersnappers practically ran me off the road in that beat-up pickup of theirs."

"Which whippersnappers would these be, Harry?" Mr. Rollins asked.

"Barclays," Harry practically spat out. "Been causing trouble most of their lives. Just like their pa and their grandpa. They breed trouble."

The Barclays again?

"Of course I can't be sure if those boards are what you're missing, but you might want to check it out."

"Thanks, Harry, I appreciate the information," Mr. Rollins said as Dave rang up his purchase on the cash register.

"Not a problem. We've got to watch out for each other."

Sarah went to find Larry and Amy. Larry had located the quality of boards he wanted and had taken them over to Dave to cut them to size. Then they popped inside the store and picked up more metal brackets and screws. Sarah also found the caulking compound she wanted for an attic window.

They checked out at the inside cash register. As Larry supervised the loading of Sarah's trunk, Sarah paid for her purchase. She noticed Gordon Leftfoot's business card lying by the cash register. "I see Mr. Leftfoot was here too."

"Yeah," Dave said and counted out Sarah's change. "He's pushing for us to upgrade our security system. If he hears about the missing lumber, he'll gloat after telling Mr. Rollins how shoddy our current system is."

"He's pretty determined to establish a business."

"I've seen the same drive in some of the veterans I've worked with. We try to help them find work or a purpose they can feel passionate about. It can give them a positive outlet for pent-up emotions or other stresses they're dealing with."

"Do you think that's what Mr. Leftfoot is dealing with? He was a policeman in Boston."

"Could be, but I don't know him well enough. I noticed his limp. Was he injured in the line of duty?"

"I think so, but I don't know the details," Sarah said. Through the window she saw Larry and Amy get in the car. "Looks like we're ready to go." She headed to the door and then paused, looking back at Dave. "I assume you don't have security cameras outside?"

"No, we don't. The gates are locked at night, but someone could come in over the fence if they're really determined. Or sneak in the back during the day when we aren't watching."

Dave joined her at the door. "Now if I were going to go to all that trouble to steal something, it wouldn't be those second-grade pine boards."

Sarah agreed after seeing how much Larry had spent on shelving. Knowing Jason, once he found out about this he would insist on paying Larry back even though the mistakes were his father-in-law's.

"I hope you find the missing lumber."

"Me too," Dave said.

Once they were settled in the car and heading home, Sarah asked, "Amy, do you know any of the Barclays?"

"Yeah, Benji is two grades ahead of us."

"Benji Barclay?"

"His real name is Benjamin but everyone calls him Benji because it annoys him."

"That doesn't sound very nice," Larry said.

"I know, but he isn't very nice either. He always teases everyone. Some kids call him a bully, but he's not that bad. Just..."

"Just?" Sarah looked in the rearview mirror at Amy.

"Just annoying. He likes to brag."

"About what?"

"Boy stuff. How he's the best in video games. He can spit the farthest. Gross." Amy made a face. "He says he's building a clubhouse in the woods and girls won't be allowed. Just *his* friends. I didn't think he had any."

A clubhouse would need wood, Sarah surmised. That would explain the boards in the back of the Barclays' pickup, but that didn't mean they had stolen them from the hardware store. Benji had to be only fourteen or fifteen, so he wouldn't be driving around a pickup truck by himself. At least not legally.

"Is his brother Tim Barclay?"

Amy shrugged. "I don't know."

Sarah turned on the radio to a station playing Christmas carols. As Larry sang along to "Santa Claus Is Coming to Town" and teased Amy that she better be good, Sarah pondered the information she had picked up. She needed to check out these Barclay boys, beginning with Tim Barclay at the courthouse.

 CHAPTER SEVEN

S arah dropped Larry and Amy back at the house and then headed downtown. She slowed as she neared Maggie's store and saw Patty through the window. She drove on past the Galleria and the Crystal Unicorn. A car pulled out of a parking space and Sarah zipped into it. She wanted to ask Annie some questions. It was almost five, dinnertime, and she hoped Annie wouldn't be busy.

The parking spot was about a block beyond Annie's shop. Sarah got out of the car and had just started to backtrack when she met up with the Helping Hands van yet again. She heard Kathleen's voice rise in an argumentative tone, "I don't carry a cell phone. You'll just have to wait until someone from Helping Hands can get there."

"But I don't know what time I can be home. I work at the Copy Shop and it gets hectic this time of year. The last time I had a charity pick something up, they were very late, and I couldn't wait. It would be much easier if you or someone could call me, and I could meet you there to pick up the sofa."

Sarah looked around the side of the van. Alison Vanter stood by the driver's door. Kathleen lifted the electronic pad and consulted it. "I can be at your place at 9:00 AM, but I can't call you ahead of time."

Alison sighed. "Okay, I guess we'll just have to try that. As long as you're there on time. If I had a truck, I'd take the couch in myself."

Alison stepped back up onto the sidewalk as the van pulled away, shooting exhaust in their direction.

"Hi, Alison," Sarah said.

"Mrs. Hart, how are you doing?"

"Doing well. How's the quilting going?" Sarah asked. Alison made quilts and donated them to a crisis pregnancy center.

"I haven't been able to quilt as much I'd like since Thanksgiving, but when things slow down at the Copy Shop in January, I plan on spending quality time at the sewing machine." She swung a brown shopping bag by her side.

"I was wondering . . . well, there've been several thefts lately at some of the businesses around town. Maybe you noticed there's been talk about improving security. I was wondering if you've been having any trouble."

"No, we've been fine, but that explains the orders for a brochure about alarm systems and a flyer advertising a council meeting about curfews and chaperoning kids."

"Did Gordon Leftfoot order them?"

"Yeah, that's him. Seemed like an okay guy. I don't know much about him, but he's very persistent." Alison grinned. "He made an appointment with me for next week to discuss our system." She glanced at her watch. "Sorry to run, but I need to get back. It was nice seeing you, Mrs. Hart. Stop by the shop sometime and we can chat some more." She took off down the sidewalk at a fast pace.

Sarah walked up the steps to the Crystal Unicorn. On the other side of the window, beyond the sparkling hanging crystals, Annie moved across the store. As Sarah opened the door, pine-scented incense assaulted her nose. She sniffed cautiously, trying not to sneeze. After a few seconds the smell grew pleasant and the tickling sensation subsided.

Annie was ringing up the purchase of a young girl dressed in faded jeans and a denim jacket. "The echinacea and rosehips should help boost your immune system and help you get over your cold sooner," Annie said.

The girl smiled and tucked the paper bag in her backpack. "Can't hurt to try it anyway."

Annie greeted Sarah. "I saw you outside talking to the Helping Hands lady. She's a little nutty, but she has a good heart, don't you think?"

"I just met her the other day, but she does seem to be zealous about helping the needy," Sarah said. "Speaking of needy, someone mentioned there was a woman who roamed the back alley. She thought the woman might be homeless."

"Homeless?" Annie set the large glass jar of echinacea and the rosehips on the shelf behind the counter.

"She pokes around in the garbage cans."

"Oh, you must mean Clara. She's not homeless. She collects aluminum cans and other recyclables for extra cash to buy food for stray dogs."

"Do you know her last name?"

"No. She's shy and the only reason she's talked to me is that I started saving my cans at home for her. I found this natural soda that's really quite good. I'm going to start selling it here in the store next summer."

"Do you think Clara would've noticed your shipment on the back step?"

Annie pursed her lips. "I doubt it. She usually comes by early before the stores are open." Her eyes narrowed. "Even if she did see the boxes, Clara wouldn't have taken one. Her aura is a lovely pink, which means love and honesty."

Aura? She was basing her assessment of a stranger's honesty on a perceived colored glow?

The skepticism must have shown on Sarah's face, because Annie let out a short laugh. "Look, Mrs. Hart, regardless of whether you believe in life force, I don't want anyone harassing Clara because of my carelessness."

"I agree. I wasn't planning to bother her."

"I don't want the police around here either. It'll scare off my customers. It's my fault for being careless. Everything's fine. I just want peace. We just all need more peace."

Sarah couldn't argue with that. She could use more peace in her life. "One other thing. Do you know the Barclay brothers?"

Annie frowned. "I only know a Paul Barclay who used to work at the Chamber of Commerce. He was totally rude to me. Sat there and read a comic book on his 'break' while I waited for twenty minutes. Then he was no help at all. I finally lodged a complaint. Apparently other people did too because I heard he got fired."

Apparently Annie's wish for peace didn't extend to all people. Sarah'd had similar experiences with Paul and Tim Barclay and she could understand her frustration.

Annie placed her hand over her chest. "Excuse me. I need to take some dandelion for heartburn."

"Dandelion works for heartburn?"

"Milk thistle too," Annie said, her back to Sarah "Besides, I'm out of Tums." She grinned over her shoulder, and Sarah laughed. As owner of a New Age store, Annie tried to project the expected image, but it was refreshing to see she wasn't totally out of the mainstream.

"You know what?" Annie said. "I should've known there was something off with Paul. His aura was the color of mud with black flecks."

"Which means?" Sarah couldn't help but ask.

"The brown could mean he's stagnating. Not growing."

"And the black?"

Annie turned to face her. "He keeps a secret."

A chill pricked Sarah's skin as she left the Crystal Unicorn, and it wasn't from the frigid air temperature. New Age businesses seemed to flourish throughout

New England, especially in places that attracted tourists. Annie's store actually sold more natural remedies and organic products now than crystals and items related to astrology. It just seemed to her that people were searching for answers and reassurance in inanimate objects like crystals when all they had to do was have faith in God.

Granted it was hard not to question God when tragedy or illness struck or when you lost someone you loved. When her father passed away, she had been more prepared than when Gerry had died from cancer. William had lived a full, happy life and when he slowly deteriorated, his death hadn't come as a surprise. But with Gerry, Sarah had struggled with her faith in dark, still moments. It wasn't fair. He was such a good man. But as the Bible text she had read the other night said, she had found peace when she let go and believed that everything was done to God's plan. She might not understand now, but someday God would explain all.

Maybe Annie really believed she could sum up a person's personality or their emotions by seeing a colored light floating around them. But how much was wishful thinking? Sarah certainly could sense when there was emotion in a room without seeing colored lights.

Like when she entered Maggie's store.

After the door chimes quieted, silence stretched taut as harp strings.

Maggie was wiping down a table, her movements jerky. She had loosened her hair today and the waves hung over her face. "Let's not talk about it now, Mom."

Patty stood watching her, twisting her hands together. "Why can't you just be happy?"

"Mom—"

"This is a great opportunity. I thought I'd explode if I kept this to myself any longer. I've got several investors, friends of mine, lined up. We'll call the place Magpie's Antiques West. You can ship antiques you find back here and vice versa. It'll broaden your stock and exposure. Someday you'll be known on both coasts."

Maggie let out a little laugh. "I'm known well enough around here."

"You've changed so much since moving here. You used to be so ambitious. Why would you isolate yourself and squander your talent when the whole world is open to you? The girls will be in college soon. Then what? I just don't understand you at all." Patty blinked rapidly and swiped her fingers at her running mascara.

"Mom, I don't want to argue." Maggie moved to a cabinet and swiped the rag over the shelves. "I appreciate how much you care, but you should've asked me before signing the deed."

"It was supposed to be a surprise. A present for you. And I just want to be with you more. So does your father. Audrey and Amy are practically grown, and I've missed them. Think about it. If you have a shop out in California, you and the girls have a reason to visit every other month *and* travel will be tax deductible. Maybe you can even move back after the girls finish high school."

"Jason doesn't want to go back to California. He's finally getting his blood pressure under control and his practice is growing."

Patty sniffed and reached for the tissue box on the counter. "But see? If the shops are successful, he won't even have to work."

Sarah bit her lip to keep herself from saying Jason would probably never agree to such an arrangement. The move from California to Maple Hill hadn't been easy for the family, but it had proved to be the right one.

Patty wiped her nose with a tissue. "Just think about it for a while. Please? This is a great opportunity."

Maggie swept her hair back with her hand and looked at her mother. "I will consider it, but I don't want you bothering Jason with this idea until I have a chance to tell him myself *if* I'm interested. I do appreciate your caring about me."

Patty smiled, her lip trembling some. "I have another surprise."

Maggie placed a hand on her chest. "I'm not sure my heart can stand another one."

"Don't be silly," Patty said, reaching into her purse. "Ta da! Tickets to *The Nutcracker* in Pittsfield."

"Oh!" Maggie's face brightened. "I've been wanting to see the ballet. When is it?"

"The only tickets left where I could get six together are for Saturday night."

"Saturday night?" Maggie frowned. "That won't work."

Patty's arms crossed at her waist. "What do you mean that won't work? I paid a small fortune for these."

"I made a commitment last month to sell raffle tickets at the Holiday Home Tour this Saturday."

Patty sniffed again. "Surely they can get someone else."

"How would it look for me to back out at the last minute to attend a play? Especially since a lot of the stuff in the raffle baskets is from my shop."

"It's not last minute. She has two days to find someone else," Patty said.

"Almost everyone I know is involved with a job or two. The rest of you can go and have a good time. It'll be all right."

"No it won't." Patty slammed the tissue box on the counter. "This was supposed to be a family outing. There has to be someone who can fill in for you." Patty finally noticed Sarah. "Perhaps Sarah could take your place with the raffle. You wouldn't mind, would you?" she asked breezily.

"I can't. I have plans for the evening," Sarah said.

"Really?" Patty's eyebrows rose. "Can you change them? It's not like Larry and I are here all the time. We need special times like this as a family."

Sarah bit back a sharp retort. How dare Patty try to guilt her into canceling her date when she should've consulted Maggie before buying the tickets? And Sarah noted that Patty hadn't bought a ticket for her. She understood Patty wanting alone time with Jason, Maggie, and the girls and she was okay with that, but Patty could've at least considered Sarah's feelings in the matter.

She opened her mouth to refuse Patty's request, but the embarrassed, pink stain on poor Maggie's cheeks changed her mind. "Maggie, don't worry. I'll fill in for you. Go have a good time."

Maggie shook her head. "I don't want to spoil your plans."

"It'll be fine," Sarah repeated. "This is important to your parents." She would just have to explain to Liam why she couldn't have dinner with him and his Irish cousins. She was disappointed, but more than anything else, Sarah wanted this first Christmas without William to be a happy one for the whole family. He would have wanted it that way.

"Now, see? Everything is fine," Patty said with a big smile.

"Thanks to you, Sarah. I appreciate it." Maggie shoved a strand of hair behind her ear and glanced at the grandfather clock. "I guess it's time to close up and go make dinner."

Patty covered her mouth with her hand. "Oh dear! I forgot. I made plans for dinner tonight. I met this lovely woman at that Unicorn shop down the road. She cooks organically and has these special pots that steam food without oil or any fat. She invited your dad and me over for a demonstration."

"But I thought you were going to make a meatless meatloaf for dinner tonight," Maggie said in a weary voice.

"I was. What a scatterbrain I am! I'll pop over there and cancel."

"No, it's okay, Mom. Go have fun. You're on vacation. I'll order pizza for tonight. It's been a while since we ordered out and the girls will like that." Maggie walked to the door and flipped the sign over to "Closed."

"We'll only be gone an hour or two. But really, dear, be careful about eating too much cheese. It can plug up your system." Patty walked behind the counter and pulled a compact out of her purse and checked her reflection. She patted powder under her eyes and then snapped the compact shut. "I'll run over and get your dad. Thanks again, Sarah, for Saturday night."

Sarah watched Patty sweep out the door. Maggie's mother was a woman of contradictions.

She wondered what aura Annie would say Patty had.

# CHAPTER EIGHT

I 'm sorry about the scene in the store earlier," Maggie said as she covered the leftover pizza with plastic wrap. Maggie had invited Sarah over for supper, and they had picked up pizza on the way home. After supper, the girls had gone to watch a Christmas program in the parlor, and Sarah wasn't sure where Jason had disappeared to.

"Once my mother gets something in her head, it's hard to shake her out of it," Maggie added.

"She means well, I'm sure."

"She does. And really the idea of a second store *someday* is not a bad idea. I love what I do and would like to expand. But California? It's so far away. Now if I could be a buyer for the store out there and leave the actual business in someone else's hands, then that might be doable. I'd have fun with that and wouldn't have to travel out there so often."

"That might work," Sarah said, although she was pretty sure that Patty's main motivation in wanting to open a shop was to draw Maggie back closer to her childhood home.

"Maybe. But I know my mother, she says she'll run the store, but follow-through isn't her strong suit. It'd depend on who her friends are and how serious they are about opening an antiques store. I suppose I should look at the paperwork she put together." She glanced at the door and lowered her voice. "I just don't want to worry Jason with all this. My mother can be somewhat pushy."

The kitchen door swung open. "Mom, Audrey won't let me watch the football game."

Maggie closed the refrigerator door. "I thought you two were watching *White Christmas.*

"It's boring and besides, we were only going to watch the movie because Grammy wanted to."

"If Audrey is already watching it, then it's not nice to change the channel. Football should still be on when it's over."

"Yeah, but then Grandma will be back, and she'll want us to do something else."

"And this is a problem?" Maggie asked with raised eyebrows. "Your grandparents are only here until New Year's. It's not like you can see them all the time."

Amy mumbled something about it not being her fault.

"Excuse me, young lady?" Maggie asked.

Amy stayed silent.

"If you can't say something nice, then don't say anything at all."

Amy clamped her lips shut, turned on her heel, and left the kitchen.

"That was scary," Maggie said. "I remember my mom saying that to me. I can hear her voice in my head. I was worse than Amy though. My mother believed in letting children have free reign when expressing their emotions. I could be really rotten."

"I can't imagine," Sarah said with sincerity. "Must've been those teen hormones."

"Oh yeah." Maggie grinned. "And Audrey and Amy are only thirteen. We're just starting."

Sarah finished wiping off the counter while Maggie started the dishwasher. "Thanks for dinner. I better head home. I have some Christmas stuff to do. I'll just say goodbye to Jason and the girls."

"I think he's in the hallway." Maggie said, leading the way to where Jason stood, hands on hips, staring at the hole Larry had created. "The doors I bought aren't going to fit."

"I know," Sarah said. "We looked at some at the hardware store but they weren't the right width either. Dave said they could order some custom doors. Larry said he'd discuss it with you."

"That'll cost a lot more than I budgeted for this project. I suppose I can frame back some of the wall." He reached down and picked up a piece of the plaster that the floor was littered with. The hardware store purchases were still in their bags at the bottom of the closet.

"He means well," Maggie said as she dragged a vacuum cleaner into the hall. "And the closet will be much more useful at this size. Consider this my Christmas present."

"Good. If this is all that it takes to make you happy, I'll take back the bracelet I got you." Jason grinned.

"Oh yeah? Take this." Maggie switched on the vacuum and stuck the nozzle on his shirt, drawing him close. He wrapped his arm around her neck, then snagged the nozzle and turned it on Maggie. They both laughed.

Sarah smiled, glad to see them enjoying each other amid the disaster. She helped Jason pick up the mess while Maggie got the dust with the vacuum cleaner.

The TV had been switched to the football game with Amy sitting cross-legged in front of the screen. Audrey was lying on the floor by the fireplace, one hand propping up her head and the other doodling on her sketch pad.

Lights twinkled on the Christmas tree in front of the window. The fresh pine scent wafted through the room, so unlike the cloying incense in Annie's shop.

Maggie's Christmas quilt hung on the wall above the couch. Sarah had started the quilt before Christmas last year to replace the heirloom Hart Christmas quilt that had disappeared. Tradition in the Hart family dictated that the recipient of the quilt embroider on the border a symbol that represented Christmas that year. Maggie had embroidered two overlapping gold hearts last year to represent the joining of two generations to continue the tradition of the quilt.

Sarah wondered what this year would bring.

At home, Sarah checked her e-mail. The letter she had sent to the mystery quilt blog owner had come back as undeliverable. That was odd. She checked to make sure she had typed in the correct address.

She quickly wrote an e-mail to the blog site moderator requesting the message be forwarded to the blog author. An automated reply arrived in her e-mail box almost immediately. Customer Service would process her request and be in contact with her as soon as possible.

She studied the piles of colorful squares. As an experienced quilter she could very easily bypass the problem and create a design herself. But the whole point of the mystery quilt was to re-create what the writer had intended. And she wanted to give the instructions and blog entries to Martha as part of the gift.

She checked that day's entry. The blurb included a story about Christmas candles and holders with typos throughout. She skipped down to the instructions. Today they were to sew the strips together to form the middle of the quilt. But again, without the order of the squares, she couldn't make the strips.

She would give the blog author another day to respond. Meanwhile she could work on the pillows for Maggie's parlor. She spread the velvet fabric on her cutting mat and measured the size she would need to cover the foam she had purchased. She pinned the fringe between the fabric edges and then ran the entire thing though the sewing machine.

Satisfied with her progress, she set the material aside. She fixed a cup of tea and got out her notebook to start a list of people she needed to investigate about the stolen merchandise. She wrote Clara on the top. Clara may have been in the alley, but had she been in the stores where merchandise had been shoplifted?

Next she jotted down Paul Barclay's name. The Barclay truck had been spotted with lumber in the back, but more significant was that Annie may have been instrumental in getting Paul fired. Would he steal from her as an act of revenge?

Who else was seen about town frequently?

Kathleen, the Helping Hands employee, traveled all over Maple Hill. Did she know more than she was letting on? Sarah really didn't know anything about her other than that she was enthusiastic in her charity work and had an aunt who had quilted.

Sarah stared at the ceiling. Who else did she need to investigate further?

The kitchen phone rang, startling her. Sarah sprang out of the chair to answer it.

"Mom, I got your package today," Jenna said. "The boys are excited and counting down the days until Christmas."

"Oh, good! I wanted to beat the Christmas rush," Sarah said, warmed by her daughter's voice. "How are you feeling?"

"Doing great. The baby is growing, and so am I." Jenna laughed. "I had to buy more maternity jeans today."

Sarah smiled wistfully, wishing Jenna lived closer so she could be more involved with her daughter's third pregnancy. "I can't wait to meet her or him!"

"Me too!" Jenna said. "How's everything there? Maggie's folks get in okay?"

"Yes, they did. They got here on Monday."

"Okay, so . . . what's wrong?"

Sarah blinked. "What do you mean? Everyone is fine."

"Oh, come on, Mom. I can tell by the tone in your voice something's not right."

Sarah laughed. Her daughter knew her so well. She also knew she could safely confide in Jenna, and it was relief to have someone to talk to. "I just worry. I want everyone to be happy this Christmas."

"I know you do, Mom," Jenna said softly and Sarah realized they were both thinking of William. Jenna let out a sigh and then said. "Spill it, Mom. You'll feel better."

Sarah told Jenna about Amy overhearing Patty's phone conversation and then Patty's business proposal. "They tend to be late for things and change their minds. Nothing wrong with that, unless it affects other people."

"Sounds like Patty's on a campaign to get her family back to California," Jenna said. "But I wouldn't worry about Maggie being pushed into anything. When I talked with her parents at the wedding I noticed how different they were from Maggie. She seems the solid, reliable one in the family. How's Jason handling all this?"

Sarah sighed. "He doesn't know about the business deal yet. He's busy repairing the closet Larry is helping with." She told Jenna about the wall demolition.

Jenna giggled. "I'm sorry. I realize it's not funny for Jason, but remember some of his disasters? There was that time Grandpa William was going to teach Jason how to build a bird house, but Jason wouldn't wait."

Sarah laughed at the memory of the crooked cube Jason had made. The side slats didn't line up well, so there were cracks in the sides and the roof sat on top lopsided. Jason told them the holes were for air conditioning. Amazingly enough a pair of sparrows adopted the ugly structure, and the crooked birdhouse had hung in the oak tree for years. Sarah couldn't bear to get rid of it until the thing literally fell apart.

"And then there was the time he and I decided to build a clubhouse out of those old fence posts. We were lucky it didn't collapse on us," Jenna said. "We couldn't agree on the paint so one half was hot pink and the other hunter green. And then Dad took up wood burning and I decided to put my name on my door? I didn't know you were supposed to burn it on a plaque of wood first."

"I called the fire department when I saw smoke at the top of the stairs," Sarah said with the shiver.

"Yeah. I got a lecture from the fire chief, but I didn't mind because I was old enough to find him cute."

"You never told me that." Sarah grinned, feeling a weight lift. All families had a little bit of nuttiness in them. "Thanks Jenna. I needed a good talk."

"Anytime, Mom. I just wish we could be together this Christmas."

"Me too, sweetie. Say hello to David and kiss the boys for me. I'll call later this week." They said good night and Sarah clicked the phone off.

The house seemed too quiet, the only sound being the soft hum of the furnace. She had been so intent on getting to work on the mystery quilt, she had forgotten to turn on the Christmas lights.

It had taken her hours to get the decorations all up. This year she hadn't waited for Jason to help. She wanted to get an early start on Christmas. And then tonight she had forgotten to even turn the lights on. Maybe she should get one of those automatic timers she had seen at the hardware store.

The kitchen clock hands edged toward eleven o'clock. Too late to call Liam and tell him she couldn't go out with him Saturday night. She would call first thing in the morning.

Sarah glanced down at her notebook. She would finish her list in the morning too, but before she closed the cover, she picked up the pencil and circled Clara's name. She would see if she could find her tomorrow. Clara may not have had anything to do with the theft of Annie's shipment, but she might have seen someone else. Looking for Clara gave her a good excuse to go by The Spotted Dog, not that she needed an excuse.

She stood and circled Clara's name one more time just for emphasis and headed for bed.

Cloud cover rolled in overnight, making the snow-covered downtown landscape bleak and cheerless. Sarah tugged on a pink wool cap and wrapped her matching scarf tightly around her neck as she ventured out onto Main Street. At seven in the morning the only shop lit with a welcoming glow was The Spotted Dog. She was tempted to dash inside for a latte and a cranberry scone, but first she needed to complete her early morning mission of checking the alley for Clara.

Her boot slid on ice as she stepped onto the more secure salted sidewalk. With the temperatures dipping back into the twenties each night, whatever snow managed to melt during the day froze again.

She ducked her head against the wind and rounded the corner to the alley. The alley appeared dark and empty. It had been worth a shot. She would check back later. As she turned to go, a flash of color caught her eye and a woman came out from behind the café dumpster. Dressed in a long denim skirt, rubber boots, an army jacket, and a shawl draped over her head, she dragged a large green trash bag as she shuffled to the next trash can.

Sarah froze, watching, while trying to figure out the best approach. A gusty wind shot shivers down her back. She turned and hurried to the café.

Karen stood behind the counter. "Two coffees to go, please," Sarah said.

"Sure thing, Mrs. Hart," Karen said. "A pot just finished brewing." She poured coffee into two paper cups and capped them. "Here you go."

"Thanks, keep the change," Sarah said, dropping some bills on the counter. She paused at the condiment station and shoved packets of sugar and creamer in her pockets.

She could hear Liam's voice in the kitchen, but she couldn't linger now. She would talk to him about Saturday night when she got back. She hurried to the alley, hoping the woman was still there.

She was behind the Galleria poking in the garbage can with a cane.

"Clara?"

"What?" The woman jumped back, nearly tripping over oversize boots.

"I'm sorry. I didn't mean to startle you." Sarah held out one of the cups. "I'm Sarah Hart. My daughter-in-law owns Magpie's Antiques." She nodded toward the shop. "I thought maybe you'd like some coffee."

The woman's gaze dropped to the cup, still looking stunned.

"I don't know about you, but I'm freezing," Sarah said. "I hope you like coffee. I could've gotten tea."

Clara took the coffee. Sarah reached into her pocket and pulled out some packets. "Cream or sugar?"

She shook her head. "Black is fine." She sipped cautiously from the cup and then took a bigger gulp. "Thank you. This is good."

Sarah drank some of her coffee and then asked, "You *are* Clara, aren't you? Annie mentioned you sometimes come back here to collect aluminum cans."

"I take whatever recyclables I can find. Every bit of change helps to feed my dogs."

"What kinds of dogs do you have?"

"Different ones. Mostly mutts. I'm on a canine rescue team and take in strays and try to find them homes. Do you have a dog?"

"Not anymore. We used to have a black lab when my kids were young. They're grown now and have children of their own."

"Do you miss him?"

"I do," Sarah said, a wistful feeling settling over her. "Hank was a great dog. We used to go to a lake in the Berkshires and he'd swim for as long as we'd let him. He liked to retrieve sticks and balls. He adored Jenna, my daughter, and would go to the end of our sidewalk and wait for her to come home from school."

"That's what I like about dogs. They're loyal, loving, and they accept you for who you are. They're true friends."

"I agree."

"I'd do anything for my dogs." Her gaze swept over Sarah. "Would you be wanting another?"

"Maybe someday. I rent out rooms in my home and it's just easier not to have pets right now. Some people are allergic."

"Well, if you ever change your mind, I can set you up with a puppy or a grown dog that's trained. Just let me know what you want."

"I'll remember that. How do I get hold of you?"

"I live out on Trinity Road. Third house on the left after you turn off Country Lane. If you can't find it, just ask people where the crazy lady with the dogs lives." She let out a laugh that sounded like a cackle.

Sarah smiled. "Before you go, Clara, I wanted to ask you some questions. I need some help."

Her brow furrowed. "What kind of help?"

"Annie had a shipment delivered to the back door of the Crystal Unicorn and it disappeared and—"

"And you think I took it?" Clara dropped her cup on the ground and the lid flew off, spraying coffee on Sarah's slacks.

Sarah jumped back and brushed away the droplets before most of them soaked in. "I was just going to ask if you saw anyone. Someone you don't usually see."

"Yeah. Right." Clara tied her garbage bag shut with jerky movements. "I mind my own business and let others mind theirs. I'm not a nosy busybody like some." She glared at Sarah.

Clara slung the green garbage bag over her shoulder and the bag caught on a piece of metal railing and ripped open. Cans rolled across the snow. Sarah bent to help, but Clara waved her away. "I got it. Don't get your hands dirty."

Clara stuffed the cans in the bag and tied the edges shut, but not before Sarah spied what looked like crystal or glass nestled inside. Apparently Clara collected other recyclables, besides cans.

Clara walked out of the alley without a backward glance.

# CHAPTER NINE

An occasional shiver shook Sarah's spine as she sat at the small round table waiting for Liam to finish in the storage room. After Clara had climbed in her battered Datsun pickup and roared off, Sarah headed back to the café as fast as the slippery ground would allow. The encounter with Clara had been unsettling, and the cold had seeped deep into her bones. She needed a mood booster and ordered a large peppermint mocha latte with extra whipped cream.

While she waited, she opened her notebook and decided to start a new list. On a fresh page she wrote "Possible Suspects" and then made three columns for names, motive, and opportunity.

She wrote down Clara's name first since the woman was fresh in her mind. Clara had said she would do anything for her dogs, which gave her motive. For opportunity, she had a truck to haul things such as lumber or boxes of merchandise, and she lurked behind the shops early in the day. On the other hand, no one had mentioned actually seeing her inside the shops. The focus had been on the teens.

She jotted down teenagers next. Motive could be for kicks, peer pressure, or simply the lack of money to buy things. They had been seen inside the shops, but then no one had seen them in the alley. And what about the hardware store? None of the girls could drive. How would they haul the lumber? Of course this was assuming that all the crimes had been committed by the same person or persons.

The Barclay brothers were next. Paul could be angry at Annie for getting him fired, and his motive would be revenge in the case of her missing box. Since he was without a job, he could be stealing other things because of lack of money. For opportunity, the Barclays had a truck. They had been seen hauling lumber. They could have used the truck to take other things. Were they desperate enough to steal?

She added Kathleen. She didn't appear to be the materialistic type and was very focused on giving to the poor. But she definitely had opportunity. Kathleen had been seen all over town with her Helping Hands truck and she was constantly in and out of the shops. Did she know more than she was letting on?

Sarah tapped her pencil on the page. Who else might have the means and opportunity?

Gordon Leftfoot. Like Kathleen, he had been in almost every business in downtown Maple Hill. What better way to drum up business than to create a need? She toyed with the idea. Gordon was an ex-cop, and he had supposedly been a good one. But what did they really know about this stranger to their town?

"What are you working so hard on?" Liam asked, causing her to drop her pencil on the floor. "You didn't even hear me when I said hello."

Sarah smiled and placed a hand over her fluttering heart as he set two lattes on the table and leaned down to retrieve the pencil. Liam looked very handsome today in black jeans and a hunter green sweater that turned his twinkling eyes emerald.

Liam settled in the chair opposite her and glanced at her open notebook. "Making lists?"

Sarah's face warmed. "Yes. I'm being a nosy busybody again and trying to figure out this shoplifting."

Liam's grin widened. "Being nosy isn't a crime. And if you do stick your nose in people's business it's only because you care and have a good heart."

Sarah smiled her thanks. It was wonderful to have such supportive friends as Martha and Liam. "Would it be nosy to ask if there've been any clues to finding your umbrella stand?"

"No such luck. I didn't have that thing very long, but I miss it." He chuckled. "When I set it up, Murphy barked at it like it was real dog."

Sarah gazed around the shop full of spotted dogs. "And he never mistook any of these for the real thing?"

"Nope. Just the stand. I suppose the Dalmatian looked too lifelike, right, Murphy?" Liam said to his corgi, who was lying on the floor in the bookstore, a miniature stuffed dog between his front paws. Murphy thumped his tail on the floor and nosed his toy over a few inches.

"So what are you doing out and about so early?" Liam asked. "Are you meeting Martha?"

"No, it's just me this morning." Sarah told him about her meeting with Clara in the alley.

"Do you think she'd steal to feed her dogs?" he asked.

"Maybe." Sarah looked down at her notebook. "I don't know."

Liam rubbed his chin. "I'll keep my eye out for her."

"Thanks," Sarah said. "Before I forget, I can't go out to dinner Saturday after all." She explained about filling in for Maggie at the Holiday Home Tour. "I'm so sorry. Her parents will be leaving right after New Year's, and it's important they have time together."

"The Home Tour? I can't believe I'd forgotten it was this weekend. Now there's an idea. I'll ask my cousins if they'd like to go, but they might not be interested. They're recently retired and touring the states."

"Are they married?"

"Nope. One never found *the* girl, so he says, and the other divorced multiple times. Told me they're free as the wind and can do as they please."

Was that a wistful note in Liam's voice? He was alone now too since his wife Jeannie had passed away. Did he wish he were free to travel?

"What time are you through volunteering?" Liam's voice broke into her pondering.

"Probably not until eight thirty."

"How about we just have a late supper, or dessert and coffee, if you'd prefer."

"Really?" Sarah said. "You don't mind waiting?"

Liam's gaze held hers. "Not at all."

Sarah felt a flush rising on her cheeks. "Thanks. I'm looking forward to meeting your cousins." *And being with Liam.*

"Good. It's settled then." He took a swig from his coffee mug, and then had to lick cream off his lip. "Now...other than tracking down old ladies in the alley and then trying to break my heart about our date," he teased with a wink, "how are you doing? Is the visit with Maggie's folks still going well?"

"Can't complain," Sarah said with a smile, although technically she *could* complain about Patty's pressure on Maggie and the girls, and the mess Larry had made for Jason to fix, but what good would it do? The holidays weren't going as well as she had hoped. Still, she was so blessed by having family and great friends around her. She was glad she wasn't free as the wind.

As Sarah exited the Spotted Dog, Maggie was unlocking the door to her store. Sarah waved and walked over.

"Mom overslept," Maggie said in answer to Sarah's unasked question. "They were late getting in last night. Mom bought a whole set of cookware and recipe books."

"Sounds like they had a good time. I'm sure Annie appreciates the sale too."

"She should. That stuff wasn't cheap." Maggie led the way inside and turned on the overhead lights and then the white twinkle Christmas lights in the window.

"I'm going to put a pot of coffee on. Would you like some?" Maggie called over her shoulder as she headed into the back room.

"No thanks, I just came from the café." Sarah picked up a long pink feather and stuck it back on the hat hanging on the rack. The smell of brewing coffee wafted into the room as Maggie reappeared, dragging a dust mop. Under the fluorescent lighting, dark circles showed up under her eyes. Sarah wasn't the only one staying up late it appeared.

"Do you need any help this morning?" Sarah asked.

"I'll be okay." Maggie ran the mop over the hardwood floor. "It usually isn't that busy until the afternoon. Mom should be here by then. What are you doing today?"

"I'm going to the courthouse. I'm still trying to find a connection among all the thefts around here."

"Well, apparently it's still going on. Last night I heard that some merchandise was stolen from the China Cup."

"I was just there yesterday. Mrs. Kloche said everything was fine. What happened?"

"I don't know any of the details, but Margie called me last night and she was in the store when Mrs. Kloche was making a police report."

The door chimes rang. "Good morning," Maggie called to a young couple wearing matching ski parkas.

The woman hung on the man's arm, giggling. "Oh, hi! We're looking for furniture for a baby's room. Do you have anything?"

"In fact I do. I have a sweet cherrywood bassinet and a really nice rocker." Maggie propped the mop against a couch. "They're back there."

"Awesome!" the young woman said, tugging the man forward.

Maggie turned to Sarah. "You're welcome to come to dinner tonight, although I'm not sure what we're having. Mom was saying something about braised gluten nuggets. So if you want to bow out, I'll understand." Maggie laughed.

"I still need to work on some things at home this evening. I'll check back with you later. Give me a call if you need anything." Sarah gave Maggie a wave and headed out the door.

Sarah's boots made faint tracks across the tile in the courthouse even though she had wiped them carefully at the door. The Register of Deeds office was at the end of the hall.

Tim Barclay slouched on a stool behind the counter. His red hair was shorter than the last time she had seen him, but it still skimmed his collar. He propped a phone between his ear and shoulder while he texted on a cell. He glanced up at Sarah and then turned his back to her and walked back toward a bank of file cabinets.

Sarah sighed and unbuttoned her coat. She had thought arriving at the courthouse right after it opened would get her in and out in a few minutes. She should've known better. Ten minutes passed before Tim returned.

"Hi, Tim, do you remember me?"

"Should I?" He shrugged. "Do you know how many people come through here?"

Sarah decided to ignore the sarcasm. "I'm Sarah Hart. I wanted to get in touch with your cousin, Paul."

"Why?"

"Does it matter?" Sarah said.

"Maybe." He glanced at an empty doughnut bag sitting by a cup of coffee on the desk.

Sarah planted her hands on the counter and leaned forward. "Look, Tim, you can get rid of me faster by giving me his phone number."

His lips twitched as if hiding a smile. "He doesn't have a phone right now. He lost his job."

"That's too bad. What's he doing for work?"

"Firewood. He and his brother run firewood out to people. Their dad cuts it. He also does odd jobs."

"Does Paul have a blue pickup?"

"When it's running. Why?"

"Someone said they saw a truck driving out of town with a load of lumber. Did you know there was a theft at the hardware store?"

Tim scratched his ear. "Not until some guy came by here asking questions about Paul."

"What guy?"

"Some security dude."

"Gordon Leftfoot. Blond and limps?"

"Yep."

Sarah took a deep breath. She wanted to get as much information as quickly as possible in case Tim's phone rang again. "Did he suggest Paul stole the lumber?"

"Like I told him, there's no crime in salvaging wood nobody wants. There's plenty around. He wouldn't need to steal any." Tim stared at his phone as if itching to pick it up. "Not that he would steal anything these days. He's changed."

"How?"

"I can't stand being around him. He's gotten all motivated and preachy about 'making something' of himself. *Boring.*"

Motivated? Paul? The last time she had talked to Paul he was a carbon copy of Tim. She focused back on the purpose of her visit. "I really need to get hold of him. Where is he living?"

"My great-great-grandparents' cabin way back in the woods. Place doesn't have an address."

"How do people get in touch with him if he doesn't have a phone?"

Tim glanced at the doughnut bag again. "He uses the post office in town for mail. Or he gets messages from his dad."

"You have his father's number?"

"Nope, don't hang with him either."

Sarah rubbed her forehead. A stabbing pain was forming over her left eye. "Paul has a brother?"

"Ben. Now there's a cool kid. I'd hang with him if Paul would let him."

"Do you know where he is?"

Tim shrugged. "He buses tables at Miss Maple when he's not in school or hauling firewood."

Sarah pulled out her notebook and jotted the info down. When she looked up again Tim had his back to her, his thumbs flying across the keypad on his cell phone. Obviously, she was done here.

# CHAPTER TEN

The cashier at the Miss Maple diner informed Sarah that Ben Barclay had picked up the breakfast shift since he was on school break, but he had suddenly left for the day. Sarah declined leaving him a message and wondered if Tim had tipped him off.

Sarah drove to the China Cup and parked. As she entered the door, Mrs. Kloche rushed out from behind the counter and exclaimed, "Sarah, I have you to thank!" She gave Sarah a quick hug.

Sarah blinked with surprise. "Me?"

"Yes, dear, if you hadn't asked me if anything had been stolen, I might not have checked my inventory until after Christmas. I just couldn't get the idea out of my head, so I got out my inventory sheets and did a thorough count. Sure enough, about eight hundred dollars worth of merchandise is missing."

"Oh no! What's missing?" Sarah asked.

"See that stoneware by the door?" She pointed to the dinnerware set that Martha had been interested in. "Four boxes are gone."

"Do the police have any clues?" Sarah asked.

"They're investigating, although I have no idea when or how the boxes disappeared. My alarm system turns on at night, so it must've been during the day. But at least now I have the missing merchandise on record for my insurance company. That helps."

Sarah followed Mrs. Kloche to the display by the door. Mrs. Kloche pointed to boxes that were stacked in several piles underneath the table. "It would be easy not to notice if some were missing."

"But how could someone get them out the door without your noticing?"

"That's what I keep asking myself. I can get busy or preoccupied, but I've never had this happen before. I haven't noticed anyone suspicious. The police did ask me about teens visiting the store recently."

"Teens," Sarah repeated, not really surprised.

"Yes, sometimes groups come in, mostly girls, but they don't stay long. It's not like I carry anything very interesting for young people. But with a big crowd like that and the store being so small, I suppose while some of them were talking to me, others could've picked up the boxes and walked out. The stoneware is right by the door. Anyway, that's what Mr. Leftfoot surmised as one possible scenario. He thinks I should get a video camera for the door."

"Yes, I suppose he would," Sarah said, studying the distance to the door. If someone parked a car right out front, they might be able to quickly tuck the items inside without Mrs. Kloche noticing.

The phone rang. "Excuse me, dear," Mrs. Kloche said, "I need to get that."

While Mrs. Kloche talked on the phone, Sarah circled the table and then lifted one of the boxes. It wasn't as heavy as she had thought it would be. She carefully set it down and stepped back, bumping a Helping Hands bin by the door. She glanced inside. People had donated lots of nifty kitchen gadgets and pretty kitchen towels. She lifted up a pasta server. A receipt had been taped to it and the price caused her to raise her eyebrows.

"I'm sorry. I need to move that out of the way," Mrs. Kloche said. "The Helping Hands Christmas campaign seems to be going really well. I see the bins all over town being filled with items. Even during tough economic times, people are still thinking of the less fortunate. It's sad people don't feel so generous the rest of the year."

"Yes, it is," Sarah agreed and glanced around the store again.

Mrs. Kloche followed her gaze. "Is there something I can help you with?"

"I was just thinking that I need to get something for Jason's mother-in-law as a Christmas present. It can't be too large because she'll be flying back home."

"Does she drink tea?"

"I think so."

"Have a look at these personal tea sets." Mrs. Kloche gestured to a colorful display of teacup and teapot sets. The cup slid into the top of the compact teapot. "They're designed for tea, but any hot beverage would do. They are great to take to work too since they're so compact, yet pretty."

Sarah lifted a colorful set with a flowery design. "This looks like something she might like." She turned it over. The price was reasonable. "I'll take it. And please add a set of those dry measuring cups to put in the Helping Hands box."

"Excellent choice and it's very kind of you to donate."

Sarah followed Mrs. Kloche to the cash register and noticed a familiar yellow flyer underneath a paperweight.

"I see you have a flyer for the mystery quilt," Sarah said. "I'm doing it as a Christmas gift for a friend."

"It sounded fun to me too, but I don't sew. I was going to tape it by the cash register but forgot."

"Who gave you the flyer?"

"A Helping Hands worker. I took it because the blog author is supposed to be someone local."

"Was it Kathleen?"

"No, it was another driver. A man dropped it off."

Sarah marched up to the door of Leftfoot Securities. The overhead light illuminated the office and she stepped into a chilly, cramped space. File cabinets lined the back wall. A metal desk occupied one end of the room. Packing crates were stacked in the middle.

Gordon leaned back in his leather swivel chair, a phone stuck to his ear. "I don't care if you *are* backlogged until after the New Year. If you can't send me what I need this week, I'll find a supplier who can."

He lowered the phone. "I'll be with you in a few minutes. There's a seat back there." He pointed to a metal chair.

Sarah nodded and squeezed between the crates. She put down a hand to steady herself and felt something greasy come off the crate.

"Do you mind if I use your restroom?" Sarah held up her black fingers.

"Down the hall."

The hallway led to two doors, both closed. She tried to open the one on the left, but the door stuck in the frame. She leaned her shoulder on it and burst into a dimly lit small room. A cot with a pillow and a rumpled blanket sat along the wall under a high narrow window. Open cardboard boxes and plastic crates were stacked around on the floor as if Gordon was in the process of unpacking. Sarah turned to leave but something caught her eye.

A small box advertising crystal stemware lay half buried in a crate filled with dishes and other kitchen utensils. Didn't the China Cup sell the same brand?

Gordon's voice carried on as he apparently still wasn't happy with the results on the other end of the call. She inched farther into the room. Books were strewn across the worn orange carpet. She noted several crime novels, a police procedural manual, a couple of fat three-ringed notebooks and three craft books, two on quilting. Sarah recognized one of the quilting books as a basic guide for beginners. The pattern looked similar to the one on the mystery quilt blog.

The noise of Gordon banging down the receiver sent her scurrying across the hall and through the other door to a minuscule restroom. She quickly washed the grease off her hand.

Surely there was a logical reason why Gordon would have books on quilting. Some men quilted, but most likely the books belonged to a girlfriend or a wife. Gordon didn't wear a wedding band, but that didn't mean he wasn't married.

The phone rang again as she walked to the front room. Sarah made her way to the chair, this time avoiding the soiled crate.

"I'll be there in a few minutes," Gordon spoke into the phone and then set it down. "Sorry about that." He nodded toward the crate. "I borrowed my brother-in-law's truck to move and didn't realize the tire he kept in the bed had grease on it."

"It's fine. I didn't get any on my clothes," Sarah said with smile. "Is your wife moving to Maple Hill also?"

Gordon looked at his watch. "I'm sorry, but I need to check on an account. Perhaps we can meet at a later time. Have you made a decision about putting in a security system?"

"I'm still thinking about it. I've been so busy lately preparing for the holidays, although my business has been fairly slow the last couple of weeks." She pulled out one of her cards and handed it to him. "I restore quilts and specialize in antique quilting. If you know of anyone who needs some sewing help, please pass on my name."

Gordon's facial expression didn't flicker. He took the card and tossed it on the table. "Mrs. Hart, what are you really doing here?"

Sarah took a deep breath and took a more direct approach. "You seem to be all over town lately. I'm wondering if you've learned anything more about the thefts."

"Actually I have. The police have a suspect."

"Who? Is it one of the kids?"

"I'm afraid I can't say."

"But since you're not a police officer anymore, it's not confidential, is it?" Sarah asked.

His jaw clenched. "Regardless."

Obviously she had hit a nerve. But it was the truth. He was no longer on the force. He was a civilian now like she was. Why was he privileged to have this information? Was he involved somehow in the crime or its apprehension?

By the time she got to her feet Gordon had walked to the door and opened it.

Sarah crossed the room and stepped outside. "I just want to help if I can."

"Leave it to the police, Mrs. Hart." He shut the door in her face.

Sarah stopped at home for a quick soup lunch. She couldn't get Gordon's evasive manner out of her head. And who was the suspect? She called Amy and Audrey and asked if any of their friends were being questioned. To her relief Audrey said she hadn't heard anything. At least Amy and Audrey weren't involved at this point.

She opened her notebook and wondered if any of the names on her list had been arrested. Surely someone would hear soon. Maple Hill was a small town and news traveled fast.

Meanwhile, she wanted to track down where the mystery quilt blog flyers came from. She still hadn't heard back from the blog site moderator and she needed to get going to finish Martha's gift.

Mrs. Kloche said a male Helping Hands employee had dropped off the flyer. Sarah was checking the yellow pages for the address of the Helping Hands charity store when the phone rang.

"I was thinking of doing some more Christmas shopping," Martha said. "What are you up to?"

Sarah tucked the phone between her shoulder and ear and flipped through the phone book pages. "Right now, I'm trying to find the address for that charity, Helping Hands."

"I've never been to the store, but…hold on a sec." The sound of papers rustling filled the receiver. "Here it is on a receipt. It's 111 Spoke Street. That's out near the highway."

"Thanks. That saves me some time." Sarah jotted the address in her notebook.

"If you're going, can I tag along?" Martha asked. "I have some more clothes and shoes I've been meaning to donate. Plus, I might be able to find some gifts for the grandkids."

"Sure, that'd be fun," Sarah said, although she would have to be careful that Martha didn't overhear her when she asked about the mystery quilt blog fliers.

Sarah drove by Martha's house and picked her up. Fifteen minutes later they were cruising winding roads on the east side of town. "I didn't see Spoke Street."

"I think we've gone too far. Maybe you should turn around," Martha said, her nose almost pressed against the passenger side window.

The narrow roads hadn't been plowed well, and Sarah's tires spun on the ice as she did a three-point turn.

"There it is," Martha said as they backtracked. "The tree was blocking the street sign."

They turned onto Spoke Street and rounded a curve to an area where businesses were struggling to survive. They passed a gas station and a tire shop, a market, and a junkyard. Helping Hands was located in an old warehouse. The faded words "Spencer's Ice" were still visible on the aged boards. A brown Helping Hands van was parked beside a ramp and warehouse doors.

A Helping Hands sign hung above the front door. A couch, an easy chair, and a rack of clothes were displayed behind a picture window to one side. The inside was surprisingly well lit. Racks of clothing lined the back of the store creating narrow aisles. Furniture was tucked along one wall. Shelves of shoes, boxes of books, and large baskets of towels and kitchen items dominated another.

"Welcome ladies." A petite young woman with Asian features and long black hair greeted them. The tag on her brown uniform shirt proclaimed her name as Lei. "How may I help you?"

"I brought some things to donate." Martha held out the bag.

"Thank you very much." A wide smile lit Lei's face. "Come over here and I'll check it into our computer system and get you a tax receipt." She gestured to a wooden counter holding up a computer, scanner, and laser printer.

"That's quite a system you've got there," Martha said. "I've been in a lot of thrift stores and haven't seen anything as sophisticated."

"It was donated by a lady whose son is some computer whiz. She insisted we modernize and gave a huge donation. To tell the truth, I think we're the guinea pigs for her son's company, not that we mind. It's pretty nifty. All donations are logged into the main system. Then when a call comes in for someone in need, we know exactly what's available," she said, her fingers flying on the computer keys in between sorting through Martha's clothing and shoes.

"I saw one of your workers using a computer pad. She does pickups downtown." Martha said, reaching over to untangle some cloth belts.

"Oh yes, that would be Kathleen Lewison. I'm surprised she was using it. She's Ms. Antitechnology," Lei said.

"I noticed she didn't seem happy about it," Martha said.

"Uh-oh," Lei looked up. "Did she give you a hard time?"

"Not really. She's just ... vocal."

Lei nodded. "It took some coaxing, but she finally learned to use the computer pad. It saves us time if the drivers log in donations while on the road, rather than let them pile up here."

Her hands paused on the keyboard. "Now how much do you think your donation is worth?"

Martha named a sum and Lei entered the number. "Ta da! An itemized receipt. Donators used to have to write out their own." The printer hummed and spit out a sheet that Lei handed to Martha. "Isn't that cool?"

"Very." Martha folded the sheet and put in her purse. She turned and surveyed the warehouse contents with bright eyes. "Where is the kids' clothing?"

"That would be on the right in the corner." Lei turned to Sarah. "Is there something I can do for you?"

As soon as Martha was out of earshot, Sarah pulled the mystery quilt flyer out of her purse. "Yes, I wanted to ask you something. Do you know anything about this mystery quilt?" Sarah pointed to the flyer. "I've been following the blog and working on the quilt. But I've run into a snag and would like to contact the owner of the blog."

"Oh, I wish I could help," Lei said. "Nobody here knows anything about it. A copy was on the counter at the beginning of the month. We have some loyal patrons, and I just assumed one of them left it or maybe it got mixed in with some items from one of the bins. I looked the address up online and it looked fun and Christmassy, so I made some copies and had Tony, one of our drivers, take the flyers and drop them at his stops. I hope it was okay."

"No one said anything to you about it?"

Lei shook her head. "Not until now." She sighed. "Now I feel bad I advertised a bogus site."

"Oh, it's not bogus." Sarah said hastily. "It's actually quite good, except for a few typos and the sewing glitch. I'm sure the owner will straighten it out once she knows."

Lei put her hand on her chest. "Oh, good."

Sarah glanced at the computer, thinking. "You said the flyer showed up at the beginning of the month. Maybe the blog owner dropped it off. Would you have a record of who came in around that time?"

"If they made a donation or purchase it would be in here." She typed on the keyboard and peered at the screen. "People did leave some items, although I don't see any of the ladies listed who I know sew." She gave Sarah an apologetic look. "I can't give you the names. Confidentiality thing. I could get fired if I did. But I can ask them if they come in again."

Sarah reached into her purse. "Tell you what. How about I give you my card and if you ever do find out who left the flyer, you can have her call or e-mail me."

Lei studied the card. "I could do that."

Martha staggered out of the racks with an armload of clothes. "For Sylvie, Ralphie, and Davis," Martha said, referring to her young grandchildren. She dumped them on the counter. "Some of the clothes still have tags on them."

Sarah picked up a pink dress with delicate tiny flowers embroidered on the white collar. It seemed like yesterday that Amy and Audrey were this small. Actually, it didn't seem that long since Jenna was a toddler and now she was expecting her third child. Where had all the time gone? That panicky feeling of time passing too quickly made her think of Patty. Was Patty's behavior simply prompted by fear of missing out on her daughter's life?

Still, it didn't excuse the way she talked about Jason in front of Amy.

Like a gathering storm, the tension seemed to be rising in that household. She hoped Maggie would discuss the idea of another store with Jason and nip the idea in the bud before the storm peaked.

"Since you donated items, I created an account under your name," Lei said to Martha. "I entered the total of your purchase too. That way in the future if you ever need a record of your donations and purchases, it'll be stored here. I've even e-mailed receipts to people at tax time."

"Sounds great! I'll have to shop here again."

Sarah browsed the store while Lei rang up Martha's purchase. She found a pile of rag-braided throw rugs. Some were slightly worn but useable. Sarah could use a new doormat for her back door. She sifted through them and found one made of blue, white, and pink rags.

Martha sidled up to Sarah. "If we stay any longer, I'll be tempted to buy more stuff than we could cram into the car. There are some real deals in here, and even Ernie can't fuss about spending two bucks on a dress. Are you going to get that rug?"

"I think so. You're right, it's a steal of a deal." Sarah took the rug to the front and paid for the doormat.

Martha turned on the radio in Sarah's car and listened to a talk show for a minute before switching to Christmas carols.

Sarah put the car in gear and they left the parking lot singing along with the radio, "Chestnuts roasting on an open fire. Jack Frost nipping at your nose . . . "

They'd sung their way through three carols by the time they turned onto Main Street. Sarah braked for a car making a right turn when Martha stopped singing. "Uh-oh."

"What?" Sarah asked.

"There's a police car parked outside of Maggie's store."

# CHAPTER ELEVEN

T hrough the window, Sarah recognized Officer Hopkins standing by the counter with another policeman. She and Martha barged through the door. The other officer spun around, his hand on his holster.

"Whoa," Martha gasped behind Sarah.

"Hi, Mrs. Hart," Officer Hopkins said. The other policeman relaxed and dropped his hand to his side. With cropped red hair, freckles, and fuzz on his jaw, he looked too young to be a cop. Sarah didn't recognize him and assumed he must be new to the force.

Patty stood beside Maggie with her arm protectively looped under her daughter's.

"Do these look like they're from your inventory?" Officer Hopkins handed a plastic bag to Maggie. She held it up to the light, turning the bag around in her hands. Sarah stepped closer. They appeared to be brooches, some with pretty stones that sparkled.

"It's hard to say. They look familiar. I normally collect these at estate auctions, but occasionally I order them online." She shifted some papers off the glass cabinet. "I keep most of them in here, but it would be impossible to tell without checking my records. It may take me some time to locate the exact items to be sure." Maggie looked at Officer Hopkins. "Where did you get these?"

"We picked up a shoplifting suspect and found them in her possession."

"Oh my," Patty said, her hand on her heart.

"Can I ask who?" Sarah asked, her heart thumping. "Was it one of the girls from the other day?"

Officer Hopkins looked at her, his stern face softening. "No, it's a woman who's been seen lurking around downtown."

"Clara?" Sarah asked.

The younger officer's eyes widened and he blurted out, "That's her."

Hopkins glared at him and he stepped back.

Patty frowned. "Clara Schmidt? No way. She wouldn't steal."

"You know Clara?" Maggie turned to her mother. "The lady from the alley?"

"Of course. I invited her in the other morning for some coffee and cookies while you were out at the post office."

"Ma'am, were you with Clara the entire time she was in this shop?" Hopkins asked.

"Of course," Patty said in an indignant tone. "Well...I *did* leave for a moment to get us coffee and cookies from the back room."

Martha and Sarah glanced at each other as Hopkins jotted something on his small spiral notebook. "When was this?"

"Yesterday afternoon. I was taking the trash out and saw her in the alley and she looked so cold. We had a lovely talk about dogs, but surely—"

"How long was she here?"

"I don't know. Ten or fifteen minutes. But she's the nicest person." She turned to Maggie. "She takes in stray dogs, you know. We're kindred spirits when it comes to animals. She wouldn't steal from us."

"We found those in her possession. She claims she found them out back. But there were some other suspicious items in her bag," the other officer said.

"Officer Jackson!" Hopkins said, a warning in his voice. Sarah didn't know if Hopkins was irritated because he was supposed to be doing the questioning or because Officer Jackson was spilling information he shouldn't. Either way it was interesting to watch.

"I still don't believe it," Patty insisted. "Who's looking after her dogs while she's in jail?"

"I don't know, Ma'am." Hopkins turned his attention back to Maggie. "If you could please check your records and get back to us as soon as possible, we'd appreciate it. Call the station and ask for Officer Hopkins or Chief Halliday." He picked up the bag. "We need these for evidence, but we do have some photos for you." Hopkins paused, waiting, and then looked at his partner and sighed. "Officer Jackson. The photos?"

Jackson reached into his pocket and set some computer-generated snapshots on the counter.

"I'll look at my invoices and get back to you," Maggie said. After the policemen left, Maggie picked up the photos and studied them again.

"This is ridiculous," Patty huffed. "I'm a good judge of people, and Clara is a nice person." She turned to Sarah. "You've spoken to her before, haven't you? Wasn't she nice?"

"Yes, at first," Sarah said. "She got a little sharp with me but—"

"You must've done something to deserve it then. She's a sweet lady."

"Mom!" Maggie said.

"I'm sorry. I'm just upset." Patty rubbed her temples as if she had a headache. Martha caught Sarah's eye and gave her a sympathetic smile.

"It's all right," Sarah said. "I probably *did* deserve it. I was pushing her for information about Annie's missing shipment."

Patty gathered up her purse and coat from behind the counter. "I'm going to go check on her dogs."

"You know where she lives?" Martha asked.

"She gave me her card." Patty dug in her purse and pulled out a simple white business card. "Here it is. Clara Schmidt.

Canine Rescue Center. It lists her phone number and address."

Sarah looked at the address. "Her place may be off-limits if the police are investigating."

"We'll see about that." Patty marched out the door.

Maggie looked at Sarah, but seemed at a loss for words. "I...uh..."

"It isn't often you see someone stand up for a stranger like that," Martha said. "I'm impressed, and I don't even know what's going on."

Maggie's lips tugged into a smile. "You'd think I'd be used to it by now." She shoved the jewelry photos into a stack. "Guess I should try to find the invoices for the police." She headed for her office.

Martha touched Sarah on the arm and nudged her toward the seating area in the back. "What's this about you talking to a woman in the alley? Did I miss something?"

"I didn't get a chance to tell you." Sarah sank down on the couch, relishing the comfort of getting off her feet. "Remember when Karen mentioned the homeless person in the alley? Well, I went back there this morning and got lucky. Her name is Clara and she's not homeless. She takes in stray dogs and checks the dumpsters and trash cans for recyclable items she can sell to buy dog food. She was friendly until I started asking about Annie's shipment."

"Do you think she took it?" Martha said.

Sarah lifted a shoulder in a half shrug. "My gut feeling is no, but then I did get a glimpse in the trash bag she was carrying. I thought I saw some crystal or glass and some small cardboard boxes."

"C.J.'s angels?"

"It crossed my mind, but I couldn't say. Anyway, the police found those brooches in her possession so...who knows?"

Maggie came out of the back room carrying a fat green file. "I'm going to take these invoices home tonight and see what I can find."

"I'm amazed that your mother would know Clara after being in town only a few days," Martha said. "I've lived here my whole life and didn't know she existed."

Maggie laughed, obviously feeling better. "My mother has always befriended strays, whether animals or people. She's worked at a dozen different charities over the years. She gets bored easily."

"It sounds like her heart is in the right place," Martha said.

Maggie nodded. "It is, even when she gets off track once in a while. She means well, but if you noticed, once she gets an idea in her head, watch out. She can be very determined. I wouldn't worry about Clara's dogs while my mother is around."

"I imagine not. I enjoyed having lunch with your folks," Martha said. "Your dad has a great sense of humor."

"Thanks. Dad's more laid back than Mom. Their differences give them some balance, which is one reason they've been married for thirty-nine years." Maggie set the file on the counter and checked the locks on the cabinets before retrieving her jacket. "I suppose I should go check on Mom and make sure she's staying out of trouble."

Sarah pushed herself off the couch, her legs protesting. Tromping through snow and ice all over town had exercised muscles she had forgotten about until now. She was going to need a long, hot bath tonight. "I can check on your mom if you'd like. I'm going in that direction anyway to drop Martha off. You're going to be busy enough tonight going through those invoices."

"That's what I'm afraid of." Maggie made a face at the invoices. "Usually there are stickers on the brooches and pins with a stock number, but the stickers seem to be missing in the photos. I'll have to go by product descriptions."

"It's settled then. I'll go check on Patty so you can head on home," Sarah said. "No argument."

"Okay, if you say so." Maggie sighed and hefted the file back into her arms. "Thanks. I appreciate it. Call me if there are any problems, okay?"

"Will do," Sarah promised as Martha and she headed out the door into the chilly, fresh air.

When they hit the sidewalk, Sarah turned to Martha. "Do you want me to drop you off at home before I head over to Clara's?

"Are you kidding? I wouldn't miss this."

Clara Schmidt's home was northeast of town where houses were spaced farther and farther apart and farmland was just beginning. Patty's rental car was by the front gate of a large, fenced yard.

Sarah parked and studied the dark, small two-story house and detached garage nestled between pine trees on the acre-size property. The growing twilight cast shadows over an old bicycle, a pile of car tires, a wheelbarrow, a kid's jungle gym, and gardening tools half-buried under the snow. Boot prints wore a path to the door and another path disappeared around the corner of the house toward the sound of barking dogs.

Martha grinned at Sarah. "Well...should we go in?"

"Looks like Patty must have." Sarah pushed the gate open and then secured it behind Martha. They tromped up to the porch and then followed the path around the corner of the house. The backyard was far neater than the front, with two rows of kennels of assorted sizes with segregated outdoor pens. The kennels needed painting and the fencing had been repaired in places, but the facilities appeared very neat and clean.

Sarah did a quick count and it looked like Clara was caring for about ten canines. Most were at their tin food bowls, tails wagging, as they munched on dog crunchies.

"I wonder why Clara didn't just turn some of them over to the humane society," Martha mused, her hands on her hips. "Dog food alone must cost her a fortune."

"Because most of these dogs would be difficult to place in good homes," Patty said, emerging from one of the kennels carrying a bucket of dog food. "And you know what happens to dogs in some of those shelters if they aren't placed in a few weeks?"

"Good point," Martha said.

Sarah moved closer to the fence and saw a cocker spaniel who appeared blind in one eye. Its pen mate, a mud-colored, unidentifiable mutt, wore a splint on its front right leg.

"Clara cares for them long-term or forever if a home isn't found," a female voice said behind them. A petite, middle-aged woman dressed in jeans, rubber boots, and a plaid barn coat stood by the corner of the house. Her flashlight beam played over the three other women.

"Oh, hello!" Patty said, setting down her bucket. "I'm Patty Roberts and this is Sarah and Martha. We came over to check on Clara's dogs."

The woman lowered her flashlight. "I'm her neighbor, Rhonda Cox. I was hoping Clara would be home by now. Are you friends of hers?"

"I consider myself her friend," Patty said firmly, "although we just met the other day."

"Have you heard from Clara?" Sarah asked.

"No, but the police were here earlier. At first I thought there'd been an accident, so I came over when I saw the squad car. They wouldn't tell me much, but from what I overheard they think she stole something."

"Which is ridiculous," Patty said.

"Clara likes to keep to herself, but she doesn't strike me as the type to either...although," Rhonda glanced over at the kennels, "I guess I can see her doing almost anything to protect those dogs."

"Was she having money troubles?" Martha asked.

"I wouldn't know. She and her group, Canine Rescue, were always soliciting donations for the dogs, but that wasn't unusual." Rhonda reached through the wire and petted the cocker spaniel who had finished his supper and planted his paws on the fence. Sarah's heart sank. What would happen to these dogs if Clara wasn't freed?

"Poor Clara," Rhonda said with a moan. "She doesn't have any family close by, and I've never seen friends visit. I told the police I'd watch over the dogs until she got home or until a decision is made about what to do with them."

Patty gasped. "They won't take the dogs away from Clara, will they?"

"They'll have to if she stays in jail," Sarah gently stated the obvious and earned a sour look from Patty.

Rhonda glanced at the cocker spaniel again. "I'm happy to help, but I can't take care of them forever."

"I'll help you," Patty said to Rhonda. "I fed them all tonight and made sure they had water."

"That's sweet of you. Thank you," Rhonda said, looking relieved. "I'll check on them in the morning."

"Does Clara ever let them out of their pens for exercise?" Patty asked.

"They're usually out when she's home."

"I'll be back tomorrow then to let them out," Patty said. She handed the food bucket to Rhonda. "You'll need that for the morning. I guess I'll be going." Patty looked at Sarah. "I suppose Maggie sent you out here to check on me."

"I was curious to see where Clara lived."

"Right," Patty said with a small smile. "Nice meeting you, Rhonda." She trudged back toward the road.

Rhonda returned the food bucket to a shed and flipped off the kennel lights. The yard plunged into darkness. "Oh, sorry. Follow me." She clicked on her flashlight and aimed the beam on the path along the side of the house.

As Martha and Sarah walked with her to the front gate, their boots crunching on the crusty snow, Rhonda asked, "How are you involved with Clara?"

"Some of the items she allegedly stole were from my daughter-in-law's store," Sarah said.

"Poor Clara," Rhonda said again. "If there's anything more I can do, let me know. I feel so guilty that I didn't make a bigger effort to get to know her. Sometimes we forget there are needs that are right in front of us."

Sarah's heart squeezed at the crack of emotion in her voice. "I'm sure she'll greatly appreciate your taking care of her dogs."

"Will you please let her know the dogs are fine? I bet she's frantic with worry."

"I'll try," Sarah said.

Rhonda closed the gate behind them. "I live right over there." She pointed to a distant ranch house on the opposite side of the road. "I can give you my phone number if you have something to write with."

Sarah retrieved a business card and her notebook from her purse. She gave the card to Rhonda and jotted down Rhonda's phone number before getting in the car with Martha.

As Sarah buckled her seat belt, Martha asked, "You think Chief Halliday will let you in to see Clara?"

"Maybe."

Especially if she had something to bargain with.

By the time Sarah got home, she was bone tired and shivering, and she smelled vaguely of wet dog. Sleet had started to fall by the time she had dropped off Martha at her home, turning the remaining snow into a slushy mess.

She hung her damp coat on the back of the kitchen chair, hoping it would dry by morning. She called Maggie who said she hadn't been able to match up the jewelry yet. Sarah declined the offer for dinner, saying she was going to have an early night.

She climbed the stairs to her bedroom, popped some soft Christmas music into her CD player, lit a candle that smelled like apple pie, and ran a bubble bath. She slipped into the hot water, determined to soak until her skin wrinkled like a sun-baked peach. She closed her eyes, willing herself to relax and not think about the day's events.

It didn't work. Her mind raced over the events of the last three days. It appeared Clara was the culprit in at least some of the thefts. She had been found with stolen merchandise in her possession. She had told Sarah she would do anything for her dogs. So why wasn't Sarah convinced of her guilt?

And then there was Patty. She hadn't been happy to see Sarah out at Clara's. Maybe she was sensing Sarah's growing frustration with her. Or maybe she was still upset about the spat with Maggie. And was Jason aware of all this? She sensed he must be. If Patty didn't let up, sooner or later there would be a showdown.

Discussing the situation with Jenna had been soothing, but it wasn't the same as seeing her father's face and relishing the tidbits of insight and wisdom he bestowed. He had taught her to laugh at herself and not take everything so seriously. Sometimes just the process of talking to him about a problem would open her to some new insight. And even though during the last few years their roles reversed some and he leaned more on her, he was always her father.

"Dad, I miss you," she said softly. The ache was still sharp, but she knew it would gradually fade. Just as it had with Gerry. She was lucky to have family to lean on, whereas Clara Schmidt seemed all alone in the world except for her dogs. If Clara was innocent, Sarah would help to prove it and try to find the person who was guilty. If Clara was guilty, she would still try to help her if she could. Decision made, she slid lower into the bathtub and closed her eyes.

CHAPTER TWELVE

S arah woke the next morning with a vague sense that
something was terribly wrong. Her nose felt like
a Popsicle. She sat up and frigid air washed over
her. She glanced at the dead electric clock on her nightstand. Groaning, she grabbed her housecoat and slippers
and padded over to the window.

Outside, ice coated everything, turning her yard into a
glittering frozen wonderland. It really was beautiful, but unfortunately with ice came treacherous roads, downed tree
limbs, and power outages. She wondered if the outage was
widespread or just affected her home.

She dressed quickly, pulling on long underwear, jeans,
and a sweater over a long T-shirt. She headed downstairs to
the kitchen and put a pot of water on the gas stove, then went
into her office and hunted for the latest utility bill to get the
service phone number.

The portable kitchen phone didn't work without electricity so she called on her cell, following the push button

instructions to report an outage. On days like this, she wished she could talk to a live person. The electronic voice assured her that her report had been noted and a crew had already been dispatched to her neighborhood. Next she called Maggie and Jason.

"We have power over here," Jason said and Sarah could hear Maggie's voice in the background. "Maggie says that the news reported that there are just a few scattered areas without power. Lucky you, you must be in one of them. Do you want me to come get you?"

"No, better to stay off the roads until they get them salted. I'm fine. I'll build a fire in the living room and I'll be warm enough," Sarah said. When she had remodeled the house, she had upgraded the gas furnace and now it required electricity for the blower to heat the house, unlike the old floor furnace. The newer furnace heated the house much faster, but the drawback was in situations like this. Maybe she should get a new generator. Gerry used to keep one around, but she had finally given the temperamental ancient piece of equipment away to someone who knew how to tinker with it to get it going.

"All right, but call if you need anything." Jason signed off and her cell buzzed.

"Good morning!" Martha said. "Ho, ho, ho, tis the season to slip on the ice. I'm tempted to get out my old ice skates and skate over to see you."

"Is is that bad over there?"

"Looks that way from my window, but I'm afraid to go out to the road to see." Martha laughed jollily. "You okay?"

"The power's out, but otherwise, I'm fine." Sarah walked into the living room. Luckily the last time she had cleaned she had piled fresh kindling and logs in the fireplace.

"Oh dear, do you have plenty of wood?"

"Enough." Sarah struck a long match and held it against the kindling. The dry tinder flared and the flames licked their way to the larger sticks, finally leaping to the bark on the logs. "I talked to Jason and they're saying on the news that power outages are scattered, so with luck they'll get to me soon."

"Well, I'm thankful for one thing, other than having electricity, and that is I'm not in charge of the home tour this year. I know that sounds selfish, but the coordinator must be going nuts with worry with the roads being this bad."

"Do you think they'll cancel it?" Sarah asked, selfishly thinking she could meet up with Liam and his friends earlier. Half of the proceeds for the Home Tour went to charity and she really should be praying it still went off without a hitch.

"Depends on whether they can get the roads cleared by tomorrow, and whether the power outage affects any of the tour homes," Martha said above the sound of running water and the clink of dishes. "I think the backup plan is to postpone until Tuesday, which means not as many tourists will be in town, but at least the locals can go."

"That would be better than nothing," Sarah agreed as she fanned the struggling fire with a magazine. The flames grew and heat bathed her face.

"The temperature is supposed to climb to forty today, so the ice should melt." They made tentative plans to meet up later in the day. Sarah still wanted to get over to the police station to see Clara and talk to Chief Halliday. And she wondered if Maggie had found the invoices she needed. She should've asked Jason when he was on the phone.

Thoughts of William from the previous night still drifted through her mind. She felt an urge to go talk to Leland. She wondered if the nursing home had power. She made the call and a staff member reassured her that the electricity had been out only about fifteen minutes there and everyone was fine. Sarah left a message for Leland that if the roads cleared she would be by sometime today.

Sarah put another log on the fire and ventured outside. The sleet that had fallen the night before was hard as marble over the top of the snow and just as slippery when wet. Seeing the cord of firewood reminded her she also needed to speak with Paul Barclay. If he did live out in the woods, the chance of getting out there today was slim.

Sarah turned back and got a hammer out of a kitchen drawer. She pounded the ice on the woodpile with the hammer to break through the surface. She grabbed an armload of wood and staggered back to the house nearly tripping over the frayed doormat that had bunched up. She had forgotten to take the new rug out of the car last night. She dumped the wood in the box on the hearth, hoping it would dry out some before she had to use it.

The teapot whistled, and she made a bowl of instant oatmeal and a cup of instant coffee. She glanced at the laptop she had left on the kitchen table. She had a couple of hours of battery life left on it, but she couldn't hook up to the Internet router without power. The house was so quiet she could hear the popping sounds of frozen tree limbs trying to free themselves of ice in the wind. She took her bowl and mug to the living room where the fire hissed and crackled softly.

The urge to sew came over her, but the next phase of the mystery quilt required the sewing machine. Besides she still needed clarification on the next step. She wondered if the blog site moderator had gotten in touch with the owner. If not, she would just continue on, making a note for Martha in the quilt blog journal she was preparing.

Sarah chided herself for just sitting there. She had gotten so used to technology, she felt almost helpless. There were plenty of other things she could do. Like scrubbing the bathrooms. Elbow grease didn't require electricity. She could grab the cleanser and some rags and really make the mirrors and porcelain shine. The upstairs would still be chilly though.

Sarah smiled. Just admit it. What she really wanted to do was work on the mystery surrounding Clara. She took her dishes to the kitchen, made more coffee, and grabbed her notebook and pencil from her purse.

After tossing another small log on the fire, she sat on the couch and tucked around her lap a cozy sea green afghan Martha had crocheted for her several years ago.

She opened to the page of suspects and studied the names. On a fresh page she made a list of suspects down one side and crimes on the other. She drew lines from Clara to Annie's shipment and Maggie. Would Clara have had access to the China Cup or the Galleria?

From Paul Barclay she drew a line to the hardware store, although Tim had insisted Paul had gotten the wood somewhere else. The hardware store theft might've been totally unrelated to the shoplifting.

The teenagers had been at Magpie's Antiques, the China Cup, the Galleria, and the Crystal Unicorn, but so far they hadn't been found with any merchandise. Sarah also needed to check out the clothing store, the Lonely Cricket.

She added Gordon Leftfoot. He had been in all the downtown stores and the hardware store, and he certainly could have been in the alley.

Kathleen Lewison, the charity worker, had also been all over town, although she said she never used the alley.

Sarah studied the spider web of lines linking suspects with crime scenes. Her mystery-loving granddaughter Amy would've enjoyed this. She stood and stretched. The living room was toasty warm from the fire. She looked out the window. Water dripped from the icicles on the eaves. The distant rumble of a snowplow grew closer and passed the house, its blades moving some of the slush that had softened. A salt truck followed. The roads would be drivable soon.

Meanwhile she could make some phone calls. She got out the phone book and looked up the Galleria.

The phone rang about six times before a woman's breathless voice answered. "The Galleria. Can you hold?" She clicked off before Sarah could answer. Sarah didn't recognize the voice. It must be one of C.J.'s Christmas helpers.

She doodled in her notebook and listened to the fire pop and sizzle while she waited until the voice came back on the line.

"Sorry to keep you waiting. How can I help you?"

"May I speak to C.J.? This is Sarah Hart."

"Hold on." The phone clicked to silence again.

"Sarah, how are you?" C.J.'s voice boomed over the receiver.

"No power this morning, but I'm fine. Thanks. I'm glad to hear you're open. Have the roads been cleared?"

"They're not too bad. They got to the downtown streets first. In fact, I see Maggie pulling up in front of her shop."

"That's good," Sarah said. "I wanted to ask you if Clara Schmidt—"

"The one they arrested for shoplifting?"

"Yes, that's the one." Sarah didn't bother asking how he knew. The gossip train in Maple Hill was reliable. "Has she been in your store?"

"Police asked the same thing. Maybe once or twice asking for donations for her cats or dogs or something."

"Dogs—"

"Hold on a sec." The phone clunked as if he had set it down, and C.J. spoke to someone else. "I need this box to go to the post office too. I'm almost done with it."

The voices faded away, and Sarah searched for the China Cup's number in the phone book while she waited.

"Okay, I'm back. What were you saying?" C.J. asked.

"Dogs. Clara takes in strays," Sarah said.

"Anyway, they figured she could've come in the back way. My new assistant sometimes leaves the door unlocked on cleaning days," C.J. said above the sound of tape being pulled from a dispenser.

"Is that who answered the phone?"

"Yeah, that's Kayla. She's here to clean, but I've been so busy, I have her answering the phone. The police cleared her if that's what you're wondering."

Sarah was, and she jotted Kayla's name down in her notebook. "So they think Clara came in the back door? I thought you said the angel ornaments were stolen from the display near the front door."

"They were. But I did some checking in my storage room and found that several boxes of vases were also gone. All Clara had to do was slip in the back, grab a box, and go out the door. You may want to tell Maggie to check her stock."

"She is, but she usually keeps the door locked," Sarah said, adding the vases to her list of stolen items. "Did the police find your vases?"

"No, but she could have sold them. Quick turnaround."

"But there's no proof!"

"What's your point, Mrs. Hart?" C.J. asked, irritation edging his words. "I'd think you'd be relieved they caught the culprit. This clears your granddaughters and their friends."

"That's true." But it was sad too for Clara and her dogs. Even though she didn't know the woman, she admired her determination to take care of animals nobody else seemed to want.

"Sounds pretty cut-and-dried to me," C.J. said as someone called his name in the background. "Gotta get to work now, Mrs. Hart. You have a great day."

Sarah thanked him and then called the China Cup. Mrs. Kloche confirmed the police had come by there too, but she couldn't confirm that Clara had been in her shop. Other than seeing her on the street from a distance, she wasn't sure she had ever met the woman.

Next she tried the Crystal Unicorn. Annie answered on the first ring and to Sarah's surprise she sounded fairly bubbly. "Mrs. Hart, I didn't make the connection you were related to the Robertses until they came over for my demonstration dinner. They are the nicest people."

"I heard they had a good time."

"Especially Patty. She talked nonstop and tried everything I cooked. I'm not so sure about Larry, but he did take seconds of my olive paté. How nice that Patty is going into business with her daughter. She's thinking of having a section of their new store devoted to natural living. She would sell my herbs."

"I wasn't aware they'd made firm plans."

"Oh yeah," Annie gushed and then hesitated, "well, that is, if Maggie's husband doesn't hold her back."

Sarah gaped at the phone. "I'm sorry?"

"Patty might not have used those exact words, but that's what she meant. You know how men can be. Always wanting to be in control. Make the decisions. It's why I stayed single all these years. I can come and go as I please. I'm a free spirit. I'm happy," Annie insisted.

"Jason isn't like that. Not at all," Sarah said softly, trying hard not to sound like an outraged mother hen defending her chick. "Maggie and he have a good relationship. He wouldn't stand in her way."

There was a long pause on the other end of the phone. "I'm sorry. Patty's enthusiasm rubbed off on me and I hate to see her disappointed," Annie finally said, sounding contrite. "I didn't mean to go off like that. What can I do for you?"

Sarah took a deep breath and tried to focus on the purpose of her call. "I don't know if you've heard, but Clara was arrested for the thefts."

A thud sounded as if Annie had dropped something on the counter. "I asked you to stay out of my business."

"It wasn't me, Annie." Sarah sighed. "The police caught her with possible stolen merchandise."

"Mine?"

"I don't know. They found some jewelry but said there was more."

"Her aura seemed so pure. I couldn't have misjudged her," Annie said.

"Clara claims she found the items in a garbage can," Sarah said. "You might want to reconsider filing a police report. It might help them find the real thief if it isn't Clara."

"I suppose you're right," Annie said. "Why do you want to help her all of a sudden?"

"I just want the truth." Sarah glanced down at the notebook in her lap. "Are you busy right now? Can I ask you a couple other questions? It might help Clara."

Annie sighed. "Go ahead. The ice seems to be keeping people away anyway."

Sarah moved her pencil down her list of suspects. "You mentioned you know Paul Barclay and—"

"He's such a jerk!"

Sarah gripped her pencil harder. "Why?"

"He's hated my guts since I reported him. He threatened me once too."

Sarah's heart rate picked up its pace. "Threatened you?"

"Yeah. Told me to mind my own business or I'd be sorry."

Sarah wrote down "threat?" by Paul's name and moved to the next. "What about Kathleen, the Helping Hands driver? Does she come in your store?"

"She's come in a couple of times, I suppose. She usually just checks the bin outside for donations. Why?"

"You ever see her in the alley?"

"Nope." A door clicked shut in the background. "Hello. Let me know if I can assist you in any way," Annie called. She lowered her voice. "Anything else, Mrs. Hart?"

"What about Gordon Leftfoot? Has he been back?" Sarah underlined his name.

"If he had, I'd have run him off with a stick. Annoying man," Annie said. "Listen, I probably should go."

Sarah was surprised that Annie had talked to her this long. "One more question. Are you sure there isn't anything else missing from your shop? Little things that you might not notice right way."

"No. Of course not. At least I don't think so ..." Annie's voice trailed away and then she asked, "How does this help with Clara?"

"Just trying to establish which other people had access to the stores where the thefts took place."

Annie let out a little laugh. "Good luck with that. Hundreds of people pass through downtown every week. What makes you think you can find something the police can't?"

"All I can do is try," Sarah said.

"Good luck, Mrs. Hart," Annie said with a smile in her voice. "Like Patty said, you might be a busybody, but you have a kind heart."

"Maybe you should talk to Patty about it," Martha suggested gently. "You'll feel better."

"I feel better already just talking to you," Sarah said. She had just gotten off the phone when Martha rang the doorbell. Her friend had braved the streets to bring Sarah a casserole dish full of savory-smelling beef stew and a bag of fresh biscuits.

Knowing Sarah so well, she had immediately noticed Sarah was disturbed, and as they ate she pried out the conversation with Annie.

"I don't mind being called a busybody. I do poke my nose in other people's business, but I don't like what Patty said about Jason's relationship with Maggie. He's not controlling. He didn't make them move here. In fact, it was Maggie who finally pushed for the move. She was worried about his health."

"It's easier for Patty to blame Jason than Maggie for something that's made her unhappy."

"Well, if you're going to be logical, you can leave now," Sarah said and they both burst into laughter.

"I know you're right. I should be more understanding," Sarah conceded.

"That doesn't mean Patty should get away with lying," Martha said. "If this continues to bother you, talk to her."

"I will but...it's Christmas."

Martha nodded. "I know."

The answering machine suddenly beeped to life and the clock on the microwave flashed. A moment later the furnace hummed to life.

"Look at that. It's a sign that the day is going to get better." Martha jumped to her feet and took their bowls to the sink. "Let's get out of here. The roads weren't too bad after all."

Sarah quickly tidied the kitchen and changed her clothes. The fire in the living room had died to coals and she secured the protective screen in front. Placing an assorted pile of Christmas cookies in a decorative tin, she was ready to go.

Martha offered to drive. The sun and salt were starting to do their jobs and water ran down the streets. A lifetime of living in Maple Hill had taught them which roads were problematic in bad weather and they maneuvered their way to Bradford Manor. The tires spun as the car climbed the knoll, but Martha kept her foot down until they slid into the parking lot of the nursing home.

They passed through the decorated lobby where residents played games and visitors signed in at the nursing station in the center of the building.

Leland's gruff voice could be heard in the hall before Martha and Sarah reached his room. "I don't have to play Monopoly if I don't want to."

"You really should get out of bed for a while," a male orderly said, his back to the door. Leland, dressed in slacks and plaid shirt, sprawled on the hospital bed.

Leland scowled. "Says who?"

"Your doctor."

"Pfftt. What does he know?"

Sarah stepped into the small room, which smelled strongly of pine cleaner. "Hi, Leland. We brought you some Christmas cookies."

Leland's face cracked into a smile. "Well, bring 'em over."

Sarah smiled. "How about we go eat them in the lobby? That way we can all sit down."

"Are you trying to bribe me, young woman?" Leland growled.

"Yes, I am." Sarah looked at the nurse. "He can have cookies now, can't he?"

"Well—"

"Of course I can!" Leland said, shoving his legs over the edge of the bed. The nurse helped him with his slippers and situated his walker. Once Leland was settled on a lobby couch, Sarah sat beside him and Martha dragged over a rocker.

"Amy and Audrey helped bake these." Sarah opened the tin and held it out to Leland.

He studied the assortment. "The peppermint ones are my favorite."

"Mine too." Martha reached for a cookie. "But then pretty much all cookies are." She laughed. "Oh, here comes the milk."

The male orderly had reappeared with small cartons and straws and passed them around.

They chatted about the twins and Martha's grandkids, Maggie's parents, and geocaching until Leland's eyelids started to droop.

Sarah patted him on the shoulder. "Don't forget that you're coming over to Maggie and Jason's for Christmas dinner if you're feeling well enough." Sarah had already cleared it with his doctor.

Leland's large hand grasped hers. "I'll be there. And good cookies."

"Anytime," Sarah said and meant it. Her heart felt lighter as she and Martha walked to the car. Even though they hadn't talked about William today, her father's love had been reflected in Leland's smile and felt in the warmth of his hand. As they reached the car, she hummed the tune to "It's Beginning to Look a Lot Like Christmas."

"You don't know how glad I am to see you." Maggie said as Sarah and Martha entered the store. "You're the first people in here today. It's given me time to go through my inventory, but it's been lonely."

"Where's your mom?" Martha asked, unzipping her jacket.

"Oh, she went out to check on those dogs. I tried to talk her out of it. The roads must be terrible out there. She's been gone for quite a while." Maggie shuffled the papers on the counter. "I'm starting to get worried. She's not answering her cell phone, but that's nothing new. Meanwhile I still can't find the invoice those brooches would've been on. I have all the invoices now filed by date, and the one for the shipment that came in earlier this week is missing."

Sarah picked up one of the sheets and looked at it. "Would the delivery company have a copy?"

"They do. I already called, and they said they'd mail a copy, but that'll take a couple of days. Guess that's the best I can do."

Sarah scanned the store. "Where did you unpack that shipment?"

"Here on the counter. I started it, but got busy with some customers, and Mom finished it for me. She was supposed to check off the items against the invoice."

The door opened and Maggie gasped. "Jason? What happened?"

Sarah and Martha turned. Jason stood in the doorway, supporting Patty with his arm looped underneath both of hers.

"I'm fine. I'm fine. I don't see what the fuss is about," Patty said. Jason held her firmly as she limped across the floor.

"She crashed her car," Jason said.

"I did not." Patty shook off Jason's hand and sat in a chair. "There wasn't a crash."

Maggie squatted in front of her, her face pale. She took her mom's hands in hers. "Tell me what happened."

"I took a turn too fast and slid off the road. It's no big deal. The paint's just a little scratched. So what? It's a rental."

"I don't care about the car. Did you hit your head? Are you hurt?" Maggie asked.

"I *told* you I just slid off the road. I was on my way back and the road looked dry."

"You were *limping*."

"I tripped when I got out to check if the car was okay."

"Let me see." Maggie pulled off Patty's boot and rolled down her sock. "Look, your ankle is swelling. You should get it x-rayed. We'll go over to the ER."

Patty shook her head. "No hospitals. It's just a sprain. They can't do anything for it that I can't do myself."

"Maggie's right," Sarah said gently. "You really should get it looked at. You could have broken something."

"Jason, run over to Annie's store," Patty said. "She has poultices I can put on my ankle, and I'll be as good as new tomorrow."

Maggie stood and looked at Jason, her eyes watering.

"It'll be okay," he said softly. "I'll be right back."

Jason went out the door and Maggie asked, "Why did you call Jason? Why didn't you call me?"

"Because I thought you might be busy with customers."

"B-but Jason might've been with a client."

Patty gave a little shrug. "Really, dear, from what I gathered about your situation, you're far busier than he."

"That's only because it's Christmas. Jason's practice is thriving." Maggie's face flushed.

"For a small town maybe. Besides, he said he didn't mind."

Maggie stepped back, her voice rising half an octave. "Of course he'd say that. What else could he do when you call him and say you've slid off the road?"

"I don't see what you're upset about. Everything is fine."

Maggie bit her lower lip and turned away.

Martha glanced at Maggie's back and then at Sarah who didn't know quite what to say. Martha pulled up a chair and sat next to Patty and asked, "How were the dogs this morning?"

"They miss Clara, but they seemed so happy to see me. Rhonda hadn't let them out, so I let them run around for a while." She looked up at Sarah. "When's Clara getting out of jail? Have they set bail?"

"I don't know," Sarah said. "I was going to go down to the police station, but Maggie hasn't been able to find the invoice with the jewelry on it."

"I find that hard to believe," Patty said. "Really, Maggie, you're usually so organized."

Maggie turned back around, her mascara slightly smudged. "I think those brooches might've been in the shipment you unpacked day before yesterday."

"Really?" Patty asked. "I don't remember any brooches being in there."

"You unpacked the shipment here, right?" Maggie patted the glass counter. "And emptied it completely?"

"Yes, of course." Patty frowned. "Oh, wait. I got tired of standing and moved the box over to that sofa. Then I brought it all back over here."

Martha was closest to the antique rosewood divan and looked under it. "I don't see anything." She dug her fingers into the back cushion and pulled out a crumbled yellow sheet. She smoothed it out and gave it Maggie. "Is this what you're looking for?"

Maggie scanned it. "This is it. Five brooches in the order and they aren't checked off."

"Impossible. Let me see that," Patty leaned forward and snatched the invoice out of Maggie's hand. She squinted at the paper. "I don't see what you're talking about."

"At the very bottom."

She peered closer. "The ink is smeared, and besides, I never saw the brooches."

Martha stood, looking around the room. "Where's the box now?"

"I don't know. I probably threw it out back," Patty said irritably, rubbing her ankle. She looked up. "If the pins were still in the box, then Clara must've found them in the garbage."

"Or she took them out of the box while you were getting her cookies," Maggie said.

"I'll look for the box." Sarah headed to the back door. Martha followed.

"When is the trash picked up around here?" Martha asked once they were outside. A breeze blew down the alley carrying the faint scent of cinnamon from the café.

"Mondays, I think. So it should still be here." Sarah pried the tin lid off the can. Several flattened boxes were lying amid packing paper. She and Martha pulled out the boxes.

"I think this is the one." Martha held up a box. "The shipping label matches the name on the invoice." She stuck her hand inside and extracted some lightweight packing paper. "Nothing in here now." Martha handed over the box and then nudged Sarah with her shoulder.

A man walked down the alley, his head bowed as if searching the ground. Sarah recognized the unruly blond hair and unsteady gait.

"Gordon Leftfoot," she murmured at the moment he lifted his head, his intense gaze landing on them.

"Good afternoon." He looked at the box in Sarah's hand. "Taking out the trash?"

"Hi, Mr. Leftfoot," Sarah said. "What are you doing in the alley?"

"Some of the shop owners want a camera back here, and I was just checking for a good spot."

By looking at the pavement? Sarah lowered the box to her side. "Really? Which shop owners?"

Gordon gave her a smile. "If I shared that kind of information, I wouldn't be in the security business very long, now would I?"

Sarah smiled back. "Guess not."

He continued on down the alley, this time studying the walls. Sarah opened the door to the store and they went back inside.

"There's something about that guy that's hinky," Martha whispered.

"I know," Sarah said as she walked back into the showroom.

Annie knelt in front of Patty. She had a white metal bowl on her lap, and was in the process of smoothing a green mixture on Patty's ankle.

Martha wrinkled her nose. "What is that?"

"Hot vinegar and sage poultice. It's used traditionally to soothe bruises and sprains," Annie said without looking up. She folded a towel over the swelling area.

"Find anything?" Maggie looked at the box in Sarah's hand.

"The box, but it's empty except for some paper," Sarah said. "You probably should take it over to the police station when you take the invoice."

"I will," Maggie said, her gaze intent on Annie's ministrations.

"If you don't feel like going, I can run it over for you." Sarah offered. "I wanted to talk to the interim police chief anyway."

"They can always come over here or call you if they have more questions," Martha added.

Maggie smiled at them. "That'd be great. I don't know when I'd be able to get over there. You make my life so much easier."

"That's what family's for," Sarah said.

Sarah caught a glimpse of Patty over Martha's shoulder. Patty was watching them, a frown pinching her face.

CHAPTER THIRTEEN

S arah and Martha decided to walk down the street to the police station. They passed the Spotted Dog where several couples were sitting near the window, but the parking spots in front of the Galleria and the Crystal Unicorn were almost all empty.

They climbed the steps to the police station and walked into the stale heat of the waiting area. Sarah strolled to the counter where a tiny, dry-looking tree sprouted out of a pot. Someone had hung a too heavy ornament on it, and it listed to the side.

Sarah gave their names to the desk clerk and requested to see Chief Halliday, explaining why they had come.

"He's rather busy this afternoon, but I'll give him your name," the clerk said.

Sarah handed over the invoice and box and then sat on one of the vinyl-coated padded chairs next to Martha.

After five minutes the frosted glass door opened and a female officer poked her head out. "Mrs. Hart and

Mrs. Maplethorpe, the chief will see you now." She took them back to Chief Weber's office where Halliday had made himself at home by shifting Weber's family pictures to the bookcase and placing his own on the desk.

"Have a seat," Chief Halliday said.

"How old are your boys?" Martha asked, lifting the picture frame.

Halliday glanced at the photo. "Sixteen and fourteen."

"You have a nice-looking family." Martha put the photo back and sat next to Sarah on the metal chairs.

The chief grunted something that sounded like "thanks," and then cleared his throat. "I saw you brought the invoice in. It confirms where Clara Schmidt got the brooches."

Sarah exchanged a look with Martha. "Well, there's a good chance that she did get them out of the trash." She explained about how Patty must've missed the brooches in the packing material and tossed them out with the box.

Halliday listened, his expression unreadable. He tapped his pen on the desk edge until Sarah finished.

"Can she be let free now?"

He shook his head. "There's other evidence."

When he didn't elaborate, Sarah fidgeted on the cold, hard chair. "Can I ask what that is?"

"No."

"That's not very nice," Martha blurted out. "We're just trying to help."

"It's not my job to be nice, ladies. It's my job to catch criminals." He stood. "Thank you for your cooperation in this matter."

Sarah and Martha rose. "Can we at least see Clara?"

"Only if she requests to see you."

Sarah and Martha looked at each other. Clara wouldn't ask to see Sarah. Not after their last encounter. But ... maybe there was another way.

"You know with a little elbow grease and fresh paint the place could be really nice." Martha gazed around the small, drab visiting room outside the local short-term jail. "Get rid of the nauseous green and maybe change to a cheerful color like yellow. Or maybe a light blue. Blue is supposed to be soothing. People are visiting friends or relatives who are in jail after all. That's bad enough. Good colors in here might make them feel better."

Sarah smiled. Trust Martha to still be entertaining after an hour of waiting to see Clara. Sarah had sent a message in that she and Martha wanted to talk to Clara about her dogs. Prisoners were allowed two visitors a day in addition to their lawyer. So far, they were the first and only ones for the day.

"It smells like stale cigarette smoke in here. I thought cigarette smoking was banned in public places. It needs a spritz of Lysol and maybe one of those room deodorizers. Cinnamon apple would be great for the holidays."

"Maybe you should write a letter to the editor at the *Monitor*," Sarah suggested.

"Actually I was thinking of Congregational Church's prison ministries group. I bet they'd get in here and fix the place up. It wouldn't cost the taxpayers a thing," Martha said.

Sarah nodded. Actually it wasn't a bad idea.

"I would suggest better padded chairs too with a nice fabric pattern, like flowers," Martha said, rocking from side to side. "My tush could use a little comfort."

"Anything else, Martha Stewart?"

Martha giggled. "Just trying to do my civic duty to raise our standards. This is Maple Hill after all."

Martha grinned at the large wall mirror and fluffed her bangs. "Do you think they can see us through that?"

Sarah glanced at her own reflection. "If it's one-way glass."

The door opened and the guard said, "Ten minutes." Clara shuffled in wearing an orange jumpsuit. Her shoulders were bowed, but when she spotted Sarah, she drew herself up and hurried over to the table.

"How are my dogs?" Clara said. "You did say you went to see them? Are they all right?"

"They're fine. Don't worry. I saw them last night and they looked happy and were eating their dinner. Your neighbor, Rhonda Cox, is watching them and so is Patty Roberts, whom you met recently. Her daughter owns Magpie's Antiques."

Clara frowned. *Patty? Yes, a nice lady. Likes dogs. And Rhonda?* "I didn't think she liked dogs. She complained about their barking once. I told her dogs are supposed to bark. It's their job."

"Well, she must've had a change of heart because she said to tell you that she'd care for them."

Clara blew out a long, relieved breath. "I was so worried."

"I would be too, but everything is fine at your house." Martha pulled out a chair. "Do you want to sit down?"

"No, I do enough sitting in there." She jerked her head to the door. "I just want to go home and be with my animals. I mind my own business and try to do good and look where it gets me."

"Clara, maybe we can help you," Sarah said.

"How?"

"Maybe we can prove that this is all a mistake. How did you get the brooches?"

Clara looked from Sarah to Martha. She opened her mouth and then closed it. She sighed. "Like I told the police and everyone else, they were in the garbage can. They didn't look expensive to me, just junk no one wanted. So I took them. No one believes me though."

"We do," Martha said. "We think there was a mistake, and the brooches got thrown out by accident."

"Accidentally?"

"Patty, who gave you coffee and cookies inside Magpie's Antiques, was unpacking the box the brooches were in. Maybe you saw it? It was this big." Sarah held up her hands to give the dimensions.

Clara shook her head. "I don't remember any box. There's lots of stuff in that store."

"Were the brooches in a box when you found them?"

"Nope. They were lying on some papers."

"Brown paper?"

"I guess," Clara said. "Did you tell the police that this was all a mistake?"

"We told the police chief the brooches could've been thrown out, but he said there was additional evidence."

"They don't know anything." Clara pressed her lips together and gazed at the table top. "They just assume the worst."

"What else did they find?" Sarah prodded gently.

"Some man gave me his watch and said I could sell it for dog food."

"Who was he?"

"I don't know. Never seen him before."

"Could you identify him?"

Clara shook her head. "He was wearing a scarf and hat that covered most of his face. All I remember is he had blue eyes and he sounded funny like he had a cold."

"But surely the police can't still hold you unless they know for sure the watch was stolen."

"I guess they can." Clara shrugged. "Can you tell Rhonda or that other woman that Molly has a doctor appointment on Monday?"

"Molly?" Martha asked.

"The cocker spaniel. She needs her ears checked. She's been shaking her head. I think she might have ear mites."

"I'll tell her," Sarah pulled out her notebook and wrote herself a reminder. "About this watch—"

"I take my dogs to Dr. White on Baker Street. She only charges me for the medicine." She moved to the door and a guard opened it.

"Wait, Clara. What's your lawyer's name?" Sarah asked.

She shrugged. "Tuddle or Toddler or something like that."

"My son's a lawyer. I'm sure he'd be willing to take your case if you want someone else. And if you need anything, have them call me."

"I just need to go home." A glimmer of tears shone in her eyes before she turned away to be led back to her cell.

In the enclosed space of Martha's van, their clothes did smell faintly of cigarette smoke. Martha turned up the air in an effort to blow the scent behind them.

"I don't think Clara was telling us everything," Martha said.

Sarah snapped on her seat belt and gazed down the street at the police station. "I don't either, but then she has no reason to trust us. If she wasn't so worried about her dogs, she never would've seen us."

"Poor woman. I can't imagine how terrible it is to be in jail, and she doesn't have anybody to bail her out."

"I wonder why the police picked her up in the first place." Sarah said. "Don't they have to have probable cause to search her belongings?"

"Someone must've reported the watch stolen," Martha said as she backed the van out of the parking spot. "Her story about a stranger handing her an expensive watch sounds weak."

Sarah agreed.

"We need to find out more about this watch and whatever else the police are holding her for."

"Chief Halliday won't tell us, but maybe..." Sarah absentmindedly tapped her index finger on her chin.

"You have an idea?"

"Let's see if we can find Officer Hopkins." Sarah called the police station and explained to the operator about the investigation at Magpie's Antiques and that Officer Hopkins had wanted to be notified if they had located the invoices.

"The operator said she'd pass on the message," Sarah told Martha.

"Where to next? Back to the store or home?"

"The store. I want to know how Patty's doing."

Sarah's phone vibrated.

"Officer Hopkins here."

"Thanks for calling back. I wanted to tell you that Maggie found the missing invoice for the brooches."

"Thanks. I'll check in with the chief later."

"But we think that the brooches got accidentally thrown out," Sarah said.

"I'll make sure it's in the report," Hopkins replied.

"Would it be possible to talk to you? In person?"

There was a pause and Sarah could hear the murmur of people's voices. "I'm on my break right now but—"

"Where are you? We can meet you there."

"Really, I—"

"It might help your case," Sarah said.

He sighed. "I'm at The Spotted Dog, but I'll be leaving in eight minutes."

"We'll be there in three."

Martha edged the accelerator down although they couldn't speed up too much with the occasional ice patch on the road. A northerly wind had started and the temperature was dropping. What had melted during the day flowed along the streets and would be solid again by morning.

Business on Main Street had picked up. They had to park farther down the street from the café than Sarah would've liked. They hopped out of the car and hurried down the sidewalk. The wind whipped at Sarah's unbuttoned coat as she dashed into The Spotted Dog.

Liam looked over from where he was working in the bookstore, a surprised look on his face. He started to say something, but Sarah gave him a little wave and strode past to the café counter where Hopkins and his partner sat, plates and mugs in front of them.

Officer Hopkins looked at his watch. "Four minutes."

"Ice on the road," Martha said, coming up behind Sarah, breathing hard. She gestured for Sarah to sit at the only empty stool left at the counter, which was next to Officer

Hopkins. Martha plopped down on a chair at a nearby table.

"Please finish your pie." Sarah slid onto the stool.

"So what's this about?" Officer Hopkins asked.

"We went to see Clara over at the jail and some things just don't make sense."

"In what way?"

"She told me about the watch. How did the police even know she had it?"

"Anonymous tip," Officer Jackson said and drained his coffee mug.

Officer Hopkins glanced at his partner. "We really shouldn't be sharing information. This is an ongoing investigation. You're not her lawyer. You're not even a relative of hers."

"No, but I did tell her I'd try to help. She doesn't have anybody else except her dogs, and they need her. Do you have a dog, Officer Hopkins?"

"Yes, I do, and don't try to play on my sympathy. There were other things in her bag that implicated her."

"But anyone who knows Clara can tell you she goes around behind the local businesses and collects recyclables. Some stores even save things for her. A good lawyer will rip this case apart, unless there is something else. Something concrete," Sarah said, although with Clara's financial situation she would get the luck of the draw when it came to a court-appointed attorney.

Officer Hopkins scraped his fork across his plate picking up the rest of the apple pie filling. He took the check from the counter and hopped off the stool. "I need to get back on duty. I appreciate your concern for Clara but let us handle it." He headed across the café to the cash register.

Sarah eyed Officer Hopkins's young partner who concentrated on finishing his pie. "I'm assuming the watch came from one of the fancy clothing stores off of Main Street by the alley."

Officer Jackson looked up. "How did you know?"

"Jackson, let's go," Officer Hopkins called. The young man wrapped the crust of his pie in a napkin and headed for the door.

Martha hopped up on the stool Hopkins had vacated. "Did you learn anything?"

"The watch came from one of the more expensive stores near the alley."

"Well, there's Harmony, but I wouldn't say their clothing is fancy. More priced in the middle range. What about the Lonely Cricket around the corner?"

"Could be. They were listed in the police blotter as having had some merchandise stolen."

Martha grinned. "Sounds like we should check it out. I think they're having a sale too."

"Good afternoon. I see you're busy scaring off the local law enforcement," Liam teased, coming around the other side of the counter. He glanced from Sarah to Martha, his smile faltering. "Are you okay?"

"Yes, why?"

Martha looked at Sarah and giggled. "If my hair looks as windblown as yours, maybe we *are* scaring people off."

"Now, now, that's not what I meant. You both look lovely, windblown or not. You gave me a jolt when you rushed past and straight to the police."

"I'm sorry," Sarah said with a little laugh. "Officer Hopkins had only a few minutes and we were late." Sarah touched the top of her head. The wind had puffed up her hair so it felt like a Mohawk. She had been in such a rush, she hadn't even noticed the wind whipping her hair.

"I just had some questions about an incident at Maggie's store."

"Nothing too serious, I hope," Liam said with concern threaded through his voice.

"With any luck it's all just a misunderstanding," Sarah said, although the fact that Clara actually had stolen merchandise in her possession didn't bode well for a happy ending. At least not yet. And who had tipped off the police about the watch? "I'll fill you in later. I better get over to the store and see how things are going."

"Okay, I'll see you tomorrow night after the tour is over."

Martha turned to Sarah when they got outside. "You have a hot date?" she teased.

"More like lukewarm. He's taking two of his Irish cousins out to dinner tomorrow night. They're only here for a couple of days. I just hope I'll have time to meet up with them. I'm filling in for Maggie selling raffle tickets and trying to raise donations for the Children's Fund."

"Why didn't you tell me? Maybe I can take your place."

"It was kind of sudden. Patty planned an outing without consulting with Maggie. It's a family thing. And besides, you have enough to do holding up Rosemary."

Martha grimaced. "Well that's true. I talked to her after I called you and she was a mess of nerves. Worse than I was last year."

"You did great last year, and remember we had that storm bearing down on us too."

"That's one of the dangers of having such a big event this time of year. But it looks like the weather will be cold but fine." Martha tilted her face to the sun and almost walked into a Helping Hands bin.

"You're going to need one of Annie's poultices if you're not careful," Sarah teased.

"Call me old-fashioned, but I'll go to the doctor. Or is that new-fashioned?" She laughed. "Give me an X-ray and a prescription from a doc I trust, and I'll be happy. My grandmother used to use poultices and they worked fine, so I'm not knocking them. But don't try giving me healing stones or magnets or pixie dust and then tell me to meditate for an hour. Good old-fashioned prayer still works the best."

"Amen to that," Sarah said with a smile.

Sarah pushed open the door to find Maggie and Audrey straightening up the store.

"How's your mother?" Sarah asked.

"I took her home and put Dad in charge of her. She's going to take it easy for the rest of the day."

"Grandma wasn't happy. She fussed about *everything*," Audrey said. "Grandpa wanted to take us geocaching this afternoon, but Grandma didn't want to be left alone. Well, she told us to go without her, but Grandpa said she didn't mean it."

"That was nice of you to wait for her to get better," Sarah said.

Maggie shook her head as she folded a hand-embroidered place mat and stacked it with a matching set. "I think I got a taste of the future. I love my mom with all my heart, but she's a terrible patient. I just hope she and Dad stay healthy for a long, long time. I'm not ready for role reversal."

"Role reversal?" Audrey asked.

"It's when the grown-up child takes care of the parents when they get old," Sarah explained.

"Someday it'll be your turn." Maggie playfully bumped shoulders with Audrey.

Audrey blinked. "I'll be so old. I can't even think that far ahead."

Martha laughed. "That's the wonderful thing about being your age. Time seems endless."

"Speaking of time, I think we can close up and go home," Maggie said. "I had only one sale today, but I suppose it's better than nothing, considering how bad the streets were this morning."

"They're much better now, at least until the temperature drops tonight," Martha said.

"I want it to snow again," Audrey said. "It's all yucky and hard now. Amy hit me with a snowball, and it really hurt. And we can't go sledding."

"I don't want you sledding on ice," Maggie said, turning off the Christmas lights at the windows as Sarah got the ones on the trees. "I already have one patient at home."

Audrey sighed. "I'm starving."

"We're having tomato soup and grilled cheese. The soup isn't organic but we just won't tell Grammy, and maybe she won't ask." Maggie grabbed her coat. "Do you want to come over for supper, Sarah? Martha, you and Ernie are welcome too, if you don't mind a really simple meal."

"Actually that sounds wonderful to me, but Ernie's been fighting the sniffles today and it's best if we just stay in."

"I was going to work on some Christmas presents tonight. I'm running out of time," Sarah said, thinking about the mystery quilt.

"Is it a present for me?" Audrey asked.

"It's funny you should ask. Someone just told me that if you reveal Christmas secrets, then you might not get any gifts. But if you insist—" She leaned close to Audrey with her hand cupped around the side of her mouth.

"No! Don't tell me." She squealed and giggled as she dashed out the door.

"I'll go warm up the van," Martha told Sarah.

Sarah followed Maggie outside. "Would you all like to come over to my place for Sunday lunch after church? It's been a while since I entertained, and it'll give me an excuse to bake more goodies."

"I'd love to," Maggie said. "I'll check with Jason to make sure he didn't commit to something else, and call you."

Audrey hopped from one foot to the other next to Maggie's Tahoe. "It's so cold!" Maggie unlocked the doors and Audrey jumped inside.

The wind took Sarah's breath away as she hurried to Martha's van. She had a hard time pulling the door shut.

"It's a good thing most of the ice melted off the trees or the branches would be snapping all over the place." Martha backed out onto the street. "Should we check out the Lonely Cricket?

Sarah glanced at her watch. It was after six, but some of the stores stayed open later during the Christmas season. "We can see if anyone is still there."

Lights shone from the clothing store. As Martha slowed to slip into a parking space, a man came out the door carrying a shopping bag.

It took a moment for Sarah to recognize the face under the navy wool cap he wore. "Interesting. What's he doing in there?"

"Who?

"Paul Barclay."

# CHAPTER FOURTEEN

S arah jumped out of the van. "I need to talk to him."
But by the time she reached the sidewalk, Paul had
gotten into a blue pickup truck and was backing out
onto the street.

"Paul!" She waved, but the truck rolled away, leaving her
in a cloud of exhaust.

Martha stood on the stoop of the Lonely Cricket. "Paul
must have expensive taste," Martha said when Sarah got
back. "There's almost nothing under fifty dollars in here."

"Tim Barclay gave the impression that Paul has been
hard up since he got fired from the Chamber of Commerce,"
Sarah said.

"Maybe he got another job," Martha said as they hurried
into the warmth of the store.

The scent of lemon-scented glass cleaner cut through the
smell of leather. A young stylishly dressed woman wiped
down a marble-topped counter. Her name tag read "Char."
"We're closing in ten minutes. Let me know if I can help you
with anything."

"We'll only be a couple of minutes," Sarah said, as she and Martha surveyed the shop.

The accessories were grouped together along the middle of one wall. Belts, purses, and scarves hung on the wall and earrings, chains, and watches were displayed on a counter. Sarah picked up one watch with a sparkly face and a pink band. She glanced at the price. Two hundred and fifty dollars. Another bracelet-style watch was three hundred. They seemed too expensive to be left out for people to handle until Sarah saw the price tag on one of the watches in the glass-enclosed cabinet—eleven hundred dollars. Sarah glanced up and noted a video camera mounted in the back corner of the store.

Martha came up beside her, holding a long silky scarf in rainbow colors. "This scarf is *on sale* for a hundred and twenty-five dollars," she whispered. "Can you imagine what it would be full price?"

The sound of heels on the marbled tile floor clicked up behind them. "How are we doing?" Char asked. "You've chosen a lovely scarf. You know it was handwoven with one hundred percent of the finest silk?"

"It's very lovely, but I need to think about it." Martha handed it to the saleswomen.

"Well, don't wait too long. Our sale will end Christmas Eve, and the scarf will go back to normal price. We also have some men's Irish wool scarves back here." Char gestured to a table. "They make very nice gifts."

Liam had mentioned that Murphy had chewed his scarf. Maybe he would like a new one for Christmas. Sarah walked over to the table and picked up an emerald green scarf with flecks of rust, yellow, lavender, and brown. The rich green reminded Sarah of Liam's eyes when they warmed with a smile.

She flipped the tag over and read that the scarf was an original, handwoven from hand-spun Donegal wool in a small Irish fishing village. The price caused her to pause, but she breathed through it remembering that the scarf was fifty percent off.

She set the scarf back on the table, but then picked it up again. This was the gift she had been looking for—especially since the scarf reminded her of how last Christmas Liam had insisted she take his scarf when they were out in the bitter cold and she had forgotten hers at home. Liam's kindness and thoughtfulness were just two of the qualities that drew her to him.

"I think I'll take this," she said to Char. Martha turned around, eyebrows lifted.

"Excellent choice," Char said, taking the scarf from her. "I'll put it over next to the register."

Martha sidled over to Sarah. "Liam?"

Sarah nodded.

"He's going to love it," Martha said with a grin.

"I hope so." Sarah paused by the watches again and focused on the reason they were at the Lonely Cricket. Had the stolen watch come from here?

Char turned her head and smiled at them. "Are you interested in the watches too?"

"Actually I am, and I realize this may seem a strange question, but did you have a watch stolen here?"

Char's smile vanished. "Who did you say you were?"

"Sarah Hart. My daughter-in-law owns Magpie's Antiques around the corner on Main."

"Oh yes, I've seen that quaint-looking shop. I haven't been in it yet though. I moved to town last summer to manage this store for my aunt. Perhaps you know her? Morgan Smithe."

"Oh, I think I met your aunt at a fund-raiser. Her husband is a banker, right?" Martha asked.

Char nodded. "Yes, that's her. I can pass on your regards, if you'd like."

"I'm Martha Maplethorpe. She may not remember me, but please tell her hello. Maybe we'll meet up again."

Char shifted her attention back to Sarah. "So why do you want to know about the stolen watch?"

"There have been a number of thefts around the downtown lately. The Galleria was hit, as well as the China Cup. I saw this store mentioned in the police blotter as having lost merchandise. Magpie's Antiques also lost some brooches."

"Actually several silk scarves were stolen, like the one Mrs. Maplethorpe was looking at. We've improved security, but then a watch and several pairs of earrings were shoplifted this week."

"Did you have that video camera when the scarves were taken?"

"Yes, but as recently explained to me by our new security consultant, our video camera is angled to give a broad view of the store and it can leave blind spots that a savvy thief can use. Too many people in the shop serve as shields, and anyone can easily slip something small into a pocket or bag."

Sarah glanced up at the camera. "Do you have the recording from the day the watch was taken?"

"I gave the memory card to the police," she said. "We're going to move the accessory section to a more central location and get another video system. That stolen watch was worth four hundred and fifty dollars. We won't get the watch back for a while, but I'm glad they caught the shoplifter, the dog lady, as some people call her."

"Did you see her in the store?" Martha asked.

"No, but that was a really busy time since it was the first day of our sale. Last Monday."

The same day Audrey, Amy, Lexie, and their friends were questioned by the police. Sarah indicated she was ready to purchase the green scarf.

As Char processed Sarah's card, she said, "We may have to invest in electronic security tags too so things can't go out the door. It's a shame to have to clip those ugly things on our lovely clothes, but what else can you do? As my aunt says, times have changed in Maple Hill."

Indeed, what could they do? Sarah glanced around the store. "Was the security consultant Gordon Leftfoot?"

"Yes, actually. Why?"

"He's been by Maggie's store too."

"Seems real competent. My aunt liked his presentation." Char handed Sarah the bag with the scarf and walked them to the door. "Do come visit again and don't forget about the sale."

Sarah paused on the steps. "I saw Paul Barclay leaving the store earlier. Does he shop here a lot?"

Char frowned. "Who?"

"The young man who left the store just before we got here."

"Oh, him. He's been in a couple of times but only recently. Hope to see you again soon." She locked the door behind them.

"Clara must've been identified on the videotape," Martha said after they returned to the van.

Sarah set her purse and the bag on the floor and snapped on her seat belt. "Maybe, but Officer Jackson said they'd received an anonymous tip about Clara. That's what led them to the watch in her bag."

Martha started the engine. "That sounds fishy to me."

"Me too. Either Clara is lying and she stole the watch, or she's innocent and being set up."

Martha gazed down the street toward the alley. "But why would anyone want to set up someone like Clara?"

The next morning Sarah parked near the hitching post in front of the white clapboard building that housed the Maple Hill Historical Society. It was after ten and to her relief the lights were on. The historical society's hours were sometimes odd, and it wasn't open every day.

Sarah yawned and checked her reflection in the rearview mirror. She had overslept that morning. Martha had hung around Sarah's after they left the Lonely Cricket. They had eaten the leftover beef stew and talked. Sarah suspected Martha was making an effort to make sure Sarah didn't get lonely during her first holiday season without William. She had done the same thing Sarah's first year without Gerry. Although Sarah loved Martha's caring warmth, she just hoped Martha wasn't missing out on time with Ernie.

Martha had left after nine, and Liam had called to tell her that his cousins weren't interested in the Holiday Home Tour, so they would just meet her for dinner. Sarah updated him on the situation with Clara and they chatted until she went to bed.

As she sat in her car in front of the historical society, Sarah smoothed her hair and decided she didn't look too scary, but she would certainly need to take a shower before the Home Tour started that afternoon.

She trotted up the steps to the historical society's door and walked inside, across the uneven, squeaky wide plank floor. A fire crackled in the main room's fireplace and the hint of wood smoke mingled with the scents of parchment and aged cedar.

A woman with brown hair twisted up in a bun bent over one of the many file cabinets popping out between the bookshelves. She looked up and her brown eyes widened. "Sarah! How nice to see you. I was just thinking about you the other day when I was at the county museum looking at a vintage crazy quilt." Irene Stuart, the head historian, set a file on top of the drawer.

"I hope it was the quilt that reminded you of me and not the crazy part," Sarah teased.

Irene laughed. "Maybe a little of both. What can I help you with today?"

"I need to locate the homestead of one of Maple Hill's families."

Irene clapped her hands together, her charm bracelet jingling, obviously delighted. Sarah knew that maps were one of Irene's favorite tools in her quest for historical accuracy.

"What's the name?"

"Barclay."

"Ah, yes, the Barclays. There are quite a few in our county."

"These would be the great-great-grandparents of Paul and Tim Barclay," Sarah said, wishing she had asked Tim their names.

Irene moved to a computer workstation in the corner that had access to the genealogy database. Her manicured red nails flashed over the keyboard as she typed in the names. Seconds later, Irene had the information she needed. "You're looking for the Charles and Gertie Barclay homestead." She walked over to a filing cabinet and pulled out a black leather-bound book.

"They would've registered it in the late 1800s." She flipped through the yellowed pages. "Here it is. The original house burned down, but I think one of the sons rebuilt nearby." Irene carried the book with her to where the society stored the maps.

Irene's index finger ran over the rolls until she came to the one she wanted. She carefully, almost lovingly, unrolled it on the counter.

"According to the records, their homestead would be in this area." Irene pointed to the northeast part of the county. "Near the state park. Actually, it looks like their property butts right up to the park boundaries. Most likely some of their land was reallocated to the state."

Sarah looked at the vast area Irene pointed to. "Is there any way to tell where the actual house would be? Tim said that they don't get mail out at the house."

"Afraid not. At least not on this map." Irene turned back to the rolls and checked several others. "They owned a lot of acreage and if I'm remembering correctly, they were a private bunch. Still are. Rumor has it that one of the Barclays robbed a bank shipment in New York City before the turn of the century and hid gold coins on the property."

"Really?" Sarah said. "I hadn't heard that one."

"No one ever claimed to have found the coins nor was anyone ever prosecuted. It could just be a tall tale. Every once in a while people tromp across the property looking for the lost gold and the Barclays run them off."

Sarah studied the map. Someone, decades ago, had handwritten the name Barclay on it, but if there were roads into the property, they didn't show up on that map or the modern one.

"Let's try using Google Earth. Chris showed me this," Irene said, referring to her husband. She walked back to the computer and accessed the Internet. "I'll type in the nearest town."

A satellite photo filled the screen. "Now watch, we can zoom in." She referred back to her map. "Now see, there's the road going into the state park." She scrolled the cursor across the screen so the photo moved. "There! See those piles of bricks? Those would be the chimneys from the original homestead and over there is another building." She zoomed in as far as it could go.

"Is that the Barclays'?"

"Must be, unless there are other structures out there not recorded in our office." She printed out the satellite photo. "Hold on while I get you a copy of this map."

As Irene went off to the copy machine, Sarah played with the computer. She typed in her address on Hillside Avenue and zoomed in on a rooftop picture of her Queen Anne.

"Pretty cool, isn't it?"

"Very," Sarah said, impressed and unnerved at the same time to think that a machine in space could spy on her home so easily. She wondered if antitechnology Kathleen Lewison knew about Google Earth.

"Here's a copy of the map. I circled where we think the house is."

"As always, Irene, I'm impressed at how efficient you are. This is wonderful. Thank you."

"Well, as I've said before, I love my job." Irene smiled as her fingers fiddled with the charms on her bracelet. "Can you tell me why you're looking for the old Barclay place?"

"Let's just say I'm not looking for gold."

With the number of tickets Sarah sold Saturday evening at the first home on the tour, there was little doubt that the raffle was a success. Maggie would be pleased.

As Martha had predicted, the director, Rosemary, needn't have worried about weather interfering with attendance. The forecasted storm had petered out before hitting western Massachusetts and only dusted the ground, adding sparkle to the Christmas settings.

When she had finished at the historical society, Sarah had raced home, jumped in the shower, and then changed into a red suit with a black collar and belt. She had slipped on soft black boots. With an ebony purse, she felt unusually coordinated, and it gave her a confidence boost. She hated to admit it but she was bit nervous meeting more of Liam's family. She was close to his daughter Caitlin who had married Travis Walsh the month before, and she had met Caitlin's Aunt Mabina from Ireland, but as her friendship with Liam had grown, so had the importance of his family's acceptance and approval.

Liam had called earlier, and Sarah had insisted he take his cousins over to The Old Mill restaurant rather than pick her up, just in case she was late. When she was done with the Home Tour raffle, she drove over to the restaurant, parked her car in the parking lot, and gazed at the lighted windows.

Sarah enjoyed visiting The Old Mill, which was housed in the original grist mill that had brought commerce to the area two hundred years before. Heavy beams intersected across the ceiling, and the old dark wood imparted a sense of history and continuity. Liam and the two men sat by a large paneled window.

As she entered the room, Liam stood, his smile instantly making her feel at ease. The other two men rose also. Sarah searched their faces trying to see a family resemblance. Both were shorter than Liam and had stocky builds. They had Liam's green eyes set in their tanned, weathered faces, but that's where the similarity ended. One cousin sported a salt-and-pepper beard and unruly hair that framed his ears. The other was clean-shaven, his hair a reddish hue with only a few silver streaks but receding off his freckled forehead.

Liam pulled out a brocade chair when she reached the table. "These are my cousins, Sean and Ronan Cassidy."

"So this is the sweet lass you've been telling us about," Sean, the clean-shaven one, said. "He's told us a lot of stories about you. Some of them quite spicy."

"Really?" Sarah said as a blush heated her cheeks. She stole a glance at Liam as he sat. "I can't imagine. What kind of things?"

"Now don't you be going telling tales on me." Liam reached for Sarah's hand resting on the linen table cloth. "He means exciting. I just told them about some of the adventures you've had around here."

"A regular female Sherlock Holmes," Sean said.

Ronan elbowed Sean in the ribs. "You'll have to forgive 'em. He's addicted to mystery novels. And here he's meeting a real sleuth."

"I just get lucky. I stick my nose where it doesn't belong."

Ronan grinned. "And a pretty nose it is too."

"Now, don't you be flirting with my girlfriend," Liam said in mock sternness and squeezed Sarah's hand.

Ronan wagged his bushy eyebrows. "Yours now? Didn't know it was so serious. Since when have you staked a claim?"

"With you two around, I better," Liam said to Sean and the men laughed.

Liam gave Sarah another apologetic look and she smiled back, letting him know everything was fine. She already liked these rugged-looking, jovial characters.

Sarah and Liam ordered the day's special of sea bass and steamed broccoli. The cousins asked for filet mignon and baked potatoes.

"We get enough fish at home," Sean explained after the waiter took their order to the kitchen.

"I think that must've been a fascinating life—being on the sea every day," Sarah said.

"Never a dull moment." Ronan reached for a roll and slathered it with butter. "But I'm glad to be grounded. No more wearing cold, wet clothes all day and night, and smelling like the brine. No wonder I never was able to catch a woman."

"Smelling like brine was the least of yer problems," Sean said.

Ronan waved his butter knife at Sean. "Says the man who was married three times. You could catch them, but you couldn't keep 'em. Sort of like yer fishing. Slippery fingers."

Sean leaned forward. "I can outfish you any day, any week, any year!"

Sarah shifted uneasily in her seat as their voices rose. Several other patrons glanced over at them. What had she started? Liam took a drink of his water apparently not finding this exchange unusual.

"Yeah, but could you hang on to them now?" Ronan set his knife down and bit into his second roll.

"Are you referring to the fish or the women?" Sean asked. He caught sight of Sarah's face and let out a loud guffaw. "Don't mind our quarreling. It's all in jest, right Ronan?"

"Huh?" Ronan was eyeing the basket of rolls again. "Oh, right, right, don't mind us. We're just two old blokes being fancy-free on our holiday. I just wish we could've booked a trip earlier for Caitlin's wedding, but Sean didn't officially hang up his waders until last week."

"Don't go blaming me because you were born first. I needed my full benefits. I worked to the last minute." He looked up as the waiter placed salads in front of all of them, and then offered ground pepper.

After the waiter left, Sarah asked, "Where are you off to after Maple Hill?"

"Hollywood!" Ronan said.

"They're flying out tomorrow for Los Angeles," Liam said.

"I think you'll enjoy southern California. My daughter-in-law's family is from that area."

"Yep, I've always wanted to see the Pacific Ocean. I hear that people can wear bathing suits on the beach all year round. Is that true?" Sean asked Sarah.

"I suppose some might if it stays warm enough," Sarah said. "I didn't get to spend much time there, and then my son and his family moved back here about a year and half ago."

"Now why would anyone want to do that?"

"Forgive my brother. No offense intended. Maple Hill is a nice town but," Ronan shifted his gaze out the window to where fat snowflakes still fell lazily, "it's just so blasted cold here."

Sarah laughed. "No offense taken." After all, she had in-laws wondering the same thing. Why move from paradise? "It doesn't stay this way. You need to come back in the summer."

"We'll have to do that," Sean said. "Now that we've hooked up with Liam after all these years, it'll seem the natural thing to do."

"You're always welcome to visit," Liam said.

"As long as I don't flirt with your girlfriend, you mean," Ronan teased. "Maybe you should be making it legal? And I don't mean how Sean did. Make it permanent."

The waiter arrived with more rolls and a water pitcher saving Liam from responding, much to Sarah's relief. Her stomach quivered. Liam and she had been taking their growing relationship slowly. She didn't want to feel pressured. Life was good right now.

She kept her head down and plowed through her salad as the topic turned to a lively discussion of distant relatives in Ireland Sarah hadn't heard about before. Sean soon had them laughing about an eccentric eighty-year-old uncle who, rain or shine, would pedal his bike five miles to town in his pajamas, pick up coffee and the paper, and then ride home in time for breakfast.

After the waiter served cheesecake and coffee, Sean leaned on his elbow closer to Sarah. "So are you working on any mysteries right now?"

Sarah set her coffee cup down. "Actually I've been looking into some shoplifting that's been going on around town."

"Sticky fingers, huh?" Sean said. "Five finger discount? Nicking as they call it in the UK. We call it stroking at home. Course, in the olden days, you weren't apt to see as much thievery when you might lose a finger." He made a whacking motion with his fork. "Worked pretty good to deter crime."

"Sean!" Ronan said. "Finger chopping is not a topic for the table, especially in front of a lady."

"I apologize," Sean said to Sarah. "I get carried away. So, have you uncovered any clues?"

"A few." Without naming any names she gave them a brief summary.

"She keeps busy," Liam said with a proud smile.

Sean scraped the last of his cheesecake off his plate. "Do you have any suspects?"

"Some. The police think they have the person though."

"And you don't?" Liam guessed.

"I'm not so sure," Sarah said. "Something feels off."

Sean nodded. "Sometimes you got to go with your gut feeling."

Ronan frowned at his brother. "Like you'd know the difference."

"Never said I did," Sean said. "But if you were trying to guess the villain in a TV show like *Murder She Wrote*, you'd pick the most famous guest celebrity. If this were a mystery novel, you'd look at the least obvious suspect." He winked at her. "If I were you, I'd start there."

# CHAPTER FIFTEEN

Sarah tugged at the collar of the mauve turtleneck she had chosen to wear under her royal blue wool suit. She had prepared for the frigid outside weather but hadn't anticipated how warm the church would be. Additional body heat came from being crammed up against Audrey.

They had been late this morning, waiting for Patty who had changed three times and moved slowly because of her ankle. By the time they got to Bridge Street Church, their choice of seating was limited. To all be seated in the same pew, they'd had to sit close and cozy.

As the deacons passed the offering plates, Sarah's mind wandered to the previous evening. Sean and Ronan had given her bear hugs good-bye, making her promise that if she ever came to the Green Isle, she would look them up.

In the parking lot, Liam had taken her hands in his and thanked her for joining them and assured Sarah she had been a hit with his cousins. She had made the evening extraspecial.

"I hope they didn't make you feel too uncomfortable about, you know, us," Liam had said with a tinge of worry in his deep voice.

Sarah's heart had beaten faster. "No, not really. They're like…big brothers. All bluff and talk."

"Good, because—"

"Hey, Liam, are you going to kiss her good-night or what?" Sean had called from Liam's truck.

"Mind your own business," Liam had said and turned his back to them. "I think I better go and put the boys to bed. Much as I enjoyed seeing them, I'm going to be relieved when they get on that plane."

Sarah had laughed. "Ah, they're all right."

Liam had glanced at his truck and then leaned forward and kissed Sarah on the cheek. "Thanks again."

Audrey nudged Sarah and she looked up to see the offering plate in front of her. She realized her hand was touching the spot on her cheek where Liam had kissed her. She fumbled with her purse to grab her tithe envelope and then passed the plate to the deacon.

"Something wrong, Grandma?" Audrey whispered.

"No, sweetie."

"Do you have any gum?"

Sarah nodded and slipped her a piece. Amy was watching and bumped Audrey's shoulder.

"Can Amy have some?" Audrey asked.

Sarah handed over another stick.

Amy let out a muffled giggle. Larry, who was seated next to Amy, was gazing at Sarah with a puppy dog expression. Sarah smiled at him and passed down one more stick.

Patty leaned forward and glared at all of them. Sarah settled back and focused on the couple getting up to sing a duet for special music. The Christmas song was one of her favorites about Mary and her baby boy. Tears pricked her eyes when it ended.

The viewing screen lowered and a mission appeal video came on. Sarah had already seen the appeal and she had sent an offering to the mission several weeks before. She suppressed a yawn. She had gotten home too late last night to work on the quilt and had gone right to bed. But before she had drifted off into sleep, she had mulled over Sean's words about looking for the least likely suspect. Granted this was real life and not fiction, but he did have a point. Someone who was guilty would most likely try hard to appear innocent. Or, perhaps, be extracooperative and helpful.

She thought about her list of possible suspects. One person *did* stand out as being right in the middle of the action.

Gordon Leftfoot.

He was an ex-cop with a supposedly good record. Who would suspect him? But, in fact, he had been at every crime scene. *And* he had a business that wouldn't thrive without crime. On top of that, he had befriended Chief Halliday and the Maple Hill police and could keep on top of the investigation. Who better to know how to frame Clara Schmidt?

Audrey nudged her again. "What are you doing?"

Sarah realized she had been holding up her hands and ticking off the reasons to suspect Gordon on her fingers. She dropped her hands in her lap. "Thinking when I should be paying attention to the service," she whispered back. "I'll be good now."

Audrey giggled.

Reverend John Peabody stepped to the podium. "Good morning. Isn't it a lovely day to come together in the name of the Lord?"

Sarah agreed and relaxed her shoulders back against the pew. She made a mental note to investigate Gordon Leftfoot as soon as possible and then turned her full attention to the sermon with relief. Time to be refreshed by the Word.

Sarah opened the oven door and pulled out the pan with the lemon-peppered roast chicken and set it on the counter. The kitchen steamed with heat, clouding the windows and blocking the view of the frozen landscape. Temperatures were still entrenched in the twenties, but inside Sarah's house her family was cozy and warm.

Sarah hummed the hymn "Blessed Be the Ties That Bind" they had sung as the closing hymn in church, as she scooped out the potatoes and carrots from the pan. She had plenty of food. She had invited Martha and Ernie to Sunday lunch, but Martha called her after church with the news that Ernie had a fever and they had left the service early to go home.

Audrey skated across the kitchen floor in her socks. "Dad's finished setting the dining room table. Are we almost ready to eat?"

"Yes, I just have to carve the chicken, and then get your grandmother's casserole out of the oven. You can take the vegetables to the table and ask Amy to pour the punch, please. The pitcher's in the refrigerator." Sarah put a towel over the vegetables to keep them warm and handed them to Amy.

Patty had made lasagna loaded with roasted vegetables, which smelled heavenly of fresh herbs, and she had also brought pumpernickel rolls from a local bakery.

Sarah had insisted Maggie visit with her parents by the fire in the living room while the rest of them got the food on the table. She wanted them to have as much time together as possible before Patty and Larry went back to California.

After the food was all on the table, Sarah called the rest of the family to the dining room. Patty sat in a chair Larry had pulled out. She ran her finger over the delicate blue flowers on the white rim of the plate. "I like your china, Sarah. Is it antique?"

"Thank you and no, this set isn't, at least not until I'm considered an antique," Sarah joked. "Gerry and I picked this out before our wedding at the China Cup gift shop. It brings back good memories, so I like using it on Sundays when guests are over. I do have my grandmother's china in the attic that I bring out for holidays."

Jason took the head of the table where his father used to sit and Sarah sat at the foot, closer to the kitchen. They'd had to add the extension to get everyone around the table. Maggie sat on the side with her mother and father and the twins took the other side.

Amy eyed the basket on the table. "The rolls are black."

"Of course they are." Audrey sent her sister a superior look. "They're pumpernickel."

"I know what pumpernickel bread is. I just never have seen it so black."

"Those are special," Patty said. "They're made with organic flour and have flaxseed oil added."

"Flaxseed?" Audrey opened her mouth to say something else, but Maggie interrupted.

"Audrey, let's say the blessing," Maggie said.

They bowed their heads, and Jason prayed.

As soon as Jason said "Amen," Patty spoke, "Flaxseed is very good for you and can help prevent heart disease. You want a healthy heart, right?"

Audrey nodded, but Sarah noted she didn't take a roll when the basket passed her.

Sarah tasted the lasagna. "This is really great lasagna, Patty. Can I get the recipe?"

"Sure, I got it out of one of the cookbooks I bought at that New Age store," Patty said with a small smile.

"New Age?" Audrey asked.

"The Crystal Unicorn."

"Oh yeah, I was in there with Lexie." Audrey turned to her mom. "Can I buy some incense?"

"Incense?" Maggie asked. "Whatever for?"

"To burn in my room to make it smell nice."

Jason looked at Audrey. "Incense requires fire, so no. Not until you're older, and not in your bedroom."

Audrey frowned and speared a baby carrot.

"They do have safe holders where you can use incense cones that are mostly enclosed by pottery," Patty said to Audrey, "I saw some in the Crystal Unicorn. Maybe we can look at them later."

Jason's jaw tensed as he forked up a piece of chicken and chewed.

Maggie glanced at her husband, and then asked, "Mom, Dad, what do you want to do this afternoon?"

"Whatever you want, sweetheart." Larry started to reach for the platter of chicken, but caught sight of Patty's frown and took another lasagna square instead.

"Let's go geocaching," Amy said. "And this time Grandma can go."

"That'd be so cool," Audrey said.

"Excellent idea," Larry said. "We'll make it a family outing. Sarah, you're going to like this."

"Well you've gotten me curious. I'd like to see how it's done," Sarah said.

"I don't know if I should go," Patty said. "My ankle is still a bit sore to be walking far."

Larry patted his wife on the hand. "Well, you can rest, darling. We won't stay out too long."

Patty sighed and pulled her hand away.

"I'll stay with you, Mom," Maggie offered.

Audrey looked at Maggie, a pout forming on her face. "But I wanted you, Dad, and Grandma to see how much fun geocaching is."

"Yes, but if we all can't go—"

"Oh, never mind," Patty said. "I'll ride along and just stay in the car. I don't want to spoil the family outing."

"Great. You're such a trooper," Larry said, and Patty shot him a glare. "We need to get on the computer and pick an area to go to."

"I have a laptop in my office if you want to use that," Sarah said.

"Excellent. Wait until you see the Web sites, Jason. You'd be amazed how seriously people take geocaching."

Jason and Larry started discussing computers, and when the topic turned to sports, Amy jumped right in.

Patty ate silently and Maggie said little. Sarah noted deepening lines around Maggie's eyes and wondered if she wasn't sleeping well. She needed her rest with all the activity at the shop lately. Sarah's mind wandered to Liam and their conversation last night.

Liam's perceptive questions about Clara and the evidence against her had convinced Sarah more than ever that something else was going on. Surely Halliday realized that too.

"Grandma?"

Sarah started. "Yes? What?"

Audrey was standing beside her. She giggled. "You were daydreaming. I asked if you were done with your plate."

Sarah smiled. "Sorry about that. Yes, you may take it to the kitchen." She looked over at Maggie. "How about we go to the living room and have dessert by the fire?"

"That sounds good." Maggie pushed her chair back. "I'll help you clean up."

"Nope. Not that I don't appreciate it, but today is your day off. We have it covered, don't we, Amy and Audrey?"

"Yep," Audrey passed Sarah with the stack of plates. "I can't wait for dessert."

"Huh?" Amy said, still engrossed in the basketball discussion with Jason and Larry. "Oh, okay." She dragged herself up and started collecting glasses while staying within earshot of the men.

"Thanks, Sarah," Maggie offered her mother a hand and helped her mother stand.

Larry blinked as if suddenly realizing Patty was on her feet. "Where are you going?"

"Living room, Dad." Maggie smiled at him. "We're having dessert in there."

The men stood and Larry turned to Sarah. "May I take you up on your offer to use your computer?"

"Sure, come this way."

Sarah got Larry set up at the kitchen table and then she and the girls finished clearing the table and stacking the china. She would hand wash the plates later. The rest went into the dishwasher. She put the chocolate sauce on the stove and started a pot of coffee while Audrey cut the eggnog cake into squares and placed them on small plates.

"Where's this?" Larry tapped the folded portion of the map Sarah had left on the table when searching for where Paul Barclay lived.

"That's near the state park northwest of us. Pretty area."

"Well, let's see if there are any geocaches up there." Larry typed on the keyboard. "You can search the geocache Web site for the area you want by entering the zip code and then selecting the range. Let's click fifty-mile radius." He sat back and Audrey and Amy crowded closer to watch. A list appeared on the screen. He scrolled through it. "Look. There are two sites near Deer Falls."

"We've been there," Amy said. "Our church youth group went to the falls one Sunday last summer. It was fun."

"The caches are called 'Watch your Step' and 'Wishing Well,'" Audrey read over her grandfather's shoulder.

"People log in here after they find a geocache and make a record. See? 'Watch Your Step' has thirty-one logs and 'Wishing Well' has twenty-three," Larry explained to Sarah.

"We logged in when we went geocaching last week," Amy added. "I have my own account."

Larry clicked on "Watch Your Step" and scrolled down the page. "Down here are descriptions that give you ideas or clues of where to look."

Amy tapped the screen. "There are other hints there, but they're scrambled."

"Encrypted," Larry added. "You just click on that spot that says decrypted and there are more clues."

"But that's like cheating," Audrey explained to Sarah. "You only do that if you're really, really stuck."

Larry leaned back. "Is it a long hike to the falls?"

"If I remember right, it's about a twenty-minute walk," Sarah said.

"It's not far," Amy said.

The last time Sarah had been to Deer Falls was with Gerry about ten years ago. She studied the map. The state park line skimmed close to the spot Irene had circled as the original Barclay homestead. It might be useful for Clara's case to go look around.

Jason walked into the kitchen with an inquisitive look. "The chocolate sauce is still warming," Sarah said before he asked.

"Jason, what do you think about a drive out there?" Larry asked, pointing at the spot on the map. "There are two geocaches we can easily get to."

Jason picked up the map. "It's about a thirty-minute drive."

"Can we go?" Amy asked her dad. "It's nice out."

"I don't see why not. The roads should be clear enough. Most of the route is state highway."

"Great!" Larry stood. "Let the adventure begin."

The sun had melted most of the snow and ice off the mountain road and only patches of white remained in the shadowed places. As they came to the turnoff to the falls, Jason switched the Tahoe into four-wheel drive, although the traction seemed adequate all the way to the parking lot.

They had all changed into boots, sweaters, and jeans and had brought daypacks, except Patty who had armed herself with a book, a pillow, and a thermos of coffee. After everyone exited the vehicle, she leaned against one door and stretched out her legs across the backseat.

"Don't worry about me," she said. "I'm going to enjoy the fresh air and my book."

Jason, Maggie, and the girls held their GPS units and Larry showed them how to tap in the coordinates from the copy of the Web site Sarah had printed out.

"We're going to make the parking lot a waypoint so we can find our way back. Normally if you stick on trails like these here, you don't really need the waypoint, but it's a precaution in case you're in an area where you can get lost."

Larry handed Sarah his GPS unit, "Now if you look at the screen, that arrow is pointing the way we want to go, and down here it says how far we have to go, which is a third of a mile."

Amy and Audrey had their units programmed and took off down the wet trail.

"Don't get out of sight," Jason called as the adults started after them.

"Be careful where you walk," Larry said. "It's tempting to just watch the GPS screen, and then you stumble or go off the trail."

The sound of water splashing over stones grew louder and suddenly the woods gave way to a wide stream. The trail turned and followed the bank.

Sarah paused. "The GPS keeps pointing across the stream."

"That's because it doesn't know we can't cross here. It looks like the trail turns again up ahead."

The twins climbed the next rise, and Audrey shouted back. "We can see the falls."

Sarah's hiking boots kept slipping on mud as she scrambled up the hill, but the climb was worth it. Melting snow had swelled the normal volume of water cascading fifty feet over a cliff into a rock-studded pool. A small rainbow glistened in the rising mist.

"Amy, Audrey, turn around." Larry pulled a camera out of his pocket and snapped some photos of the girls in front of the pool.

Sarah studied the GPS unit. The arrow pointed straight ahead into the falls and indicated the geocache was ten feet away.

Larry checked his printout. "The first hint is 'don't look to the right, don't look to the left, be sure to watch your step.'"

"Do you think it's in the pool?" Amy asked.

"If it is, you're not wading in that ice cold water," Maggie said. "You don't want to get sick before Christmas."

"Watch your step," Sarah murmured, repeating the clue. She moved close to the rocky edge. The GPS arrow kept pointing straight ahead. Large boulders dotted the pool.

"Neither to the right nor to the left," Amy added. She and Sarah both said "Oh!" at the same time.

"You find something?" Jason asked.

Sarah pointed. "Look at these rocks. They go straight out in a line."

"Like a bridge," Amy said.

Jason reached out and caught Amy's arm as she stepped forward. "Let me go first." He took off his daypack.

"Be careful," Maggie said as Jason put his foot on the first boulder to check its stability.

He looked back at Maggie and grinned. "Solid as a rock, just like our marriage."

Maggie groaned. "Is that your way of sweet-talking me?"

"Hey, I get points for effort, don't I?" He winked at her.

Audrey rolled her eyes. "Da-ad."

Jason stepped to the next flat boulder and looked down between the rocks. "Eureka! Or whatever one says when you find treasure."

Audrey jumped up and down. "You found it!"

"Can you bring it up?"

He pulled on something. "Yep. There's something on a chain wedged between the rocks." Slowly the dripping chain emerged, followed by a plastic box.

"Well, this is a new one for me," Larry said. "I've found geocaches hanging from a bridge, under a pier, and floating by a dock, but never one underwater."

"It wasn't totally under, only halfway. It's hooked to the chain by a clip." Jason unfastened the box.

"Oh, let me see!" Audrey said, bumping Amy out of the way.

"Hey!"

"Sorry," Audrey said with a glance at Maggie. Her mother was engrossed in watching Jason pull off the airtight lid and didn't notice. Sarah just smiled, enjoying the excitement.

"Why is there a big rock in there?" Maggie asked.

"To keep it weighted down, I imagine," Jason said.

Maggie reached into the box and pulled out a ziplock plastic bag full of small objects.

"Now you can take whatever you want, but it's considered proper to leave something in its place," Larry reminded everyone.

"I brought some stuff." Audrey patted her jacket pocket.

"Me too," Amy said.

They set the bag on a flat rock. The bag contained some baseball cards, which excited Amy, a key chain with the Eiffel Tower, several small plastic toy animals, a rubber duck, and a plastic boat. Larry picked up the key chain with a small dog tag attached to it. "This is a travel bug!"

"Cool!" Amy said. "Maybe it's from Paris!"

Larry grinned. "Should we take it or leave it for someone else?"

"Take it!" Audrey exclaimed. "You can take it back to California and put it in a geocache out there."

"We could. I like that idea." Larry beamed at her.

"I wonder where it's been." Maggie dangled the Eiffel Tower between her fingers.

"We can find out by checking the Web site when we get back," Amy said. "Isn't this fun?"

Maggie nodded. "I thought geocaching sounded like a strange hobby when your grandpa first told us about it, but it's kind of exciting. It *is* like treasure hunting."

Larry sorted through the items in the bag and extracted a small notebook and golf pencil. "This is the log book. You can sign in that you were here." He wrote the date, the Roberts and Hart names, and the number six indicating how many had been there. He replaced it and then asked, "So what are you going to take back with you?" he asked the girls.

"I want the rubber duck and..." Audrey reached into her pocket, "and I'm going to leave this." She dropped in a sparkly pencil eraser resembling a ladybug. Amy looked the baseball cards over but took the plastic boat. She left behind the geocoin they had found at the courthouse. Larry pocketed the travel bug key chain and left a pin with the LA Lakers logo.

"Anyone else? Sarah?"

Sarah shook her head. "Maybe next time we go geocaching, I'll have to think of something special to bring and leave behind."

"Next time?" Audrey grinned. "See? I knew you'd like this."

"That's because it's like a mystery," Amy teased.

Sarah tugged Amy's braid. "I think you're right."

"Jason was telling us about some of your adventures," Larry said.

"Good things," Maggie emphasized.

"Of course." Jason smiled at Sarah. "The good stuff."

When Sarah had first taken it upon herself to pursue some mysteries, Jason had assumed the role of protector and disapproved of her poking around trying to uncover clues, but now he seemed to take a small measure of pride in some of her discoveries. But then he didn't know *everything* that had happened over the last year and a half either. If he had, she might get lectured again about being careful.

"Grandma helps people," Amy said.

"I think that's great," Larry said.

"I do what I can," Sarah said. She had also made some enemies along the way, but when people do bad things, they should suffer the consequences.

Larry regarded her with interest. "You ever consider being a PI?"

Sarah laughed remembering Sean's comparison of her to Sherlock Holmes and imagining herself wearing a deerstalker hat like the great detective. "No. My quilt restoration business keeps me busy enough. The mysteries just sort of fall in my lap. It's not like I look for them." Like Clara and the shoplifting. The whole situation started with Audrey and Amy being questioned by the police, which automatically brought Sarah into the picture.

"Let's get this back to where it belongs. Don't we have one more geocache in the area?" Jason repacked the plastic box, attached the chain, and lowered the box back between the boulders.

"We do." Larry pulled out the sheet again. "Wishing Well."

"There's an old homestead site around here," Sarah said, thinking about the Barclays. "Maybe there's a well on it."

"We'll soon find out," Larry said. "Let's program in the coordinates."

Everyone gathered around with their GPS units. Larry let Sarah use his and had her input the information. "See, you're a pro already."

The arrow pointed west, back in the direction of the parking lot and the Barclay land.

# CHAPTER SIXTEEN

The hike through the woods took twenty-five minutes. In the parking lot Patty was still stretched out in the backseat of the car, contentedly reading her novel.

"We won't be long," Larry assured her and led the way back into the woods in the opposite direction from the falls. They came to the stream again and followed it, keeping their eyes on the GPS arrows.

Sweat dampened Sarah's turtleneck under her coat by the time they reached a clearing. A historical plaque on a tree proclaimed it as the homestead of the Charles Barclay family from 1819 to 1875 when a fire swept through the forest and destroyed the house. The land now belonged to the state park.

A stone foundation poked out of the leaf-covered ground with the piles of bricks on both ends that Sarah had seen on Google Earth. Amy hopped up on the wall and walked along it. Sarah stepped inside. Patches of snow lingered along the inside wall and around the crumbled fireplaces on each side of the house.

"The hint reads "Wish I may, wish I might, the treasure is fifteen paces to the right," Larry said.

"If there really is a well," Maggie said, "then you'd think it'd be outside, close to the house. At least that's the way I'd want it if I had to haul water."

"You would?" Jason said. "Just think, though, of the muscles you'd develop carrying water every day."

Maggie poked Jason in the ribs. "Now why would I haul water when I have you?"

"Hey, I'd think it'd be cool to have a well," Audrey said. "No chlorine taste."

"Yeah, right." Amy rolled her eyes. "You'd carry in water? You don't even like picking up your clothes."

Audrey stuck her tongue out at Amy and hopped down off the foundation as Larry yelled, "I found it." He lifted two rocks. Underneath was a steel box.

The girls ran over to Larry with Maggie and Jason following, while Sarah turned slowly, getting her bearings. Where was the building she had seen in the satellite picture? The Barclay land must be close by.

Sarah called to Jason. "I'm going to take a look over there." She pointed to a small tree-covered hill. A faint, narrow trail went to the top.

He shot her a puzzled look but nodded. Sarah trudged up the hill. A muted smell of wood smoke hung in the air. She was breathing heavily as she reached the top.

A cabin graced the middle of a meadow. Smoke dribbled out of the chimney. A satellite dish hung on the roof corner. A blue pickup was parked by the front door. It had to be the Barclays'.

"Who are you spying on?" Jason said in Sarah's ear. She jumped, her hand over her pounding heart.

"Don't do that!"

"I thought you heard me coming."

Sarah shook her head and glanced behind her. "Where did everyone go?"

"Audrey was getting chilled, so they're heading back to the car. What are *you* doing?"

"I heard that Paul Barclay was staying out here. I've been wanting to ask him some questions." She explained about Annie getting him fired, the missing shipment, and what Mr. Graham at the hardware store had said about seeing lumber in Paul's truck.

"Didn't the police question him?"

"I don't know. Chief Halliday thinks they've caught their culprit."

"Maybe they have."

"Martha and I saw him coming out of the Lonely Cricket, which is a high-end clothing store, at least for Maple Hill. So he seems to have money, although his cousin Tim said that Paul was hard up."

Jason leaned against a tree, crossing his arms over his chest. "So what's the plan here? You think this guy will just tell you he stole Annie's shipment or the lumber?"

"Of course not, but you never know what you might learn by just talking," Sarah said with a huff.

"Do you want to go down to the house? It'd take us at least fifteen minutes to get down there and longer coming back because of the hill."

Sarah studied the distance. "Yes. No. Everyone's waiting for us at the car."

"If you want to come back later, I'll come with you. Don't do it alone."

Sarah was actually thinking of bringing Martha. She could use more firewood, so she *did* have an excuse to seek Paul out. A tapping sound caught Sarah's attention. "Do you hear that?"

"The woodpecker?"

"Sounds more like hammering."

The tapping came again. "It *is* a hammer." Jason cocked his head. "And it's close." He veered off the trail and they walked through the woods. They passed the markers for the edge of the state park, and when they climbed a small rise, Sarah gaped at the sight of a man on a platform that circled the top of a giant oak tree.

"Hello there!" a male voice said. Paul Barclay walked toward them with a plank under his arm. "Observation deck isn't open yet."

Sarah tilted her head back. "Deck?"

"You're geocaching, right?" Paul looked pointedly at the GPS unit in Jason's hand.

"Yes, we were," Jason said. "What's this about a deck?"

"Oh, I'm sorry. Some geocachers listed our project in their logs and we've had some people come by and ask about it already," Paul said. "So many people come this way to see the old homestead or find the geocaches, we figured we might as well get in on some of the action. The view up there is incredible."

Sarah watched Paul talk about the landmarks you could see. She almost didn't recognize him as the bored, insolent, almost useless young man who had sat behind the Chamber of Commerce desk. His red hair had been clipped short. He walked with a spring in his step and his sweaty face was animated with enthusiasm.

"We're using all recycled materials so the project is 'green' and costing us next to nothing. We figure we'll charge a small fee for people to access the deck and make a profit."

Jason gazed at the treetop, and Sarah sensed he wanted to climb right up there. What was the huge attraction for boys, even grown ones, for tree houses?

"That's my brother up there," Paul said. "Say hello, Ben."

A grunt descended from above.

"My granddaughters know your brother. They call him Benji."

"He hates that nickname, but it seems to fit him." Paul laughed. "I think I've seen you two around town, right?"

"I'm Jason Hart and this is my mother Sarah." Jason shook Paul's hand.

"I've been at the Chamber of Commerce to see you before," Sarah said. "I just talked to your cousin Tim the other day."

"I don't hang with him much anymore." He cleared his throat and a sheepish expression crept over his face. "Actually, Tim was a bad influence on me. We kind of brought out the worst in each other."

Paul turned to Jason. And you're a lawyer, right? I've seen you at the courthouse. I almost consulted with you when I got fired. But now I realize it was the best thing that could've happened to me. I've been meaning to thank that nasty woman who constantly complained about me."

"Annie Harper?"

"That sounds about right, but like I said, it doesn't matter now. I'm finally taking responsibility for my life and I like it."

"You sound happy. I'm glad for you." Sarah smiled. "Is that your home down the hill?"

"Right now it is. The house is a family hand-me-down."

"Tim said you sold firewood."

"We did in the fall when I was looking for work, but then I started my own Web design computer business. Now we deliver just if someone calls. Do you need wood?"

"I could use another quarter cord. With this nasty weather we've been having lately, I'm running through my supply quickly."

He felt around his pockets. I have nothing to write with. "Where do you live?"

"Hillside Avenue," Sarah said. "How can I get in touch with you? Your cousin said you don't have a phone out here."

"We do now, but it's easier if you just go to my Web site, Barclay Solutions. You can e-mail and you'll find my cell number there too."

"How do you get Internet out here?" Jason asked. "Satellite?"

"Yeah, not my first choice, but it gets the job done. All those years playing computer games and fooling around on the Internet is paying off."

"I could've used your computer skills the other day to find the real e-mail address of a blog owner I'm trying to get in touch with, Sarah said, half-joking.

"Send me the information. I may be able to help."

"Hey, bro, it's getting cold," Ben called.

"Just chill, Benji," Paul said with a grin. "I'm coming."

Jason and Sarah said good-bye and retraced their steps back over the rise and to the trail to the parking lot.

"Did you find out what you needed to know?" Jason asked.

"I suppose," Sarah said. Since Paul didn't appear angry at Annie anymore and didn't need the money, there went his motive.

So now what? She still needed to find out more about Kathleen Lewison and Gordon Leftfoot, but maybe she was wasting her time. Maybe Clara was guilty after all.

Sarah awoke Monday morning with sore legs and a nagging feeling that time was running out. She stared at the ceiling trying to decide if the feeling stemmed from Christmas being four days away and she still hadn't finished Martha's quilt, or that she hadn't made any progress on proving Clara's innocence.

At Patty's insistence, they had stopped by Clara's home on the way home and checked on the dogs. Rhonda Cox told them that county services had stopped by and the dogs would be taken into custody if their owner wasn't released within the week. This had upset Patty, which in turn upset Audrey and Amy. The day had ended on a downbeat.

By the time Sarah got home, she was dead tired from all the hiking and limped into bed after a hot bath. She really needed to get in better shape. Maybe she could talk Martha into joining a gym with her after Christmas, or at least start walking again.

She pulled on her fuzzy robe, red and green for the holiday season, and her slippers and padded downstairs. She flipped on the TV as she passed through the living room and turned the volume up so she could hear the morning news.

She decided on Holiday Tea and oatmeal with dried cranberries and walnuts to see if she could get back into a Christmas mood.

While the kettle heated, the meteorologist warned that a strong winter storm was approaching and nobody needed to worry about having a white Christmas. Several feet of snow were expected in the next couple of days, but the roads should be adequately cleared by Christmas Eve.

Sarah placed two tea bags in a large mug and poured boiling water into it. The tea would steep while she made the oatmeal. She poured the quick-cooking flakes into the pot and mixed them into the bubbling water. She added the dried cranberries next, to give them time to soften and plump up. The walnuts would be sprinkled on top when it was almost done.

As she stirred the oatmeal the local news anchor said, "And here's some breaking news. Last night the China Cup, a gift store in downtown Maple Hill, was broken into and cases of china and Waterford crystal were stolen."

Sarah dropped her wooden spoon and raced to the living room as fast as her stiff legs would move. She skidded to a stop just in time to see a live shot of the scene. Poor Mrs. Kloche, looking pale and shaken, stood in front of the store. Police cars lined the curb.

"The store's alarm went off and the police arrived eight minutes later, but the merchandise and the thieves were already gone," the reporter said.

*That might mean the thieves knew exactly what they wanted beforehand*, Sarah thought. As the camera swept the scene again, a man appeared in the background, his shoulder resting on the corner of the building, watching the scene with an intense gaze.

Gordon Leftfoot.

Why wasn't she surprised?

She sniffed. What was that smell? Oatmeal! She dashed back to the stove, groaning at the pain moving caused her muscles.

The cereal was on the edge of scorching and she yanked the pot off the burner and dumped the oatmeal into a bowl.

Walnuts next and then milk. She grabbed the bowl and her mug of tea and headed back to the living room, but the news had shifted from local news to sports. She sat on the couch anyway, sinking into the soft cushions. It was going to be a long day if she stayed this stiff. She had places to go and people to see. First the man who seemed to be everywhere crime was.

Sarah drove past the Leftfoot Security office on her way to the China Cup. She wanted to take another stab at finding out what Gordon Leftfoot knew about the store thefts, but the lights were out and the shades were lowered. A mob scene came into view in front of the china store. It seemed everyone in Maple Hill had seen the news and popped in to see how Mrs. Kloche was doing. Sarah decided to return later when the crowd had thinned.

She stopped at Maggie's store. Patty's white rental car was parked in front. A long, ugly scratch marred the entire driver's side of the door and something had dented the corner of the front bumper.

Sarah opened the store door to hear Patty saying, "I don't care. It was the right thing to do."

Maggie leaned back against the counter, her arms crossed over her chest. "But what if the woman takes off? You'll lose all that money."

Patty shook her head. "She won't leave her dogs."

"How do you know? She's a stranger. Besides, she could take the dogs with her if she leaves." Maggie gave Sarah an apologetic smile. "Good morning. Please ignore our difference of opinion."

Patty kept her attention on her daughter. "You worry too much, Maggie. Have a little faith in people. You've changed, you know that?" Patty grabbed the purse at her feet. "And you used to respect my opinion. I know when I'm not wanted." She swept out of the store.

"Mom, you left your coat." Maggie grabbed it and rushed to the door. Patty's car door slammed and she backed into the street.

Maggie's shoulders slumped as she came back. "Sorry you had to hear that."

"It's okay. I gather your mother bailed Clara out of jail."

"Yeah. It really is a kind thing to do, but we know nothing about this woman. If she runs, my parents are out five thousand dollars."

"Clara has been in the community for years. Chances are she'll stick around," Sarah said, although she wondered now if Clara had been involved with the break-in at the China Cup. Even if she hadn't been, she might be tempted to leave the area. "When is her court date?"

"January third. My parents will be back in California by then, although my mom's now talking about staying here longer." Maggie tucked her mother's coat behind the counter. "This argument wasn't even the worst thing about this morning. Mom was talking about that second store in California when Jason came into the kitchen. She acted like he knew all about it and it was a done deal. Poor guy. He looked so confused and unhappy when he left."

"The whole thing probably just took him by surprise."

Maggie nodded with a small smile. "It wasn't as if I was concealing something from him. I was going to tell him about Mom's plans for a new store, but I thought she might change her mind after she saw how much work is involved in running this kind of business. I certainly can't be flying out to the West Coast every month, even if it could be a justified expense, but yet, I hate to discourage her if this is really what she and her friends want to do.

"And I love searching out bargains. A second store could be fun and profitable," Maggie said. "I know I'm sounding wishy-washy. I just don't want to rush into anything, and I certainly don't want to be pressured."

"Have you told her what you're telling me?" Sarah asked gently.

"I tried, but you can see how well she took it," Maggie said. "And there's more. She's been talking to the girls about California and all the good times they've missed. She probably doesn't mean to, but she's making them homesick all over again."

Sarah was tempted to tell Maggie about Patty talking in front of Amy about Jason making a mistake moving here and how she was encouraging the girls to go to a

California college, but it wouldn't help the situation. Maggie was already aware of Patty's not so subtle campaign.

Sarah waited quietly as Maggie paced in front of the counter.

"I'm used to my parents and their wild ideas. Jason is trying so hard to be nice and patient. He's been up late with my dad working on that closet and then putting in a full day of work. He's tired." Maggie lifted her head and turned to the window. "What was that? Sounds like a bus."

Sarah looked out the window as the sound of air brakes filled the street. A *New England Tours* bus rolled to a stop in front of The Spotted Dog. A stream of brightly clothed people poured down the steps to the street. Most headed into the café, but a group of about six tromped straight toward Magpie's Antiques. The chimes rang on the door as they streamed in.

"Oh, Mom, look. What a quaint shop," a middle-aged woman exclaimed to an elderly woman beside her as they swarmed around a table of goods with a forty-percent-off sale sign.

Happy voices filled the store, and Maggie jumped into action as the gracious shop hostess. Sarah glanced at the grandfather clock. It was almost eleven. Maybe Gordon Leftfoot was back in his office. The anxious feeling of time quickly passing was accented by the radio switching songs to a rendition of "Jingle Bells."

Sarah's gaze shifted back to the shoppers as another man strode in. A woman was waiting by the cash register, her fingernails tapping on the glass as Maggie showed another couple a lamp.

Sarah took off her coat and stowed it next to Patty's behind the counter. She smiled at a customer clutching several antique tree ornaments. "May I help you?"

Gordon Leftfoot would have to wait.

# CHAPTER SEVENTEEN

Sarah checked the mystery quilt blog as soon as she got home. Two more entries had been added. While they printed out, she checked her e-mail. No response from the blog's Customer Service.

She took the sheets off the printer and read yesterday's blog. At the bottom there was a note that a correction had been made to Day Four with apologies. She clicked on Day Four and the blog entry had been updated to include instructions on how to align the strips. So the author either had gotten Sarah's or another quilter's message or discovered the mistake herself.

The anecdote on the previous day's blog was about Christmas dinner—the joy of bringing families together, using your best tablecloth, and breaking out the special chin@ and gl@sses.

Sarah's gaze froze on the typos...was it possible? Hadn't the news reporter said that china and Waterford crystal had been stolen from the China Cup?

She flipped back through the blogs and her excitement grew as she discovered that quite a few of the recently stolen items were mentioned in the blog anecdotes.

She felt certain that there *had* to be a connection. But what? And why use a blog?

She studied the stream of letters and numbers on the bottom of each page until her eyes blurred. Were they a clue?

She *had* to find out the identity of the blog's writer. But she needed help from someone who knew the intricacies of the Internet. Someone like Paul Barclay.

Paul had mentioned that the Web site for Barclay Solutions had his e-mail address. She quickly composed a note with a link to the mystery quilt blog and asked if there was some way to discover the correct e-mail address or the identity of the blog owner.

Sarah pushed Send feeling a weight lift. Chances were that the creator of the mystery quilt would remain a mystery, but doing something made her feel productive. If Paul couldn't find the blog owner, maybe Chief Halliday could. But before going to the police, she needed to mull this over and make sure she wasn't just conjuring up something that didn't exist.

She pulled up news articles about the burglary at the China Cup and learned nothing new. The fact that the store had been burglarized at night broke the pattern of the other thefts that had occurred during the day. The police might be dealing with a different thief.

She cupped her chin in her hand and studied the screen. Her head ached, but she couldn't quit now. She still hadn't found out much about Kathleen Lewison. Maybe Lewison was the woman's married name. She had mentioned that her great-aunt had left her a house. She opened the white pages and got Kathleen's address: 1891 Blue Bird Avenue. Most of the houses in that area were older homes built fifty-plus years ago. She wished she'd had this information when she had visited Irene at the historical society. It was after seven, so most likely Irene would be at home with her husband. Even though that pesky growing sense of urgency still bothered Sarah, she didn't want to disturb them by calling. She composed an e-mail asking for information about the house, and whether there was any family history associated with it. Specifically, she wanted the name of the last occupant and any family names associated with her.

She fired off the e-mail and then turned to the next name on her suspect list. Gordon Leftfoot. He hadn't been at his office when she had left Maggie's store. She searched online and read three newspaper articles about the police shooting that had ended his career. One of the articles mentioned that Officer Leftfoot was recovering in New England Memorial Hospital with his family by his side.

Who were Gordon's family? She ran Leftfoot through the online white pages for Boston and got twenty hits. She had to narrow it down somehow. She looked up the address of New England Memorial Hospital, which was in Newton, a suburb of Boston. She ran Leftfoot again for Newton.

Sheila Leftfoot popped up. Sarah looked over at the column that listed people associated with this address.

"Eureka!" she said out loud, just as Jason had yesterday. G. Leftfoot was on the list.

But...Gordon hadn't been wearing a wedding ring and he had evaded her question about his wife. She clicked the link for the full listing. Sheila Leftfoot's age was noted as being thirty to thirty-four years old. Around the same age as Gordon. Maybe they had been having problems and had split up. That would explain the odd assortment of household items, like the stemware and quilting books, in his office's spare room.

She jotted this down in her notebook next to Gordon's name. This was an interesting tidbit, but she wasn't sure how it would help her figure out if Gordon was somehow involved in the strange happenings in Maple Hill.

She went to his Web site again. Nothing new or helpful there, except...she peered closely at the bottom of the page. He used the same blog engine that the mystery quilt blogger used. Which could mean...what?

Sarah sat back and laughed at herself. She was starting to think like Kathleen and imagine conspiracy on the Internet. Maybe she just wanted Clara to be innocent, so Patty would get her money back and go home happy.

She rubbed the back of her neck and decided to concentrate on finishing the quilt strips tonight. That would give her three days to add the border and machine quilt. The quilt would be ready for Martha on Christmas.

She set to work and was completing the last row of stitching when the phone rang.

"I have the information you needed on Kathleen Lewison's house," the caller said.

"Irene? I didn't expect you to get back to me tonight."

"Is it late?" Irene said with a surprised lilt to her voice. "I guess it is. Sorry."

"Oh, no problem. I was sewing. I just didn't want to disrupt your evening."

"Actually I was glad to have something to do. Chris got a new computer program that creates digital photo albums. He's obsessed about getting one done before Christmas."

A sound of shuffling paper filled the background and then Irene continued, "The house on Blue Bird Avenue was built in 1925 by John Williams, and he passed it on to his daughter, Gertrude Williams Black. She owned it for over thirty years but lived in Florida for the last eighteen of those, after she was widowed. The house was rented out until she died and left it to family. Survivors include one great-niece, Mable Jenkins of Oakland, California. I assume that may be Kathleen's mother," Irene said. "Does this information help with whatever you're looking for?"

"It may. Thanks so much, Irene." Sarah finished furiously scribbling names.

"Not a problem. I do love my job."

After Irene disconnected, Sarah stared at the notes she had jotted down.

Kathleen Jenkins. If she had grown up in the Oakland area, she most likely had gone to high school and possibly college there. She had been involved in protests, but there had been a lot of protests, marches, and sit-ins in the sixties and early seventies.

Sarah ran an Internet search for Kathleen Jenkins paired with Oakland. Several references popped up but nothing that seemed to relate to the woman who worked at Helping Hands.

Maybe she had been called Kathy in her younger days. Sarah futilely ran the search again and was about to give up when she hit a link that took her to the alumni news archive of Riverdale Center High School in a town not far from Oakland, California.

In the *Remember When* section of the newsletter was a story about how Kathy Jenkins and Janet Bullough had broken into the school cafeteria and stolen a trunk load of milk cartons and potato chips to take downtown to give out to homeless people. They were protesting town budget cuts to the local homeless shelters. Although they had been arrested for breaking into school property, their actions helped draw attention to the shelter situation. Eventually, changes were made to local policies to expand services to the less fortunate.

Sarah leaned forward and studied the photo of a much younger Kathleen Lewison at the bottom of the page.

So...Kathleen was no stranger to breaking and entering. Could she be using those skills here in Maple Hill?

Sarah had just finished breakfast when the phone rang.

She was greeted by Martha's bubbly voice. "Hi! I was wondering what you were doing this morning." "I'm heading out to Clara Schmidt's again. I want to talk to her." Sarah updated Martha on Clara's being released on bail. "I would've called you, but I thought you still might be nursing Ernie."

"I gave him some of the cough medicine the doctor prescribed, and it finally knocked him out. He really needs to sleep. He was snoring peacefully when I tiptoed out. He'll probably sleep until supper. I left the phone by his bed with a note to call me. I figured I'd get some fresh air while I can."

"Do you have time for a latte or some tea?"

"Always! I'll meet you."

The breakfast crowd at The Spotted Dog had thinned and Sarah and Martha were able to walk right up to the counter. Karen Bancroft took their orders for the special drink of the day, eggnog latte.

"Here you go. I put extra whipped cream on both." Karen set two paper mugs on the counter and a white bag. "Blueberry muffins. Compliments of the owner."

Sarah looked from Karen to Liam working behind the counter in the bookstore with a customer. "Thank you," she mouthed. He smiled and winked.

Martha bit into a muffin as they walked outside. "Yum! If I'd known about the perks we'd get with you dating the owner, I'd have tried to set you up long ago," she teased.

On the road to Clara's, Martha asked, "How was the dinner date?"

Sarah grinned at the memory of Liam's Irish cousins. "Entertaining." She relayed some of the conversation with Sean and Ronan.

Martha laughed so hard she almost spilled her latte and had to set it in the cup holder. "They sound like a riot. I'd love to meet them."

"They're already on their way to Los Angeles. They're taking a couple of months to tour the US, and might come visit Liam again before they go back to Ireland."

"At least they'll have better weather in California," Martha said, scanning the gloomy sky.

Sarah sighed. Just the mention of that state gave her heartburn, thanks to Patty and her well-meaning desire to draw her family back out there. Underneath the image of holiday festivity the tension continued to swell with each passing day.

"You know what?" Martha shifted in her seat so she could face Sarah. "I wouldn't want to give up a white Christmas in Maple Hill for anything. Christmas wouldn't be the same without all the pretty lights in the snow, caroling, shopping downtown, going to church on Christmas Eve, and then spending Christmas surrounded by family and friends. It's home!"

Sarah smiled. Martha knew just the right thing to say. "I knew there was a reason you're my best friend."

"Oh, you mean besides my good looks and charming personality?" Martha fluffed her hair and giggled.

"Yes, even more than that." Sarah turned the car onto the road that headed out of town as snowflakes began to fall.

Martha gazed at the passing scenery. "So what are we trying to accomplish out here today?"

Sarah quickly updated Martha on Paul, Clara, and Gordon. The information was deliberately sketchy since the mystery quilt was still supposed to be a surprise, but Martha didn't seem to note anything amiss.

"So it looks like Paul is off the suspect list," Martha said as Sarah slowed to park in front Clara's house. "Or at least on the very bottom."

They exited the car and walked through the nearly frozen mud to the chain-link gate. Sarah stopped with her hand on the latch. "Listen."

"What? I don't hear anything."

"Exactly. Where are the dogs?" The place was eerily quiet.

The hollow feeling in Sarah's stomach grew as they approached the front door. She pushed the doorbell, and when there was no response, lifted the knocker on the door and banged it.

"I don't think she's home." Martha peered in a front window. "It's dark in there."

They descended the steps and rounded the corner of the house. As Sarah suspected, the dog kennels were empty.

"Looks like she flew the coop."

"Maybe Clara just took them to the vet?" Martha suggested.

"All ten? I suppose she could have," Sarah said, but judging by Martha's expression, she didn't believe it either. If the county had taken them away, where was Clara?

"Do you think maybe the police rearrested Clara on suspicion of breaking into the China Cup?" Martha voiced Sarah's fear.

"Maybe."

"I still don't believe it was her." Martha glanced around them. "She has a good heart."

Sarah went to Clara's back door. The screen was unlatched and as she used her fist to pound on the door, it gave way and swung open. Sarah stepped back in surprise and bumped into Martha. "The door's unlatched."

"Looks like she's inviting us in," Martha said, pushing the door farther open with her foot.

"Clara?" Sarah called into a small, dated kitchen.

"Maybe she's lying in there hurt." Martha took a step inside. "Clara? Are you home?"

"We probably shouldn't go in," Sarah said.

"But the door is open, so it's not like we're breaking and entering. And her truck could be in the garage."

Martha had a point even if it was mostly rationalization to justify snooping. "Let's take a quick look to make sure everything is okay." Sarah walked inside the kitchen and down the hall. The downstairs had a basic floor plan. Dining room and bathroom on either side of the hall, which led to the front living room. Stairs ascended to a second floor.

The living room furniture was shabby and the floors badly needed refinishing, but the house was neat and smelled like Lysol. An ancient desktop computer covered a student's desk in one corner.

"Looks like she has Internet access. Dial-up." Martha pointed to a phone line snaking to the back of the console. She picked up several sheets of paper stacked next to a dot-matrix printer. "Advertisements seeking homes for dogs and a flyer for Canine Rescue."

Sarah stepped over to the staircase and called Clara's name. Still no answer. She trotted upstairs and glanced in the two bedrooms. One was obviously a guest room judging from the smooth blanket on the twin bed. A sewing machine sat on a card table in the corner. The larger bedroom consisted of an unmade double bed and a dresser with the drawers pulled out. A shirt and some socks lay on the floor as if they had fallen from the dresser. Sarah stared at the quilt on the bed. Was the pattern similar to the mystery quilt's? Could Clara be the author of the blog?

She hurried downstairs and met Martha coming in from the back door. "I checked the garage and no truck."

"She's not upstairs either," Sarah said. "Looks like she pulled some clothes out of her dresser in a hurry."

The screen door banged in the kitchen. Martha grabbed Sarah's arm and pulled her toward the front door. "Someone's coming."

"I thought you might be in here." Rhonda Cox walked down the hall toward them. She was dressed in blue overalls covering a thick grey sweater. "I saw your car out front."

"The back door was open," Martha said, releasing Sarah's arm. "We wanted to make sure Clara wasn't in here hurt or something."

"I haven't seen Clara all morning. And then when I didn't hear the dogs when I went out to my mailbox, I got worried," Rhonda replied. "You beat me here."

"Where do you think she may have gone?"

"I have no idea really. I—"

A loud knock on the front door caused the three women to jump and sent Sarah's heart rate into overdrive again.

"Police. Open up."

Sarah unlocked the dead bolt and yanked open the door to reveal Chief Halliday and Officer Hopkins standing on the step. They looked as surprised as Sarah felt.

"Mrs. Hart. What are you doing here?" Chief Halliday demanded, his frosty gaze sweeping over them.

"I have a key." Rhonda stepped forward and waved it in front of their noses. "Clara gave me a spare, so I could look after her house in case something happened to her again."

"Is Ms. Schmidt here?" Officer Hopkins asked.

"No." Rhonda glanced at Sarah. "She's ... out at the moment. What's this all about?"

"Afraid we can't say," Halliday said.

"Does this have anything to do with the China Cup burglary?" Sarah asked.

"Can't discuss that with you." Chief Halliday's expression remained passive, but Officer Hopkins's lips twitched. Sarah assumed she was correct. Officer Hopkins turned and went down the steps.

Halliday opened the screen door. "Now if you'd let me in—"

"Do you have a warrant?" Martha asked Halliday and then whispered to Sarah, "I've always wanted to say that."

"Not yet. I'm just here to ask questions," Chief Halliday said, his piercing gaze analyzing them again. "You aren't trying to interfere in a police investigation, are you?"

"Of course not." Sarah stepped back and let him into the living room. "We just stopped by to see if Clara was all right."

The chief turned his head to look around the living room. He didn't make any attempt to move in farther.

Officer Hopkins appeared at the door again. "Looks like her truck is gone, and so are the dogs."

"Did the county take away her dogs?" Martha asked.

"Wouldn't know. Dogs are the least of my worries at the moment," the chief said. "Whose is the silver car out front?"

"Mine," Sarah said.

"I walked over. I live across the street," Rhonda offered before he asked.

"And I came with Sarah," Martha added as the sound of tires crunched on the street. Patty's rental car, with the long, dark scratch on its side, parked behind Sarah's. She got out and limped toward the porch.

"What *is* this? A hen party?" Chief Halliday asked with a snort.

Sarah bristled. "We're worried about Clara."

"What's going on here?" Patty asked, her gaze shifting from the police to the women. "Is Clara all right?"

"Who are you?" Halliday asked.

"Patricia Roberts. I'm a friend of Clara's."

"Ah yes, I saw your name in the file for posting bail. Do you know where Ms. Schmidt is?"

"She's not here?" Patty asked, her eyes widening.

Halliday snorted. "All of you need to go. Now. If you hear from Ms. Schmidt, have her call the police station. It'll save everyone a lot of trouble." He spun on his heel and strode to the porch.

He paused on the steps. "Remember, interfering with a police investigation is a criminal offense. We'll be back. Do not remove anything from the premises. Don't think I'd hesitate to arrest you."

"Y-yes, sir." Rhonda's voice quavered.

It wasn't until the police car did a U-turn and sped off that all four women let out a collective deep breath.

"Why do I feel so guilty?" Martha fanned her face with her hand. "I know nothing."

Rhonda shut the door and leaned against it. "They'll probably come back with a warrant to search the place. They had one the first time they arrested her."

"What's going on?" Patty sat on the couch and rubbed her ankle.

"Looks like Clara may have taken her dogs and skedad-dled," Martha said.

Patty shook her head adamantly. "She wouldn't do that. She promised me she'd be in court. Jason is going to repre-sent her if we don't find someone better."

Patty meant someone who had more experience in crim-inal law, Sarah reminded herself, but the dig at Jason felt like a sharp stick in her side. Martha caught her eye and winked. Sarah let out a deep breath and let the agitation go.

"Did she mention any relatives or friends to you? People she might go to visit?" Sarah asked.

Patty shook her head. "That's why we had to bail her out of jail."

"That was *you*?" Rhonda asked. "That was the kindest thing I've ever heard of. You must be an angel."

Patty's face pinkened. "Not really. I felt partly responsi-ble for getting her in trouble since I wasn't careful when I unpacked Maggie's stock. The brooches wouldn't have been in the garbage bin if it hadn't been for me."

"She wasn't arrested only for the brooches," Sarah said.

"I realize that!" Patty snapped. "But they didn't help. The police might've believed her about the watch if she hadn't had the brooches. Too coincidental."

Sarah pressed her lips together. She had only been trying to make Patty feel better. Patty was correct though. Maggie's jewelry being found in Clara's bag had helped the prosecu-tor establish a pattern of conduct.

"Well, she's not here now and neither are her dogs. We'll just have to wait and see," Rhonda said as Patty got to her feet and followed Martha out to the porch.

Sarah hesitated at the door. She wanted to go on Clara's computer, but Chief Halliday's warning rang in her ears. Still...Sarah crossed the room to Clara's computer and turned it on. It was password protected. She turned it off and rubbed her fingerprint off the button.

She quickly wrote down the multiple phone numbers on the Canine Rescue flyer before she joined Martha and Patty outside. They turned at the gate to look at the house as Rhonda locked up.

"If she did run, it's going to be bad. Everyone is going to assume she's guilty," Patty said.

Sarah sighed. "I'm afraid so."

Martha's cell phone rang. "Hi, sweetie." She listened for a moment. "Sure I can buy some more juice. What are you doing out of bed? Get back under the covers. I'll be there soon."

"Someone's sick?" Patty asked after Martha slipped her phone back into her pocket.

"My husband has a terrible cold. The doctor's worried about it becoming bronchitis if he doesn't take it easy."

"We'll head back now." Sarah yanked her keys out of her coat pocket. "Try to beat the worst of the storm." The snow was falling heavily now, blanketing the yard and street.

"Have you tried echinacea?" Patty asked as she opened her car door. "It's a natural immune system booster. I think

I may have some tea packets. I carry it with me when I travel in case I feel a cold coming on."

She dug deep in her big purse and extracted three packets. "Here, these have vitamin C in them too. You may want to check with your doctor first of course, but I don't think there's anything in it that would react with other medications."

Martha took the tea and squinted at the tiny ingredient list. "Thank you, Patty. He might like this."

"Add honey. That'll soothe the throat. If you want more tea, the Crystal Unicorn carries some. Not this brand, but I saw one in there for colds." Patty tossed her purse on the passenger seat and slid into the rental car. She backed up and did a three-point turn, the wheels spinning before the car roared off toward town.

Sarah and Martha buckled up and waved to Rhonda as she crossed the street. As Sarah turned the car onto the main road, Gordon Leftfoot passed them going toward Clara's. What was he up to now? Sarah gripped the steering wheel more tightly. She wanted to whip the car around and follow him, but Martha needed to get home to Ernie. She glanced at her friend who was staring at the tea packets she kept absentmindedly turning over in her fingers.

"Ready for Christmas?" Martha asked, breaking the silence.

"Almost," Sarah said, thinking about Martha's quilt that still needing finishing. She also needed to wrap gifts.

A heavy cloak of frustration settled on her shoulders. It was hard thinking about Christmas looming three days away with the case against Clara still unresolved. Was Clara guilty? Had she acted alone or was Gordon involved somehow? Had Sarah hit a dead end?

Maybe she should just concentrate on getting ready for Christmas. Let the authorities handle Clara or Gordon or anyone else involved. Chief Halliday seemed confident about his case against Clara. He probably had enough evidence lined up. Jason would just have to dispute it in court, if he could. Assuming they found Clara.

Sarah would focus on her family, and after Christmas she would see if she could help Clara if she still needed it. Assuming she resurfaced.

There.

Decision made.

Sarah waited. No sense of peace followed. She sighed. Her conscience wouldn't let the mystery go. The heat was off the twins, but she couldn't let another innocent person be accused. Assuming Clara was innocent, of course. She wondered what was on that computer of hers. Was she behind the thefts after all?

She tapped down on the gas pedal, inching up their speed. Maybe there was still something she could do.

# CHAPTER EIGHTEEN

Sarah walked into her house, tossed her keys and purse on the kitchen table, and grabbed the phone. She shrugged out of her coat and got the numbers she had copied off the flyer at Clara's house. The first one from the list was a local number. She dialed and Clara's answering machine picked up. Sarah left a message for Clara to call her when she got home. She tried the next number.

"Canine Rescue East," a nasally male voice said. "This is Bernie."

"My name is Sarah Hart, and I'm trying to locate Clara Schmidt."

"Clara? Did you call her home number?"

"I just did, and she wasn't home. Your number was on one of her flyers."

"Sorry, can't help ya. I haven't heard from Clara in weeks. She only calls when she's trying to place a dog."

"Can you have her call me if she does contact you? It's important."

"Does this concern a dog?"

"It might," Sarah said, thinking about Clara out there with ten dogs. What if the police picked her up on the road? Where would they take those dogs? "If she gets in contact with you, tell her to call Sarah Hart." Sarah gave the man her contact information and then tried the next phone number on the list.

No answer.

The third number resulted in a woman answering, "Canine Rescue North. Judy here. How can I help you?"

Sarah began to explain about Clara when Judy interrupted her. "A policeman already called here, and I'll tell you the same thing I told him. Clara dropped her dogs off here about two hours ago and said she'd call when she found out how long she would be gone."

Police? That was quick. Surely Chief Halliday and Officer Hopkins hadn't had time to get their warrant and search Clara's house. Unless, of course, they had taken down these numbers the last time they arrested her.

"Do you remember the policeman's name?"

"Leftfoot or something like that," Judy said, raising her voice over a sudden din of barking. "Clara is in some kind trouble, isn't she?"

"How well do you know her?"

"We go back a ways. We used to volunteer at a shelter together, and then a couple of years ago, several of us formed Canine Rescue. We're trying to help the overload at the shelters by finding volunteers to foster dogs."

"Sounds like a very worthy cause."

"Someone has to care for the creatures that can't fend for themselves."

"Do you know of any family or friends who Clara might go to?" Sarah asked.

"No family, at least no one in this part of the country. I think she may have a cousin in Wyoming, but the way she talked, they haven't seen each other for a long time. As far as friends go, Bernie and I are it, as far as I know. Clara is a loner and relates to animals better than people. I'm the same way. Is there something I can do for Clara? I'm worried."

"If she gets in touch with you, please have her call me." Sarah gave the woman her house and cell number.

Sarah took a deep breath, dreading the next call. She dialed the police station and asked to speak to Chief Halliday.

The desk clerk asked her name, and after making sure it wasn't an emergency, asked her to hold.

Sarah opened a can of soup while she waited. About five minutes later Chief Halliday's gruff voice came on the line.

"What is it, Mrs. Hart? Haven't you interfered enough today?"

Not quite. Sarah decided to ignore the question. "I'm worried about Clara Schmidt. Have you located her yet?"

"Nope."

"What do you know about Gordon Leftfoot?"

"Leftfoot was a good cop who got a raw deal on the wrong end of a gun. Why?"

"Because I have reason to believe he's out there looking for Clara." She told him about passing Gordon on the road to Clara's and what the Canine Rescue lady had reported. "Impersonating a police officer is against the law," Sarah pointed out.

"I'm aware of the law, Mrs. Hart. It was probably just a misunderstanding."

"Clara may have a cousin in Wyoming."

"We know about the cousin. She passed away."

So Clara really was alone out there.

"Is there anything else, Mrs. Hart?" Chief Halliday asked. "You may have time for idle chitchat, but I don't."

Idle chitchat? Sarah felt her blood pressure rise. She figured since she already had the chief all riled up, she might as well go all out. "Actually, there is. I've been following a Christmas mystery quilt blog?"

"Blog?"

"Yes, it's sort of a diary where—"

"I know what a blog is, Mrs. Hart, I just don't understand why you're telling me about this. I need to go—"

"I think it may be connected to the thefts."

There was silence on the other end which Sarah took as a good sign and pressed forward. "The blog started about two weeks ago and the woman, or whoever is writing it, tells stories or gives advice and refers to things like china, crystal, televisions, and other items—things that have been stolen in Maple Hill." Sarah paused. Silence again, but she thought she heard Chief Halliday breathing.

"I know it sounds far-fetched, but it really is uncanny. I can show you my list of stolen items and the blog entries. What if someone is using the blog to convey information about what they've stolen?"

"Clara Schmidt has a computer," the chief said.

Sarah's heart tripped. There had also been a sewing machine and a quilt in Clara's house. "Gordon Leftfoot has a computer and a Web site."

"And almost everyone else in Maple Hill has access to a computer too, including those kids," Chief Halliday added.

"This type of operation would take some organization. I can't see any of those teen girls going to so much effort. Gordon had a quilting book in his office which you have to admit seems unusual for a man. Also he's been all over town wherever there's been trouble."

"So have you."

Sarah struggled to hold back her sharp reply at his sarcastic tone. "You can access Clara's computer and get information on Gordon Leftfoot that I can't. And maybe as a police officer, you'll have better luck contacting the owner of the blog. They won't answer me."

She heard scratching noises as if Chief Halliday was taking notes. Encouraged, she continued. "Also some of the flyers that advertised this blog came from the Helping Hands charity shop. But they don't know where it originated. One of their customers could've brought it in, or it could have gotten mixed up in one of their bins. They have computer records of the people who donated, but I can't access those either."

Sarah took a deep breath to slow down. She knew she had dumped a lot of information on the chief, but she was hoping it would speed up finding out who the thief was.

A sigh drifted over the phone. "I guess some of this is worth checking out. What's the blog address?"

Sarah gave it to him. "Look for words with typos." At least he was listening to her. She just hoped that she didn't come out looking like a fool. Even so, it was worth it if they found the truth.

"Mrs. Hart, if Clara Schmidt contacts you, let me know immediately." He hung up without even a good-bye. Sarah would be glad when Chief Webber got back. Even if he did seem to find her a pest at times, he was at least more polite.

Sarah set the phone on the table, feeling drained. Now what? She pulled out her notebook and looked over the list of suspects. She had crossed off Paul Barclay's name. She wondered if he was having any luck finding the blog owner. Maybe Chief Halliday had resources Paul didn't and would find it first.

Kathleen Lewison. She stared at her name. Kathleen had said she didn't own a computer or even a cell phone. Nor did she sew. But hadn't she mentioned that her aunt quilted? Was that the same aunt who had left her the house? Something else, a memory, kept nagging at the back of her mind. That first day Sarah met Kathleen, she had told Vanessa that the bin was missing appliqué scissors. How many people who didn't sew would know what appliqué scissors looked like? There hadn't been a label on them.

A hissing sound filled the kitchen. The chicken noodle soup on the stove bubbled over the pan's edges and spilled onto the stove top. She grabbed a pot holder, yanked the pan off the burner, and turned off the gas. She poured the soup into a bowl and found some crackers in the cupboard.

After she had eaten, her spirits and determination rose. Maybe she was wrong about the blog, but she would give it another shot. She spread all the printed sheets out on the kitchen table and then accessed the Web site.

Another entry was up. She printed it out. At the top of the page was a photo of a Christmas tree with opened gifts underneath.

She scanned the anecdote.

*Today we come to the end of our journey together. I hope you enjoyed making the quilt as much as I did. If your quilt is meant as a gift for someone else, they will receive a blessing.*

*Gifts can be tricky things. I remember when I was young and my mother wanted a microw@ve and new can opener for Christmas. My father, having been trained by his mother never to give women appliances as gifts, gave her jewl&ry instead. The day after Christmas, she took the br@celet and rings back to the store and bought the things needed by the family.*

*A quilt can be a thing of beauty as well as a practical item and after you finish today's stitching, you or a lucky someone will have something to treasure.*

The instructions for machine quilting the border followed and then the weird set of numbers.

If her suspicion was true, then a microwave and jewelry had been stolen recently and possibly the shoes, purse, or toys in the photo. But what did the numbers at the bottom of the page mean?

*20111222%20:20&&132###&&N42°XX24.910\*\**
*W078°++12.667*

Sarah got out a pencil and began fiddling with the numbers. The first eight numbers were obviously today's date. The circles over the 42 and 78 could mean degrees. But what did the 20:20 represent?

She leaned her head on her hand and stared at the sheet. She had the feeling she was missing something obvious. Surely there had to be someone around who could crack this code if indeed it was one. She gathered up the sheets.

She knew just the man to help.

With all the time Sarah seemed to be spending at the Spotted Dog lately, the café was starting to feel like a second home. She greeted Murphy, threw his ball a couple of times for him, and then settled at a table. She ordered a chai tea and spread out the sheets of paper.

Karen Bancroft was on waitress duty again. "What are you working on?"

"I'm trying to crack this code, if it *is* one," Sarah said, showing her the numbers. "I thought since Liam likes puzzles so much, he might be able to help. Wanna take a crack at it?"

Karen set her coffee pot on the table and leaned over to take a closer look. "Cool."

"I already figured out that these numbers are the date, but I'm not sure what the rest is. Would you have any idea?"

Karen studied the line for a moment. "Let me finish getting my orders out and I'll take a look again.

"Military time," Liam's deep voice said over Sarah's shoulder.

Startled, Sarah looked up at him. "Just the man I was looking for. I didn't see you when I came in."

"I was in the back." He pointed at the 20:20 she had circled. "That would be 8:20 PM."

"Thanks." A shiver sent goose bumps down her arm. Something was happening at 8:20 tonight, but what? And where?

"I'll be back." Liam stepped away as a man with a book in his hand headed for the cash register. The door opened and Martha bustled in, her hat and shoulders covered with snow. She spied Sarah and headed straight to the table, shaking off her hat.

"You're here *again*?" Martha asked.

"I could say the same about you. How's Ernie?"

"Better. Christine and Lexie stopped by and are babying Ernie this evening. I needed to get more Scotch tape and wrapping paper so I ran by the store and then decided to pop by here." She gazed down at the sheets. "So what's all that?"

"It might be just my overactive imagination, but I think it could be a key to the burglaries and shoplifting around town." Sarah gestured to the chair opposite her. "Want to help?"

Martha's eyes widened. "As if you have to ask." Sarah explained about the date as she copied the string of numbers into her notebook and pushed it over to Martha. Luckily Martha was intrigued with trying to break the code and didn't question where the numbers had come from.

They were so busy talking, Sarah didn't see Patty until she was standing by Sarah's chair.

"Sarah, can we talk?" Patty glanced at Martha. "In private?"

"Um, I can go over there," Martha gestured to another table and started to shove back her chair.

"No, please stay. I'll go." Sarah stood, wondering why Patty was sounding so rude. She took a good look at the woman. Patty's normally neat hair needed a good brushing, and dark smudges under her eyes suggested she may have been crying.

"Let's sit over here." Sarah gestured to a table beside the empty counter. Patty asked Karen for some water, and Sarah waited as Patty twisted her paper napkin in a tight coil. Finally she looked up. "I just had a fight with your son."

"A fight?"

"Okay, a heated discussion," Patty said. "I was hoping you'd talk to him."

"What's going on?"

"He accused me of lying."

And you did, Sarah wanted to say, but she just asked, "Why would he think that?"

Patty waved the napkin in a dismissive gesture. "Oh, one of the girls overheard me talking on the phone and misunderstood something I may have said about Jason and told him."

Sarah recalled what Amy had said about Jason giving up a good job and being lazy. How did one misunderstand that?

"He also told me to stop trying to manipulate Maggie." She sniffed. "I'm not trying to manipulate my daughter. I just want what's best for her. I simply presented her with a great opportunity."

"You didn't try to make her feel guilty?"

"Of course not!" Patty said, bristling. "And then Maggie overheard us and got in an argument with Jason."

"I think you need to stay out of it," Sarah said bluntly. She knew Maggie well enough to know that she probably wouldn't appreciate Jason trying to fight her battles.

Patty took several deep breaths. "You can't point a finger at me for trying to spend more time with my daughter and grandchildren. You talked Jason into moving back to Maple Hill."

"Patty, I did no such thing," Sarah said, her voice rising. Liam and Martha looked over at her, concern on both their faces. She couldn't believe that after all this time Patty was accusing her of interfering in Jason's life. Sarah lowered her voice. "Jason asked my opinion, but it was totally his and Maggie's decision. And that's what I told him."

Patty pressed her lips together in an expression of disbelief. "I'm just trying to save my family. Ever since Maggie and the girls moved across the country I can feel us all growing further apart every day. I try so hard to keep things interesting for Larry and me. We're trying new things and planning trips, but I just feel like we're treading water, growing stale and old. Surely you can understand that."

Sarah almost laughed at the sling, but knew that Patty probably didn't realize what she had just said. And even if she did, Sarah was starting to feel sad for her. Moving across the country to a small town had been a huge change for Maggie and the twins, but over time they had all adjusted and seemed to be thriving. No one seemed to remember how hard the change was for those they left behind.

"I can see you're upset, but all I can suggest is that you try talking to them again," Sarah said gently. "I would only muddy the waters. I usually stay out of their personal affairs unless they ask me to get involved, and even then I have to be careful. You raised a great daughter, and you can trust her to make the right decisions."

Patty seemed to consider what Sarah was saying and then shrugged. "I should've known you wouldn't help."

Sarah was spared a reply by Karen. "Sarah, I think I've got something!" The waitress had taken Sarah's vacated seat and held up the blog printout.

"Just think about what I've said," Sarah said to Patty as she got to her feet. She hurried over to the other table.

"Watch." Karen took the pencil. "If you cross out the symbols, you get this." She showed her the line from the blog.

*132 N42° 24.910 W078° 12.667*

"I don't know what the 132 means but the rest of the numbers look like coordinates," Karen said.

"Coordinates?" Martha asked.

"Like for a map. Longitude and latitude. We use maps in some of my architecture classes." She looked over at her boss. "Liam, do you have any of those Massachusetts maps behind the counter?"

"I do." Liam strode across the store and handed the map to Karen. She unfolded it and spread it across the table.

"Look—they correspond to somewhere just east of Maple Hill. Over by the county park."

"That's still a pretty wide area," Sarah said.

Karen nodded. "It's hard to pinpoint the area without a more detailed map or a GPS."

"I have one in my car," Patty said walking over. She picked up the sheet of paper. "All I have to do is plug in the numbers." She turned to Sarah and Martha. "Well? What are we waiting for?"

Sarah looked at Martha who nodded and said, "Let's roll." They grabbed their jackets and purses and headed for the door.

"You'll tell me if you find anything, right?" Karen asked, following them.

"Of course," Martha said.

"Be careful," Liam called, his gaze seeking out Sarah's. He gave her a smile that warmed Sarah from the top of her head to the tips of her toes.

Sarah stepped outside and put on her jacket as Patty retrieved the GPS unit from her car. "You can drive while I program the GPS."

Patty got in the passenger seat of Sarah's car, and Martha took the back. As Sarah started the car her phone vibrated and then chirped. She didn't recognize the number on her caller ID.

"Hello?" Sarah said.

It was Paul Barclay and what he told her made her smile.

Darkness had fallen early, wrapping Sarah's car in a swirl of black mist and driving snow as she pulled into the park. Signs indicated that the park closed at dark except in designated camping and fishing areas.

"Make a left up here," Patty said, watching the tiny screen on the handheld GPS unit. We have about five hundred yards. The spot should be around the next curve."

Martha leaned forward from the backseat. "That would be the parking lot for the creek. Ernie used to launch his boat from there to go fishing."

Sarah turned off her headlights and edged around the bend.

The narrow parking lot was empty. The clock said it was eight thirty, past the time relayed in the blog. So where were they?

"Could you have gotten the coordinates wrong?" Patty asked.

"There's a road that runs along the creek. The bank is really high on this side so you can't see the road from here," Martha said. "Over there! See the lights?" She pointed to where a gravel road dipped behind the high bank. A faint glow spread out across the water.

"I'm going to take a look," Sarah said, unbuckling her seat belt and opening the door.

"I'll go with you," Martha said.

"Wait. Isn't this dangerous?" Patty asked.

"I have a pretty good idea who's down there," Sarah said, thinking about Paul's phone call. She had already tried to contact Chief Halliday, but she'd had to leave a message. She hoped the police chief or Officer Hopkins would call back soon.

"Why don't you stay here?" Sarah said to Patty. She still wasn't sure why Patty was helping them after her outburst in the café, but Sarah had decided not to question her motives and just let all the emotions Patty had stirred up lie dormant for a while. "If I wave at you, call the police again."

Patty nodded, holding up her phone. "I can do that. What do you want me to tell them?"

"Tell them where we are and that we've found who's been stealing from the stores." She opened the door. "And to hurry up and send someone out here."

Martha and Sarah got out of the car, careful not to bang the doors. The clouds hung low and heavy as if wanting to be as close to the ground as possible to dump their load of snow. There was a break in the snowfall for a moment and the ground felt spongy under Sarah's feet as they kept to the perimeter of the parking lot, away from the lights.

"Could just be some guys fishing," Martha whispered.

"At this time of night?"

"Ernie loved night fishing. Ice fishing too. I didn't enjoy it, but now I wish..."

Sarah nudged Martha's shoulder. "Hey, just remember all the stinky fish that had to be cleaned."

"Oh yeah." Her smile returned, but with a tinge of wistfulness. Ernie hadn't been fishing as much since being diagnosed with Parkinson's disease. It wasn't as if his condition prohibited it, but he just didn't go.

They fell silent. The only sound was their breathing as they neared the bank. Sarah's steps sank into the sand as she used her hands to clamber up to the top of the bank. Martha followed, both of them keeping low as they peered over the top.

The bank dropped straight down to the gravel road below that led to a boat launch area and then continued along the creek.

A paneled van was parked on the road with a pickup truck backed up to it. The van's doors were open and two people were moving items to the back of the shelled pickup.

Martha gasped and covered her mouth.

Sarah backed away and stood, waving at Patty in the Grand Prix. Patty stuck her arm out of the window and gave them a thumbs-up.

"Now what?" Martha whispered.

"We go back and wait for the police."

"Okay." She started to move back and the sandy earth beneath her shifted, sliding down the steep bank.

Sarah gripped her arm and for a moment everything stabilized. Then the ground crumbled away beneath both of them, and they tumbled down the bank landing by the pickup's bumper.

A dark figure, holding what looked like a tire iron loomed over them. "Hey! What are you doing here?"

Sarah rolled off Martha. She opened her mouth, but no sound came out.

"Don't move or someone will get hurt!" he said.

Sarah held up her hands. Martha glanced at her and did the same.

"Oh, for Pete's sake. Chill out. I know these people." Kathleen Lewison rounded the truck. She shook her head as if not believing what she saw. "Mrs. Hart. Mrs. Maplethorpe. What are you doing here?"

"I was going to ask you the same thing." Sarah used the side of the truck to assist her getting to her feet.

"These friends of yours?" the man asked in a low guttural voice.

"Not really, but—"

The hooded man dropped the tire iron and jumped in the cab of the pickup. The engine roared. Sarah grabbed Martha's wrist and yanked her away from the spinning tires. Sand kicked back in their faces.

"Hey, you jerk, you didn't give me my money!" Kathleen yelled and heaved a rock at the receding lights. The rock bounced off the tailgate as the truck tore up into the parking lot.

Kathleen turned, hands on her hips. "Thanks a lot, Mrs. Hart!"

The sound of screeching brakes drowned out Sarah's reply, followed by a resounding crash.

# CHAPTER NINETEEN

Sarah charged up the incline to the parking lot. Her Grand Prix was turned sideways across the road with the truck's hood smashed into one side of the trunk. Sirens sounded in the distance, nearing, the police cars' red lights reflecting off the low clouds.

Patty stood beside the car, calmly watching the man in the truck fighting an airbag.

Sarah ran to her. "Are you okay?"

"Just dandy." Patty's eyes widened as she took in the woman walking up beside Martha. "Is that Kathleen?"

"Yes," Sarah said. "Or maybe as she is more commonly called, RobinHood38."

Kathleen gaped at her. "How'd you know?"

"An acquaintance uncovered your username."

Kathleen gave her a wry smile. "Go figure. Betrayed by technology again." She shrugged. "I'm not ashamed of what I did. I only skimmed the excess. A little here. A little there."

Sarah nodded. "You just dropped the stuff into the Helping Hands bin when no one was watching and picked it up later."

"It was easy until those teens aroused suspicion and then that security guy wanted to put up video cameras everywhere. Made my mission harder." Kathleen scowled at the squad cars rolling into the parking lot. The sirens switched off. Doors slammed.

"So that's why you broke into the China Cup the other night?" Sarah asked.

"I didn't break into the China Cup. It was that jerk over there." She nodded to the man being surrounded by police. "It was also his idea to frame that poor homeless lady when that security guy started poking around. Got too greedy. Wanted to keep stuff for himself. I told him tonight to stay away from Maple Hill and that I wouldn't do any more business with him. I have other contacts who can process the items."

Not any more, Sarah thought. The scheme was over. "Pretty clever how you conveyed information through the blog. The quilting part of it came from your aunt, didn't it? The one who loved to quilt?"

"She was a saint! A hard worker for her church and for the poor. I looked up to her. She was the only one who ever really understood me and my causes. She was taking a load of quilts and food supplies to a needy family when she was killed in a car accident." A tear rolled down Kathleen's cheek.

Martha placed her hand on Kathleen's arm. "Your aunt sounds like she was a special person."

Kathleen nodded. "She was working on the mystery quilt blog the Christmas right before she passed away. I thought it'd be a tribute to her to post it, although I didn't own a computer anymore. Then Helping Hands gave us those computer pads for work, and I got the brilliant idea to continue her cause of helping the needy. E-mail is too dangerous, but this way my friends and I could communicate despite the Internet spies. I was going to edit out the codes later."

"But why did you put copies of the flyer out everywhere?" Martha asked. "Didn't that make it more dangerous?"

Kathleen sniffed and wiped her nose with her sleeve. "I made only a few copies to give to people helping the cause. That way it would seem like public information even though it was meant for only a few. I must've dropped one at the store. I didn't realize Lei made more and sent them out until it was too late."

Kathleen took a deep breath and looked at Sarah. "I wasn't hurting anyone. I just wanted to help people, especially now at Christmas."

"I know you did," Sarah said as Officer Hopkins came up behind Kathleen.

"I just wanted to carry on her work. Helping the poor. All the money went to families who really need it. I promise you that!" Kathleen put her hands behind her back for Officer Hopkins to clamp on the handcuffs.

Officer Hopkins led her away, reciting her rights. Kathleen turned her head and called out, "Merry Christmas!"

A weight squeezed Sarah's chest. She should be happy that the mystery was solved. Clara was in the clear now. Audrey and Amy didn't need to worry about their friends being accused of shoplifting. And Gordon Leftfoot...well maybe he couldn't help being the way he was. But her heart ached for the woman who wanted to do good, even if she had gone about it in an illegal, warped way.

"I'm sorry about your car," Patty said, staring at the crumbled trunk. "I saw the truck coming and reacted on impulse."

"As long as you're okay, it doesn't matter," Sarah said and then grinned. "In fact, you're the heroine of the night. You stopped the bad guy from getting away."

"I did, didn't I?" Patty said with wonder in her voice.

"Just think what you can tell people when they ask what you did on your vacation." Martha laughed and after a stunned moment, Patty joined in.

Sarah called Jason and explained the situation. He said he'd be right out and arrange for a tow truck.

"Okay, I'm a little confused," Martha said. "How did you find out about the blog in the first place?"

"It's a long story." One Sarah planned to share with her best friend on Christmas Day when she unwrapped her present.

The fire crackled merrily. The Christmas tree lights twinkled, and holiday music played softly in the background as Sarah relaxed alone on Maggie's parlor sofa.

Christmas Eve had finally arrived and Sarah had dressed in her new Christmas sweater and warm black slacks to attend the special service at church. She took a sip of the peppermint hot cocoa that Audrey had brought her as she waited for her family to get ready.

As usual Patty and Larry were running late. Patty had spent the afternoon at the Crystal Unicorn. Despite the fact that Annie typically shied away from religious traditions, Patty had somehow gotten through Annie's shy reserve and convinced the lonely woman to attend the Christmas program with them.

Patty was also instrumental in getting a local women's group to "adopt" Clara and her cause. They were already planning fund-raisers for Canine Rescue.

Clara had returned to town after all. She had only been trying to protect her pets. The police took Kathleen's confession about her partner's giving Clara the watch to the judge and the case had been dismissed.

Kathleen would probably be doing jail time, although her lawyer was already preparing a plea bargain, citing her mental instability. Sarah wondered how the judge would interpret the plea. Kathleen's mind had been sharp enough to concoct the code in the blogs to communicate about the merchandise she had gotten from the stores and Helping Hands. But then again, she had been motivated by her zeal to help the poor and wasn't a danger to society.

Some of the stolen merchandise had been recovered, including Liam's Dalmatian umbrella stand, which he promptly gave away after Murphy started chewing everything in sight again. Apparently the life-size dog gave the corgi territorial anxiety. Liam didn't care what the vet called it as long as Murphy stopped attacking his shoes.

Gordon Leftfoot was still ever-present, trying to make Maple Hill more secure. He grudgingly congratulated Sarah for solving most of the recent thefts, but there was still enough crime in town to keep him busy. It turned out he was married after all, but separated. Because some of his estranged wife's belongings, including some quilting books, had gotten mixed up in Gordon's packing boxes, his wife was coming to Maple Hill to retrieve them the day after Christmas and to talk. Sarah prayed that she and Gordon might be able to work things out.

Despite all the good things happening in Maple Hill, there was still a cool wall of reserve between Patty and Sarah. It could stem from the fact that Maggie had finally put her foot down and made it clear to her mother that she wasn't going to consider helping start a second store for at least another year. Jason and the girls needed her right where she was.

Patty probably found it easier to blame Jason and Sarah for Maggie's "stubbornness," but Sarah could live with that and the temporary sense of peace it brought to the family.

Sarah had finished Martha's quilt and Maggie's pillows earlier that day. They lay wrapped along with the scarf for Liam under her tree. For Patty, in addition to the pretty teapot, she had found a fun but meaningful gift, an antique sheriff's star in remembrance of Patty's bravery in stopping the bad guy from getting away.

Sarah glanced at the clock. They needed to leave in a few minutes to make the program in time. Liam was going to meet her at the church, and Sarah was looking forward to spending more time with the kind man who had come to mean so much to her.

She set her mug on the coffee table as footsteps pounded down the stairs. Audrey and Amy rushed into the parlor and plopped down on both sides of Sarah.

"Ready for Christmas?" Audrey asked, her scrubbed face pink and shining.

Sarah smiled. Gerry and William might not be here, but she could still feel their love, *family* love, radiating from the two precious girls beside her.

She wrapped her arms around their shoulders and gave them a squeeze. "Yes, I am. It's going to be the best Christmas ever."

# ABOUT THE AUTHOR

From her first introduction to the beginner readers with Dick and Jane, award-winning author Kelly Ann Riley has wanted to be a writer. She started penning stories at an early age and received special recognition for her short stories. Later, she became a reporter and the editor for her high school newspaper.

Now Kelly Ann enjoys writing romantic suspense and cozy mysteries. Her past hobbies of quilting, cross-stitching, and crocheting make *Patchwork Mysteries* particularly fun to write. She loves watching fabric, string, and yarn transform into art. She is a member of American Christian Fiction Writers and Romance Writers of America, and lives in Alabama with her family. You can contact her through her Web site at KellyAnnRiley.com.

# TORN IN TWO

## BY KRISTIN ECKHARDT

 CHAPTER ONE

A car horn blasted and Sarah Hart dropped her beeping cell phone, cranked the steering wheel with one hand and narrowly avoided the blue Impala that shot out in front of her. Her tires hit an icy patch on the road, the tail end of her car careering dangerously close to a towering oak tree on the corner.

She gripped the wheel with both hands as her tires found traction on the slick street. The Impala sped away, its windows covered with winter grit and grime, making it impossible for Sarah to see who she had almost collided with.

"Thank you, Lord," she prayed aloud, "for protecting us both."

The speeding car had come from the Maple Hill High School parking lot, which was Sarah's destination. When her cell phone beeped again, signaling another text message, she ignored it, keeping both hands on the steering wheel. She pulled into the high school parking lot, the yellow parking stall lines obscured by the packed snow and ice.

She finally found an empty spot near the auditorium and switched off the ignition. Then she sat there a few moments, waiting for her heart to resume its normal rhythm.

That had been a close call and all due to her carelessness. She had heard Jason lecture the twins about the dangers of distracted driving and they weren't even old enough to drive yet. Now, here she was, letting a text message distract her.

"Never again," Sarah vowed, leaving the cell phone in her pocket. It was probably Martha texting her that she and Ernie were on their way to Boston to visit Ernie's sister.

She didn't have time to open the messages and read them now anyway. She was due to give a quilting presentation to the home economics class.

Sue Gormley, the home ec teacher, had approached Sarah last week after Sarah had given a workshop on vintage fabrics at the library.

She had never met Sue before but had been impressed by the woman's astute questions and knowledge about textiles. They had exchanged a few e-mails since the workshop to discuss the presentation, and Sarah had suggested several different quilting topics, hoping to find one that would interest teenagers. She knew they bored easily and wanted to find a subject that would keep their attention during the fifty-minute class.

Sarah closed the car door, then rounded the car and opened the trunk. She lifted out a green plastic tote box, balancing it against one bent knee as she reached up to close the trunk. Then she gripped both handles of the tote box with her gloved hands and lugged it into the high school.

As soon as she walked into the building the smells and sounds greeted her like an old friend. She inhaled the spicy scent of chili soup and the sweet aroma of cinnamon rolls from the cafeteria. They mingled together with the musky aroma of physical exertion from the gymnasium.

The old high school had been torn down ten years ago and a new one built in its place. A lot had changed in the forty-plus years since she had attended high school, but her nose told her that some things stayed the same.

Chatter emanated from the cafeteria where the students had congregated for lunch. She and Gerry used to share a table by the window in the old high school, along with their friends. Some of them, like Gerry, were gone now, but the memories were precious to her.

With a sigh, Sarah turned toward the office. She set her tote on the bench just outside the door and then pulled off her winter gloves and stuffed them into her coat pockets. When she walked into the office she saw Sandy Turner, the school secretary, seated behind a desk covered with files and papers and a mug that read *School is cool!*

Sandy had worked at the high school as far back as when Jason and Jenna were teenagers. She loved kids although she had never had any of her own.

"Hello there, Sarah." Sandy nudged her glasses up on her nose. "What brings you here on this fine January day?"

"Mrs. Gormley invited me to give a presentation to her home ec class."

"Oh, that's right." Sandy shifted the papers on her desk until a large datebook appeared beneath the clutter. "I have you on the calendar. Sixth period?"

"Mrs. Gormley told me one o'clock."

Sandy nodded as she pushed her chair back and stood up. "That's sixth period. Mrs. Gormley is probably still on lunch break so I'll take you to her room."

Sarah grabbed the tote box on her way out of the office.

"I can get one of the kids to carry that for you," Sandy offered. "It looks heavy."

"No, I'm fine. It's more awkward than heavy. I wanted to bring some of my quilts to show the kids."

Sandy led her down a hallway, then turned and headed down another long wing. Next year, Amy and Audrey would be walking these halls. They were growing up so fast.

The halls were empty now, giving Sarah a chance to admire the artwork on the walls by Liza Cullen's art students. Liza attended Bridge Street Church and loved to talk about her students. When Sarah mentioned at church that Sue had invited her to speak, Liza had invited Sarah to stop by her classroom after the quilting presentation so she could show off their latest projects.

"Here we are." Sandy stopped in front of a closed door and pulled a key ring from her pocket. "We keep the classrooms locked during the lunch period, otherwise some of the kids sneak in looking for mischief."

Sarah smiled as she remembered some of the pranks her classmates used to pull on the teachers.

"That's strange," Sandy said as she easily turned the door handle and pulled it open. "Looks like Mrs. Gormley forgot to lock her door."

"Maybe she was expecting me," Sarah said, noting that the classroom lights were on. She set the plastic tote box on the desk nearest to her.

"Is there anything else you need?" Sandy asked.

"No, I should be fine until Mrs. Gormley gets here. Thank you, Sandy."

"My pleasure," she said as she walked out the door.

Sarah took a moment to look around the home ec room. It was a bright classroom with cheery yellow curtains adorning the bank of windows along the south wall. On one side of the classroom were three rows of sewing machines and long tables that would be perfect for cutting fabric. On the other side of the room were two identical kitchenettes, each one complete with a white stove, a white refrigerator, and a stainless steel sink.

Sue's large walnut desk sat in the middle of the room, a half circle of students' desks surrounding it. That's where Sarah would give her presentation.

She lifted the tote box and carried it to Sue's desk. That's when she saw the spilled coffee. A large puddle of dark coffee pooled on the walnut desktop. Sarah recognized the paper cup with The Spotted Dog logo. The liquid had spilled onto a bundle of fabric and dripped onto the floor underneath the desk.

But as she looked more closely, she realized the bundle of fabric was actually a quilt. She set the box down, well away from the spilled coffee and then carefully lifted the quilt off the desk. Dark wet stains obscured the faded cotton prints, but she could see it was a child's quilt—at least forty or fifty years old.

The bell rang, the shrill sound startling Sarah. She gently laid the quilt on the other side of the desk, not wanting the coffee to do any further damage.

A moment later, students began spilling into the classroom. Their laughter and easy chatter quieted when they saw her and she noticed several of them exchanging curious glances with each other.

Ian Carper, Martha's grandson, gave her a subtle wave as he passed by on his way to a desk. Ryan Palladino sat next to him and Amber Lewis, who sang in the Bridge Street Church choir, greeted Sarah with a wide smile as she entered the room.

"Are you our sub today?" Ryan asked her. "Is Mrs. Gormley sick or something?"

"No, she's here," Amber interjected, parking herself at a desk close to Sarah. "I saw her in the hallway right before lunch."

"Then why do we have a sub?" another boy asked.

"I'm not a sub," Sarah clarified. "I'm Mrs. Hart and I'm giving a presentation to your class today." She pointed toward the spilled coffee on the desk. "Mrs. Gormley is probably getting something to clean that up. I'm sure she'll be here soon."

"Cool." Ryan leaned back in his chair, his long legs stretched out in front of him. "That means we don't have to do anything today."

One of the girls walked up to Sarah. "Mrs. Hart, would you mind if I studied for my grammar test during your talk? I can still listen while I study."

"I'll leave that up to Mrs. Gormley," Sarah said, looking toward the door. "In the meantime, why don't you all sit down and I'll show you some of the quilts I brought with me today."

The bell sounded again as a few stragglers entered the classroom and headed for their desks. Sarah opened the lid of the tote box and pulled out the folded quilt on top.

She waited until the students had settled into their seats before she began to speak. "This is a Log Cabin quilt from 1911 that I bought at an estate sale for five dollars. At that time, it had water and mildew stains all over it. Some of the cotton batting was missing and several of the quilt blocks were torn and frayed."

A boy in the back row raised his hand, then started talking without being called on. "You're here to talk about quilts?"

"That's right," Sarah said, "I restore vintage quilts. Some of them are quite valuable." She opened up the Log Cabin quilt for them to see. "Does anyone want to guess how much this quilt is worth now that I've restored it?"

"Ten dollars," Ryan guessed.

"Higher," Sarah said with a smile.

"A hundred dollars," Amber said.

"Higher," Sarah said.

"Ten thousand dollars!" someone shouted from the back of the classroom.

Sarah smiled. "That's too high. It's now valued at five hundred dollars, but its real value is the history in these fabrics and these stitches. They tell a story about the quilt maker, the fabrics used to make the quilts, and even the place this quilt was made."

Ian leaned forward. "So what exactly did you do to make it worth so much money?

Sarah glanced toward the door, wondering what was keeping Sue. It shouldn't take that long to find a mop. "The first thing I did was give it a good cleaning. Then I repaired the torn or missing quilt patches by finding vintage fabrics that matched the ones in the quilt."

"Is that one of your quilts on Mrs. Gormley's desk?" Amber asked, pointing to the coffee-stained quilt. "Are you going to show us how to clean it?"

"No, that one's not mine. It must belong to Mrs. Gormley."

Sarah glanced at the clock, beginning to grow concerned and then turned to Martha's grandson. "Ian, would you go to the office and see if they can locate Mrs. Gormley?"

"Sure." Ian unfolded his body from the small desk and ambled to the door.

A few minutes later, he returned with Principal Rod Wagner. Sarah hadn't met the new principal before today, though she had heard his name already. He reminded her of a young Gregory Peck, with wavy, dark hair and gentle brown eyes.

"Hello, Mrs. Hart," he said, reaching out to shake her hand. "Ian tells me that Sue didn't show up for class."

"*She's in trouble,*" Ryan crooned under his breath.

Principal Wagner gave him a warning glance and then turned back to Sarah. "Have you seen her at all since you got here?"

"No," Sarah said. "Sandy brought me to her room, which was unlocked. Sandy found that a little unusual."

"It is." He turned to the class. "Did any of you see Mrs. Gormley at lunch?"

"I saw her in the hallway right before lunch," Amber said.

"How did she seem?" he asked.

Amber shrugged. "Fine, I guess. I mean, I didn't talk to her or anything."

"Where was she headed?"

"I don't know. I wasn't really paying attention."

"She had a planning period right before lunch," he mused, "so she didn't have any students."

"Did she look ill?" Sarah asked Amber, trying to find some reason for her absence.

"No," Amber said. "She looked like she always does."

The students began to talk in whispers to each other as Principal Wagner walked over to Sue's desk.

"What happened here?"

"I don't know," Sarah said. "The coffee was spilled when I got here. I assumed Mrs. Gormley had gone to find a custodian or a mop to clean it up." She moved beside the principal and reached for the child's quilt. "This had coffee spilled on it too so I moved it out of the way. Does the quilt belong to Mrs. Gormley?"

"I don't know," he said. "I've never seen it before."

"Do you find this as strange as I do?" she asked in a low voice.

"I certainly do." He reached into his suit jacket and pulled out a cell phone. "Maybe she went home for lunch and something happened."

Sarah waited while he dialed Sue's number, then saw him shake his head.

"No answer on her home phone," the principal said, "let me try her cell."

"Do you think something bad happened to her?" Amber asked Sarah.

"Not necessarily," Sarah said. "If she did go home for lunch, maybe she had car trouble on the way."

"But wouldn't she call the school to say she'd be late?" Amber said.

Sarah had thought the same thing, but she tried to stay calm for the kids.

Principal Wagner sighed as he lowered the cell phone. "Her cell phone isn't in service, so either the battery died or she turned off the phone."

The door opened and, for a moment, Sarah thought Sue had finally arrived. Instead, Sandy Turner walked inside the classroom.

"I checked the rest of the school, but no Mrs. Gormley," Sandy said. "Then I checked the parking lot and her car is gone. Do you want me to try to call her?"

"I already did," Principal Wagner replied. "She's not answering."

None of this made sense to Sarah. Why would Sue abandon her classroom? And why wouldn't she answer her phone?

*Unless she couldn't answer it.*

Sarah thought about her near accident on her way to the high school.

"What kind of car does Mrs. Gormley drive?"

"It's a blue Chevy Impala," Sandy said. "Why?"

"Because I almost hit a blue Impala when I was pulling up to the high school. It shot out of the parking lot right in front of me."

"Was it Sue?" Principal Wagner asked.

"I don't know. I didn't see the driver and the car sped off while I was still trying to regain control of my car." Sarah tried to remember any details that might help. "The car had a Massachusetts license plate, but I didn't catch the number. It all happened so fast."

"It had to be Mrs. Gormley," Sandy said. "None of the other teachers drive a blue Impala."

"But her behavior seems strange. It sure doesn't sound like her," Principal Wagner said, looking at Sarah. "Sue would have stopped to make sure you were all right. And she wouldn't have been speeding in the first place. At least, not the Sue Gormley I know."

"Then what do you think happened?" Sarah asked him.

"I don't know," he said, reaching for his phone once more. "But I think it's time we call the police."

# A Note from the Editors

We hope you enjoy Patchwork Mysteries, created by the Books and Inspirational Media Division of Guideposts, a nonprofit organization that touches millions of lives every day through products and services that inspire, encourage, help you grow in your faith, and celebrate God's love in every aspect of your daily life.

Thank you for making a difference with your purchase of this book, which helps fund our many outreach programs to military personnel, prisons, hospitals, nursing homes, and educational institutions. To learn more, visit GuidepostsFoundation.org.

We also maintain many useful and uplifting online resources. Visit Guideposts.org to read true stories of hope and inspiration, access OurPrayer network, sign up for free newsletters, download free e-books, join our Facebook community, and follow our stimulating blogs.

To learn about other Guideposts publications, including the best-selling devotional *Daily Guideposts*, go to ShopGuideposts.org, call (800) 932-2145, or write to Guideposts, PO Box 5815, Harlan, Iowa 51593.